A FLAME IN THE WIND OF DEATH

ABBOTT AND LOWELL FORENSIC
MYSTERIES

A FLAME IN THE WIND OF DEATH

JEN J. DANNA
WITH ANN VANDERLAAN

FIVE STAR
A part of Gale, Cengage Learning

GALE
CENGAGE Learning·

Farmington Hills, Mich • San Francisco • New York • Waterville, Maine
Meriden, Conn • Mason, Ohio • Chicago

GALE
CENGAGE Learning®

LIBRARY OF CONGRESS CATALOGING-IN-PUBLICATION DATA

Danna, Jen J.
    A flame in the wind of death : Abbott and Lowell Forensic Mysteries / Jen J. Danna ; with Ann Vanderlaan. — First Edition.
        pages cm. — (Abbott and Lowell Forensic Mysteries)
    ISBN-13: 978-1-4328-2809-7 (hardcover)
    ISBN-10: 1-4328-2809-6 (hardcover)
    1. Policewomen—Fiction. 2. Serial murder investigation—Fiction. 3. Forensic anthropologists—Fiction. 4. Halloween—Salem (Mass.)—Fiction. I. Vanderlaan, Ann. II. Title.
PR9199.4.D365F53 2014
813'.6—dc23   2013041355

First Edition. First Printing: April 2014
Find us on Facebook– https://www.facebook.com/FiveStarCengage
Visit our website– http://www.gale.cengage.com/fivestar/
Contact Five Star™ Publishing at FiveStar@cengage.com

Printed in the United States of America
1 2 3 4 5 6 7 18 17 16 15 14

ADDITIONAL COPYRIGHT INFORMATION

DEDICATION

In memory of Dave Giblin (1945–2012), who spent his entire adult life in service to others—six years as a member of the US Navy, and forty-five years as a firefighter and district chief. Also, to the men and women of our fire departments who put their lives on the line each day to protect us. They are our friends, even though we may never meet.

ACKNOWLEDGMENTS

This book could not have been written without the help of Captain Lisa Giblin of the South Placer Fire Department. Lisa was our guide into the world of firefighting, sharing everything she knew about fires, offensive and defensive firefighting, rescues, investigations, incendiary devices, and the day-to-day life of a firefighter. But firefighters are a family, and assisting Lisa was her South Placer family: Dave Giblin (Chief), Bob Richardson (Butcher Bob), Dan Ward Sr. (Doc), Donny Gray, Erik Garside, Austin Kimbrell (A.K.) and Matt VanVoltinburg (Van). Sincere thanks to you all.

We were also very grateful to be assisted by numerous experts in their field in the Salem and Boston area. The support from the Salem Fire Department was nothing short of outstanding: Deputy Chief Gerry Giunta for going above and beyond, not only hosting a personal tour of headquarters and sharing his knowledge and experiences, but for being available for multiple phones calls and emails, and then arranging connections with other experts and providing materials as needed; Communication Supervisor Jeff Brown for discussions and a demonstration into the inner workings of how the Salem Fire Department responds to emergencies, and for assisting with collecting radio calls so our communications lingo was accurate; Lieutenant Erin Griffin, for sharing her experiences as Salem's fire marshal. Captain Jeanne Stewart of the Massachusetts Department of Fire Services, Fire and Explosion Investigation Section, for ensuring that our fire investigation was realistic. Steve O'Connell of the Essex County District Attorney's Office for continually facilitating our research within the district attorney's office and the Essex State Police Detective Unit. Detective Lieutenant Norman Zuk of the Essex Detective Unit for his unending patience and willingness to share departmental life and protocols with us. Salem Witches Laurie Cabot, Memie Watson, Sharon Bradbury and Gypsy Ravish for assistance with our questions concerning the Craft in Salem. Dr. Tara Moore at Boston University for always being willing to answer any of our questions concerning forensic anthropology research at the university. We've taken a few minor liberties with Salem for the sake of storytelling, but, beyond that, any mistakes are ours alone.

We were thrilled to be joined again by our wonderful critique team. Lisa Giblin, Marianne Harden, Jenny Lidstrom, Margaret McMullen and Sharon Taylor: Once again we hardly know how to convey our thanks to you for all your hard work. To say that we wouldn't be able to write to the best of our abilities without you is an understatement. Sincere thanks for all that you continue to do for us, and for the generous gift of your time and talents. Thanks as well to our wonderful agent, Nicole Resciniti, for always being there for us and for continuing to support us on our writing journey. And to our editor, Gordon Aalborg, who uses each manuscript as an opportunity to teach his authors how to improve their craft overall, thank you for your continued efforts and encouragement.

J.J.D. and A.V.

Thank you Paul and Shelly—still the best daughter-in-law any mom could ever have—for your unstinting enthusiasm when Jen and I decided to wade into the writing maelstrom yet again; and Paul, whose phenotype is one hundred-percent engineer, even read some poetry to find out more about the title of the first novel in this series. Don and Margaret Newman, whose help was invaluable after Spike Thundertail broke my ankle, continue to be great neighbors—even if Don won't let me build him a computer. Angel, Love-A-Bull Pit Bull rescue alumnus, still greets me every morning with a big pittie grin while pretending he does not hog the middle of the bed. Meanwhile his fur brother Spike, a deaf dog from the same rescue, taught me to get out of the way when he's got the zoomies (which are not diarrhea, btw). R Kane—that's shorthand for Raising—is the newest member of the Thundertail tribe. This alumnus of Don't Bully Me Rescue in Lago Vista, Texas, is the perfect "stubby dog": big heart, big head, and a tail that never stops wiggling his butt.

A.V.

Thanks to my husband for good-naturedly putting up with my crazy nonstop work habits that allowed a project like this to be completed outside of my day job's regular work hours. Rick, without your support, I'd never have been able to pull this off. And to my daughters, Jess and Jordan, who started the journey of this book with me by accompanying me on a research trip to Massachusetts. You two were my support team, my sounding board, my fellow explorers, and my photographer and sidekick. To top it off, you patiently listened to my continual plotting during the entire trip with only minimal eye rolling. Let's do it again soon!

J.J.D.

PROLOGUE:
IGNITION

Ignition: the start of a fire; the deliberate human act of starting a fire to produce light, heat, or pleasure.

Saturday, 4:07 a.m.
Uniquely You Antiques
Salem, Massachusetts
As if cast by magic, flames suddenly burst in midair, slicing through the smothering darkness. Writhing tendrils of fire greedily reached out as they fell, finally tumbling to the floor below. With a whoosh, the fire found sustenance—wood, cloth, paper.

And human flesh.

The flames flickered and danced, hungrily consuming everything they touched. Smoke rose in dark billows to fill every crevice in the room as the fire grew stronger and brighter. Wood charred, cloth scorched, and paper crumbled to ash.

A figure skulked in the shadows, safely observing from the far side of a pane of glass. Cool eyes watched as the face of the victim was lit by flames, then kissed by them, the skin blistering before shrinking and splitting to reveal pale bone beneath.

It was a nightmare in shifting shades of grey, black, and red. But the killer felt only elation as the victim's identity was obliterated. Washed clean by the scouring flames. Erased.

Satisfied, the killer turned and melted into the gloom.

CHAPTER ONE:
FIRE POINT

Fire Point: the temperature at which a fuel produces enough vapor so it continues to burn after ignition.

Sunday, 1:24 p.m.
Harborview Restaurant
Boston, Massachusetts

Sunlight sparkled in lightning-quick flashes on the open ocean as a lone black-backed gull soared on outstretched wings, motionless on the breeze. In the harbor, sailboats unfurled yards of canvas to the cool fall winds, while high above the water, the historic Customs House Tower stood watch over the busy port below.

Inside the restaurant, wide panels of sunlight fell across linen-draped tables set with china and silver. The air was fragrant with garlic and peppercorn as a low buzz of conversation filled the room, punctuated by bursts of laughter and the clatter of dishes.

"And then he jammed his gun in his pants to make a run for it. But while he was wedging it under his belt, it went off and he shot himself in the foot." Leigh Abbott paused to sip her mimosa. "After that, the foot chase was pretty much a technicality, what with all the limping and whimpering."

Matt Lowell chuckled as he set his knife and fork on the edge of his empty plate. "I shouldn't be laughing, should I?"

"Because he's a murder suspect?" One corner of her mouth

14

tipped up in an almost reluctant smile. "Welcome to cop humor; it's how we survive the job. This guy was a mistake waiting to happen from the second it occurred to him he could have the family business all to himself after his father died. He just needed to kill his brother to get it. He left a trail of clues a blindfolded rookie could follow."

Matt's smile slowly melted away, his face growing serious. "You deserve an easy case. After the last few weeks . . ."

His voice trailed off, but Leigh understood, even without words.

A Trooper First Class with the Massachusetts State Police, Leigh was a member of the Essex County Detective Unit, headquartered in Salem. When a single human bone was found in a coastal salt marsh the previous month, she'd approached Dr. Matthew Lowell in his capacity as a forensic anthropologist at Boston University to help identify the victim. What began with a single set of remains rapidly spiraled into ten murder victims, all dead at the hands of a man determined to see how far he could twist the human mind. Their teamwork solved the puzzle, but the case nearly cost them their lives. Mere weeks later, they'd joined forces again for their second case together, a chilling tale of trust gone horribly wrong.

"This case couldn't have been more different," Leigh stated. "You're right—it was a welcome change of pace after Bradford. Still, I'm sorry I had to cancel dinner last week. Between court and this case—" She broke off as Matt covered her hand with his.

"Don't worry about it. I understand the job takes priority sometimes. Besides, we traded dinner for Sunday brunch, so it all worked out."

With a quick flick of his head, he shook his untrimmed dark hair out of his eyes, briefly exposing the thick ridge of scar tissue running into his hair from his temple.

At a sudden shriek, Leigh jerked her hand free, reaching for the weapon that normally rode her hip. But even as her fingers touched soft wool instead of hard metal, her body relaxed as she quickly assessed the harmless scene across the room where a young woman had knocked over a glass of red wine.

Leigh's gaze drifted back to Matt to find his eyes fixed on her. "What?"

He sat with his elbows braced on the table, watching her over his steepled hands. "You can't turn it off, can you? You can't just go out socially and let it all go. Even when a case is closed."

Embarrassed heat flushed her cheeks at his continued examination. "It's not like it's a switch you throw when the clock hits five. Cops are always on duty." Stubbornness stiffened her spine and she met his gaze head on. "Apparently you can't turn it off either. You're studying me like I'm one of your bones."

"Just trying to figure you out, that's all." Reaching out, Matt tucked a loose strand of hair behind her ear. As his hand pulled away, he ran his fingertips along the curve of her jaw in a subtle caress. "You're an intriguing puzzle."

Her eyes locked with his and her stomach gave a slow, sexy roll of anticipation at the heat in his expression. "No one's ever called me 'intriguing' before."

"I like to think of you as a gift that needs to be unwrapped one layer at a—" Matt frowned as a muffled ring came from the suit jacket draped over the back of his chair. "Sorry, I need to see who's calling."

Leigh's senses instantly went on alert when he froze, his gaze fixed on the name of the caller displayed on-screen. "What is it? What's wrong?"

"I think I have to take this."

The edge in his voice made the back of her neck prickle in alarm. "Is it one of your students?"

"No, it's the Massachusetts State Police."

"Calling you?" The words burst out, cutting through the buzz of conversation around them. Leigh purposely lowered her voice when several heads turned in their direction. "Why are they calling you?"

"I'm as baffled as you are." He answered the call. "Lowell."

Leigh leaned forward, trying to catch any trace of the other end of the conversation.

Maddeningly, Matt relaxed back in his chair even as he cocked an eyebrow at her. "Sergeant Kepler, what a surprise," he said into the phone.

Only her white-knuckled stranglehold on the edge of the table kept Leigh from leaping to her feet to listen in on why her superior officer was calling Matt. If it was something to do with the Bradford case, he'd have surely gone through her instead.

Matt was silent for a long time as he listened, his hazel eyes fixed on her. "This request comes straight from Dr. Rowe?"

Rowe? Someone had to be dead for the medical examiner to be involved, but the remains must be in bad shape if Rowe was personally requesting Matt's expertise.

"Whose case is it?" Matt's eyes suddenly went arctic-cold as his casual air of relaxation dropped away. "No." The single word was whiplash sharp. "That's exactly what I mean. I'm not working with him. If you and Rowe want me on this case, you need to transfer it to Trooper Abbott."

Leigh recognized that stubborn tone; she'd run headlong into it several times—Matt was digging in his heels and wasn't about to budge.

"Actually my request is quite logical," he continued. "Trooper Abbott and I had a rough start, but we learned how to work together. She's familiar now with how my lab operates, and she knows my students and how we process evidence. It would waste my time to have to train a new officer." There was a pause, and Matt's eyes narrowed to slits. "Those are my terms,

Sergeant. If you want my help on the case, have Trooper Abbott call me with the details." He abruptly ended the call, his expression grim.

"What was that about?" Leigh demanded.

"Kepler wants me to consult on another case. There's been a fire in Salem in one of the historical shopping districts. You probably know it—Wharf Street? The body recovered is so badly burned that Rowe needs a forensic anthropologist. He asked for me specifically."

"That's no surprise—you work well together. But why do you need me?"

"It's Morrison's case," Matt said shortly. His open palm slapped down on the table hard enough to rattle silver and crystal. "I've got the right guy, don't I? Isn't he the Neanderthal who gives you a hard time at the detective unit?"

Leigh let out a resigned sigh. "Yes. That's him." She met his eyes to be sure he understood without question. "Don't interfere, Matt. I can handle him on my own."

"I'm sure you can. But I'm not working with him. And that's my call to make."

"Look, you don't have to—"

Her phone rang.

Matt crossed his arms over his chest, his eyebrows raised in challenge. "Better get that."

Leigh pointed an accusing finger at him. "You stay quiet. Kepler doesn't know we're seeing each other. He wouldn't approve of me—"

"Fraternizing with your consultant? Too damned bad." When her glare threatened frostbite to delicate parts of his anatomy, he mimed locking his lips and tossing the imaginary key over his shoulder.

She rolled her eyes and answered the call. "Abbott. Yes, sir." She slipped a hand into the breast pocket of her jacket, pulled out a notepad and pen, and scribbled quickly. "Yes, I know where that is. I'll let him know and meet him there." She clicked off and gestured to the waitress for the check. "Kepler's pissed."

"He's used to giving orders, but he's not used to someone refusing them." Matt pulled his jacket off the chair and shrugged into it. "Look, I understand they need help, but I'll be damned if I'm going to work shoulder-to-shoulder with Morrison. You and I, we've developed a rhythm. On top of that, you value my students. If I'm going to bring them into another case, I need to know they'll be treated well. And I know you'll work as hard as me to keep them safe."

"You're still thinking about the salt marsh."

He bristled, his shoulders pulling tight and his mouth flattening into a thin line. "I took them into the field and they were shot at. They could have been killed."

She lightly brushed her fingertips over the back of his hand. "We'll keep them safe. Are you bringing them in now? Or do you want to see the site on your own first?"

"I'll bring them in now. My students are familiar with the concepts of burned remains from class, but this will take them from theory to practice. To do that properly, they need to see the remains *in situ*. And the extra eyes will help." He met her gaze. "Have you ever dealt with remains like this before?"

"No."

"Then you need to be prepared. They can be horrific, both by sight and smell."

She grimaced. "Thanks for the warning. Are your students going to be able to handle it?"

"They'll be fine. They held up before, didn't they?"

"They were great." Leigh looked out over the harbor. Suddenly the day seemed so much darker than ten minutes ago. "I was really looking forward to getting out on the Charles this afternoon," she said. "It's the perfect fall day for it—not too cool and not so breezy that the water would be rough and I'd tip us."

"If I can't keep the boat upright, then I need to put in a lot more time at the oars. I promise I'll take you out in the scull first chance we get." The waitress approached but before Leigh could reach for the bill, Matt slid the young woman his credit card. When Leigh objected, he simply held up a silencing finger. "My treat. You're not going to insist on splitting everything down the middle, are you?"

"No. But you shouldn't have to pick up the check every time we go out. You paid the last time."

"We've only been out a few times, so your representative sample is too small to be statistically significant. I chose this place and it's not cheap, so I should pick up the tab. Also, I suspect a professor's salary beats a cop's, so it's not fair to stick you with the check when I picked the expensive restaurant."

She glared at him, but remained silent.

"As I thought. You get the next one, okay?" He tucked his card back into his wallet and stood. "Rowe must be using this as another demonstration. Will he still be there when we arrive?"

Leigh rose from her chair. "I'm not sure, but I'll find out. He may not be able to stick around that long."

"It's a good thing we came in two cars. You head back now; I'll go pick up my students. We'll be there by two-fifteen or two-thirty at the latest. They'll hold the scene until then?"

"Yes. When remains are found in a fire, it's officially designated a crime scene and nothing gets moved until the crime scene techs and the ME get there. The techs are probably on their way right now."

"Then let's go." He circled the table to lay his hand at the small of her back as they headed for the exit. "We've got a scene to process."

Chapter Two:
Overhaul

Overhaul: the process of putting a structure in the safest possible condition after a fire. During the *cleaning-up* phase, firefighters verify that the fire has not extended into unknown areas and that hidden *hot spots* are extinguished.

Sunday, 2:21 p.m.
Wharf Street
Salem, Massachusetts

Matt nodded to the Salem officer who waved them through the barricade. He led his group around the silver and blue police car blocking the street, bar lights flashing in bright bursts of color. Resettling the equipment bag on his shoulder, he glanced back at his three graduate students—two young men and a woman, their faces set in determined lines as they headed toward another horrific scene. Matt slowed his steps until they caught up to him.

Around them, smiling ghosts peeped playfully around the corner of a toy shop while gaudily decorated Witch hats filled the window of a ladies clothing store. Despite the Halloween window dressing, the shops lining both sides of the street were eerily silent and deserted, their doors locked tight even though it was mid-afternoon.

"What's that stench?" Paul, tall and gangly in baggy jeans and a faded sweatshirt, grimaced, his nose wrinkling in distaste. "That's not just burned wood. Something really reeks."

"From what I understand, it's the plastics and synthetics that really stink in a fire like this." Kiko glanced sideways at Paul, her pretty Japanese face serious. "This is a commercial area, so who knows what was in the stores that burned. And then there's the victim."

Paul's face flushed with color. "I didn't mean it that way," he stuttered. "I—"

Kiko put him out of his misery with a fluid shrug. "I know," she said easily.

Paul hunched his shoulders, but gave her a grateful half smile.

Juka trailed a step behind them, his dark eyes fixed on the surrounding stores. "These buildings are over a century old. A fire could easily spread due to the old-fashioned construction."

"That's what it sounded like to me from what I've heard so far," Matt said. "But we'll find out more when we get there." He glanced over, seeing feet start to drag and recognizing the hesitation in the young faces—they were dreading what was to come, but delaying wouldn't make it any easier. "Come on, guys. Leigh's probably waiting for us by now. It looks like all the action is around that corner." He indicated the bottom curve of the U-shaped street. "Over there."

The group picked up their pace, falling silent as they approached their destination.

The street curved out of sight, but over the roofs of the untouched shops, steady streams of thick, dark smoke drifted sluggishly skyward. A red fire truck was parked just before the curve in the middle of the street, its massive white ladder extended high over a building around the bend. Perched atop the ladder was a firefighter wearing a black helmet and a heavy beige coat with SALEM on the back in white block letters.

"What's he doing up there?" Kiko asked.

"Looks like he's got a camera," Juka said, shading his eyes with his hand as he squinted up into the cloudless sky. "He's probably documenting the scene."

The cool fall wind suddenly gusted, skittering in chill wisps under Matt's jacket. He pulled the collar a little tighter against his skin. But even the wind couldn't drive away the reek of smoke and devastation.

They rounded the curve into organized chaos: Firefighters shouted to each other as they jogged in and out of the burned building. Smoke rolled out of broken windows, and the sound of falling debris came from deep within the structure. Two engines were pulled up to the curb across the street from the fire, their running motors adding to the din. A thick hose connected the engines, and smaller hoses ran from the closest one toward the building, crisscrossing the sidewalk in fat lines. A firefighter stood beside the second engine, draining water from hose lines and meticulously folding them into compact piles to be stored in the back of the vehicle. Other firefighters carrying axes and long, hooked pike poles disappeared through a door near the end of the line of shops.

A burned-out shell was all that remained of the building. Daylight spilled through gaping doorways over charred contents and fallen rafters. Glass from storefront windows sparkled like diamonds strewn across the sidewalk, the tiny shards catching and reflecting sunlight where they lay in pools of water. The roof was burned away and only a few feet of charred rafters and shingles outlined the perimeter, allowing sunlight to flood the carnage within.

"Whoa . . . ," Paul breathed. "Not much left."

Matt's gaze roamed over the scene, cataloging every detail. "Yeah, it looks bad. But you knew it would be."

"Because they need us?" Kiko asked.

"Exactly. If the fire wasn't that bad, Rowe would have handled the remains on his own."

A yell punctuated by a loud crash came from the nearest

doorway. Two firefighters tossed sodden debris from the store onto a growing pile atop a large canvas tarp spread across the sidewalk.

A flash of yellow caught Matt's eye. Across the street, a soot-smudged golden retriever jumped into the back of an SUV with the Massachusetts state crest emblazoned on the door. A man wearing navy pants and a white uniform shirt with an emblem on the sleeve slammed the hatch shut behind the dog.

Matt smiled in greeting as Leigh came around the opposite bend of the street, striding past an antique lamppost, the base obscured by a shock of scorched corn stalks. "Looks like our timing's just right. Here comes Leigh." He waved and she smiled in return as she started toward them.

Leigh's smile vanished as a stocky man stepped into her path, his tan sport coat pulled tightly across his stiffly set shoulders.

"What the hell are you doing, Abbott?" His raised voice sliced through the haze like a jagged knife, making Leigh jerk to a stop. "This is *my* case. Now Kepler's telling me to stand down."

"Kepler assigned the case to me," Leigh said as Matt strained to hear her words over the continual noise. "Now, if you don't mind getting out of the way, I need to meet with my team."

"What's going on over there?" Paul asked. "Who's the guy hassling Leigh?"

"I bet that's Morrison." Matt swung the bag off his shoulder and shoved it unceremoniously into Paul's arms. "Be right back." He strode across the asphalt toward the two officers.

"Your *team*," Morrison practically spat at Leigh. "Is that how you weaseled onto this case? Telling Kepler no one could work with these people but you, the golden girl?"

"She didn't kick you off the case. I did." Matt purposely stepped between them, going chest-to-chest with Morrison and physically forcing him back a step. "*I* wanted Trooper Abbott."

Leigh's hand wrapped around Matt's upper arm, giving him

a rough jerk, but he didn't budge. "I've got this," she hissed from behind his shoulder.

Matt threw her a sidelong glance. "The decision to bring you onboard was mine." He turned back to Morrison, drawing himself up to his full height. At over six feet, he topped Morrison by a full three inches, while Morrison easily had him by fifty pounds. But Matt knew all the hours spent rowing gave him a physical advantage. Morrison's bulk wasn't all muscle and his face was an unhealthy shade of crimson that hinted at high blood pressure. "If you want to blame someone, she's not your mark. I am."

Over Morrison's shoulder, Matt saw Paul and Juka drop their gear and jog across the street toward them.

"Fine, then I'll hassle you. This is my case. You don't get the department pet to sit up and bark at your command. You get the officer on call." He stabbed at his own chest with a meaty index finger. "That's me."

"I get who I want," Matt shot back. "And since Dr. Rowe asked for me specifically, the department is willing to oblige me."

Morrison's face pinched into a mask of pure spite as he took a menacing step forward, using his bulk to crowd Matt backward into Leigh. "Look, I don't care who you are. You don't just waltz in here and—"

"Hey! Not at my scene!" A sharp voice rang out, and all heads turned to see a tall, lean woman headed their way, her cold gaze fixed on them. She was dressed in full firefighting gear and a white helmet. "Which one of you is the responding officer?"

"I am," Leigh said. "Trooper Morrison has been relieved."

"Then Trooper Morrison can go." The woman jerked her thumb over her shoulder in dismissal. "Only people working the case are allowed back here. No gawkers."

Morrison glared at Leigh and mumbled something that sounded like *"I'll be talking to my rep,"* as he stalked away.

Kiko hurried over, weighed down with all four backpacks. "What happened?" she asked breathlessly as Paul and Juka helped her lower everything to the ground.

"That's what I'd like to know." The woman pulled off her helmet, revealing short-cut blond hair. Tucking the helmet under her left arm, she held out her right hand to Leigh. "Trooper Brianna Gilson from the State Fire Marshal's Office, Fire Investigation Unit. This is my investigation."

"Trooper? You're not a firefighter?" Paul blurted.

Trooper Gilson froze, her hand still extended, but her gaze drilled into the young man. Paul stared at his hightops and shuffled awkwardly, clearly wishing the ground would swallow him whole.

"Members of the state fire investigation unit are all members of the state police," Gilson said crisply. "City fire departments can investigate property fires, but when a death occurs or arson is suspected, the case comes to us. But don't worry; you've lucked into both cop and firefighter with me."

Leigh clasped Trooper Gilson's hand, pulling attention away from Paul. "Trooper Leigh Abbott. My apologies for the earlier commotion. Trooper Morrison was originally called to this scene, but there's been a change of officers."

Matt stepped forward. "Trooper Gilson, I'm Dr. Matt Lowell. Dr. Rowe asked that I consult on this case as the forensic anthropologist. Since Trooper Abbott and I have worked together before, I specifically requested her." When he held out his hand, Gilson shook it firmly. "That should be it for the dramatics."

"Good. And just 'Bree' will be fine. I hate formality when it's not needed." At Matt's raised eyebrow, she elaborated. "I like things straight up and have a low tolerance for BS." She fixed him with a steely stare. "And dramatics."

"Just like scientists. I think we'll get along fine." Turning, Leigh held out an arm toward the group. "Meet the rest of my scientific team. These are Matt's students—Kiko Niigata, Paul Layne and Juka Petrović."

Bree's gaze swept over the young people, lingering for several extra beats on Paul. "Do they all need access? We try to keep the number of people entering the scene to a minimum."

Matt opened his mouth to respond, but Leigh spoke first. "They're all contributing team members, so they all need to be here." When Bree looked skeptical, Leigh said, "I had the same concerns when I first worked with them. Trust me—you won't regret having them around."

Bree stared at the young people for a moment, then nodded. "Then let's suit up and get in there." She scanned the group quickly. "I'm going to find you some alternate gear. If you go in like that, you'll never wear those clothes again."

Matt nudged the bags at his feet. "We brought disposable Tyvek coveralls. We always suit up at forensic scenes so we don't contaminate any potential evidence."

"Great. But you'll still need boots. Everything's down in there, so you need better protection than what you're wearing." Bree turned to Leigh. "What about you?"

Leigh shrugged. "This is all I have." She looked down at the old jeans and T-shirt she wore under her jacket. "It's old. It's not a big deal if it gets dirty."

"Dirty is an understatement," Bree said. "You don't need full turnout gear like this—" She tugged on the edge of her heavy white coat, pulling it back far enough to reveal red suspenders over a smudged white uniform shirt. "—but you'll at least need a pair of bunkers."

"Bunkers?"

"The pants." She patted the thick beige pants she wore,

rimmed at the cuffs with reflective tape. "I'll scam some boots and a pair of bunkers from the truck or one of the guys. And helmets." Putting on her own helmet, she jogged toward the engine at the far end of the scene.

Leigh turned back to the students. "Good to see you guys again. Well . . . not given the circumstances, but you know what I mean."

"Sure," Paul said, his gaze shifting back to the wreckage. "Where's the body?"

Leigh scanned the burned-out husk before pointing to a doorway. "In the middle store—the antique shop."

"Let's suit up over there, out of the way." Matt pointed at the far side of the street, away from the chaos and cacophony of the fire scene. An open green space hugged the shore, a forest of tall sailboat masts clustered behind it. In the distance, sunlight glinted off the open water of Salem Harbor.

The students grabbed their bags and started carefully picking their way over fire hoses and around equipment. Matt moved to follow them but Leigh grabbed his arm. He turned to meet green eyes glinting with anger.

"I don't need you to fight my battles for me." Thankfully, she pitched her voice low enough that his retreating students couldn't hear. "I have to deal with Morrison on a daily basis. You standing in front of me doesn't help one bit. All it does is destroy my credibility."

Matt's temper flared, but he tamped it down in favor of reason. "I know you, Leigh. You're more than capable of handling that bastard. But, in this case, it wasn't your fault; it was mine. And I'm not going to stand by and watch you get harassed by someone who likes to throw his weight around when I caused the problem. If Morrison's got issues about who's assigned to this case, he can take it up with me. Or Kepler. But not you, because you're just following orders." He forced himself to stop and really look at her: she held herself stiffly, her jaw locked and her hands balled at her sides as if expecting an attack from him as well. "Look, I'm sorry if I overstepped. But at the time, I didn't think I did. What the hell has he got against you anyway?"

"I'm sure he could recite you a laundry list," Leigh said flatly, her defensive stance deflating. "He's never liked the fact that I'm the daughter of the unit's past sergeant. He thinks I get special treatment." Defiance flashed in her eyes. "Which I don't."

Matt held up both hands, palm out. "I'm not saying you do. But that at least explains the 'department pet' comment, which irritated the hell out of me." He stepped closer. "Truce?"

"Are you going to leave Morrison alone next time?"

"I can't promise you that. If he's going after you—"

"You'll leave him to me."

Matt swallowed the curse that sprang to his lips and tried to meet her halfway. "I'll do my best. But no promises if I think he's way out of line."

Leigh sighed. "Fine." She glanced over toward the students. All three had their bags open and were pulling out disposable white jumpsuits. "Come on, you need to get ready."

They started toward the harbor's edge. "I'm confused," Matt said. "What exactly is Bree? She's a firefighter *and* a cop?"

"Sort of. I've never worked with her before, but I've heard about her from one of the guys in the Unit who went through the academy with her and later worked a murder case with her. She was a firefighter, right here in Salem. She worked up the ranks to lieutenant and was the city fire marshal for a few years. But I guess she wanted the meatier cases because she quit the fire department and went to the police academy with the express purpose of getting into the fire marshal's office. She's been there a few years now and has a good rep."

"Having been a firefighter, I'll bet she has instincts cops don't have. Sounds like a good person to have on the case."

A few minutes later Bree and a second firefighter returned, their arms full of equipment they unceremoniously spilled onto the grass.

Leigh pulled on the bulky bunkers and boots Bree offered her, awkwardly readjusting the waistband around the Sig Sauer service weapon at her hip before pulling the suspenders over her shoulders. Holding out both arms and turning in a slow circle, Leigh glanced over her shoulder at Kiko. "Tell me the truth. Does my ass look big in these pants?"

Kiko laughed. "Nah. Just ask the guys. I bet they think the lady firefighter look is sexy."

"Oh yeah," Paul agreed, zipping up his jumpsuit and tugging on a pair of latex gloves. "It's . . . uh . . . hot." He glanced at Bree. "No pun intended."

This time Bree's eyes held a glint of humor. "Like I haven't heard that one before." She turned to Leigh. "Do you know what happened here this morning?"

Leigh shook her head. "Just that a victim was found after the fire was extinguished."

"Let me give you a quick rundown. Someone called nine-one-one at four-thirty-two this morning."

"Who spotted the fire at that hour of the morning?" Matt asked.

Bree turned to the boats bobbing in the dark-blue water of the marina. "Someone heading back to his boat after an evening with the boys at an after-hours club. We agreed not to ask too many questions about that in return for his statement."

"That's some evening," Paul muttered.

"Headquarters responded and the first trucks arrived at four thirty-eight—two engines, a ladder truck, and Deputy Chief Baldwin as the incident commander. When a working fire was

30

confirmed, they sent two more engines and a second ladder truck so they had five attack lines going at once. The building was fully involved by the time those trucks arrived, but they managed to keep the fire contained to this one building, saving the surrounding structures. With simultaneous attacks to both the front and back of the building, the fire was extinguished by six a.m."

"When was the victim discovered?" Leigh looked up from her notepad, her pen poised over the paper.

"Just after ten. When the guys started overhauling, they began with the outside stores and worked their way in because the seat of the fire was the center store. They needed to let that area cool down, preferably without dousing it again."

"Sorry," Leigh interrupted. "Overhauling?"

"Once the fire is out, they check for extensions—places where the fire spreads into walls or attics where they can't readily see it—and hot spots, to make sure the fire is really out. For safety, they also took the time to shore up the walls of the middle section with two-by-fours. The roof collapsed into the structure during the fire, so they had to clear a lot of debris for the investigation. That's when they found the victim and called the state police, the medical examiner's office and the fire investigation unit."

"You've worked with Dr. Rowe before?" Leigh asked.

Bree nodded. "Yes. Good man, Rowe. Never had him at a scene though. Usually I'm on his turf, not him on mine."

"He's trying to get additional funding for on-scene body processing by showing that having an ME at murder scenes improves conviction rates, so he's running some cases himself on his own time. He's not still here, is he?"

"No, he left about an hour ago. He said something about enough hands coming that he wouldn't be needed. I'm sure he'll be in touch—" She looked back and forth between Matt and Leigh. "With one of you. But he called for techs to transport the remains. They should be here shortly." She glanced around the group. "You guys look ready to go. The Crime Scene Services guys were here earlier with Rowe, but they went for coffee and will be back in a few minutes. Grab whatever gear you need."

Matt and the students put on their backpacks, and then Bree led the group across the street to where the dark maw of the fire scene beckoned.

CHAPTER THREE:
BLEVE

BLEVE: pronounced "blev-ee," an acronym for Boiling Liquid Expanding Vapor Explosion. This type of explosion occurs when the contents of a closed container boil and vaporize when the container is heated, even if the container was not pressurized prior to the fire.

Sunday, 2:43 p.m.
Wharf Street,
Salem, Massachusetts

A charred beam slanted down from the roof, partially blocking the gap that once marked the store's front entrance. They had to duck as they moved from blazing sunlight into a steamy haze of rancid smoke and stifling humidity. Paul misjudged the distance and scraped his helmet against the rough wood, causing a shower of charcoal shards to rain down on him.

"Step carefully in here," Bree directed. "We've cleared a path but the floor is uneven and the water makes it slick. And watch the wiring overhead—it came down when the ceiling collapsed. The power's off, but you can still get caught in the wires."

Matt, Leigh and the students paused as they took in the devastation.

Debris was piled high all around while open blue sky soared above their heads. Water puddled around their boots on the scorched antique tongue-and-groove floor, and more steadily dripped from the remnants of the roof. Wisps of smoke rose from scorched piles of charred timber, shattered china and twisted metal, and the acrid air reeked of burned wood and plastic.

Leigh's face was pinched and she blinked rapidly. Matt's own eyes stung and watered from the bitter smoke. He let her precede him around what looked like the remains of a glass-topped jewelry display, tipped over in the rubble, its treasures lost in the surrounding chaos. "Try to breathe through your mouth," he murmured, drawing her gaze. "It's like being around decomp. You learn how to make it easier on yourself."

"Thanks." She took a cautious shallow breath through her mouth. "Better. My lungs still burn, but at least it's easier on my nose." She glanced at Bree who stood a few feet away, hands on hips, surveying the damage and totally oblivious to the stench. "How does she do it?"

"I'll bet she's so used to it, she doesn't really notice anymore." Matt turned to study the space around them.

The shop was about twenty-five feet wide. The front of the store was mostly intact, the walls which framed the bottom of the doorway revealing the original cream-colored paint. But from several feet above the floor, the paint was darkly stained with soot and smoke. Heavy soot outlined pale rectangles on the wall, marking where antique paintings and photos hung until fire and blasts of pressurized water displaced them. The front window was shattered, the glass blown outwards to scatter over the sidewalk leaving a rim of vicious teeth biting from the sill.

Juka picked up a twisted piece of metal balanced on scraps of wood and shingles. It was scorched and bent but the original cylindrical shape was still discernible. "I wonder what this was."

Kiko lifted it from his hands and examined it. "A lantern? Maybe one of those old-fashioned punched tin ones that hold a candle? How hot did it get in here that metal melted?"

"It was plenty hot," Bree said. "Somewhere between fourteen hundred and sixteen hundred degrees. But the temperature would have varied around the room. It would have been hottest at the seat of the fire."

"How can you tell where it started?" Matt asked.

"I look for the area of deepest penetration of the fire and the most widespread thermal damage. The longer materials are exposed to heat, the greater the damage. A lantern made of a soft metal like tin would begin to melt at less than five hundred degrees." She pointed at a blackened wall sconce that hung beside the door. "But that lamp on the outside wall didn't melt. It looks like brass, which melts at about sixteen hundred degrees. And the hurricane glass on it would have melted at fourteen hundred degrees. It's only crazed."

"Crazed?" Leigh asked.

"You see the pattern of micro fractures in the glass?"

Matt leaned in to examine the crisscrossing spiderwebs of tiny fractures spanning the glass shade. "That's from heat?"

"It's actually from the sudden change in temperature between the heat of the fire and cold water from the hoses. Depending on the temperature change, the glass might craze or it may simply shatter." She indicated the front window. "Like that."

"That's why the glass is all outside?" Juka asked. "From the water streams inside the store?"

"Yes. We had two attack lines coming into this store—one from the front and one from the back. And then additional lines overhead from the ladders. It wasn't actually the force of the water that shattered the window, although two hundred psi packs a hell of a punch. It's the sudden drop in temperature that weakens the structure. Knowledge about how heat affects materials also helps me determine the point of origin."

"Where's the body?" Matt asked. "I thought I might be able to smell it, but there's just too much sensory overload."

"That's typical. There's a lot of wood in here, but the real stench comes from the polyurethane foam in cushions, and from plastics and other chemicals."

Matt looked over sharply. "Chemicals?"

"They refinished antiques, and the chemicals used were all highly flammable. When we get to the back, you'll see the damage they did. The body is there too." Bree picked her way toward the back of the store. "It was while the guys were clearing debris in here that they found the victim. That's when we called Bailey in."

"Bailey?"

Bree grinned. "Bailey is always my spot of sunshine in a scene like this. She's part of our K-9 unit—an accelerant detection dog. We always use the K-9 team when there's a fatality or if we suspect arson. Unfortunately, there was so much background from all the refinishing chemicals in the store, she alerted multiple times but never in the place I've identified as the point of origin."

As they moved toward the back, light flooded in from the rear of the building. Blackened studs outlining a doorway marked the separating wall to a back room. Inside, the crumpled remains of a garage-style door lay in strips on the floor, the freshly cut edges razor sharp. The rear wall of the store was almost completely destroyed.

"As you can see, the fire had a really strong foothold back here," Bree said. "Unfortunately, as we often see in historic buildings, there was no centralized sprinkler or fire detection system in place. Since it's not required by law, many owners skip retrofitting because of the cost. Add to that a single common attic stretching the length of the building, and the fire spread unchecked in all directions."

The smell hit Matt in that instant—the sickly sweet scent of roasted flesh that made saliva pool in his mouth even as his stomach rolled. It had been years since he'd run experiments at the University of Tennessee's Body Farm using burned cadavers, but he never forgot the smell. He'd gone off Canadian bacon for years afterwards as a result. As he scanned the surrounding debris, his gaze finally came to rest on blackened flesh camouflaged by scorched wood.

The burned bulk of a large wooden box—perhaps a cabinet or a wardrobe—lay on the floor, but there was no mistaking the body partially pinned underneath. The victim lay on its side, the upper body charred deep black. One forearm was curled up and pulled into the chest, but it ended abruptly at the wrist. Instead of a hand, the exposed flesh had split over the ends of the long bones in the arm, curling away to reveal glimpses of white. The torso was a mass of striated muscle and charred intestine disappearing underneath the wardrobe.

Leigh gave a choked gasp from behind him and he turned to see her eyes fixed unblinkingly on the victim, her sheet-white face tinged with green. He reached out to touch her arm, stopping at the last second as he realized his gloved fingers were black with soot and grit from maneuvering through the debris. Instead, he rubbed the back of his hand against her upper arm. "You okay?"

It took her a moment to answer, and she swallowed audibly first. "Yeah." The word came out as a half croak. She sucked in a breath, her eyes going wide as the putrid smoke filled her lungs. She coughed raggedly several times. "You warned me it was going to be rough."

"First burn victim?" Bree asked.

"Yes." Leigh's voice wobbled but she doggedly stepped forward to take a closer look.

"Rowe did an initial examination but said right away that he'd need a forensic anthropologist," Bree said.

Matt stepped into the debris, skirting the rubble along the

very narrow area around the body. He squatted down beside the torso. "This is CGS-3. Definitely outside his expertise."

Bree crouched down across from him. "That was my estimate too."

"CGS-3?" Leigh asked.

"It's the Crow-Glassman standardized scale for burned bodies. One is the least severe and five is the worst—essentially a cremation. Three means there is significant loss of tissue, including disarticulation of some body parts, and a visual ID isn't immediately possible from the remains." Matt looked up at Kiko. "We're going to need to do a skull reconstruction."

"I agree," Kiko said, "but it's going to be a challenge. Even if we can find all the pieces, the bone is going to be calcined."

Leigh slid in beside Matt, bracing her hand on his shoulder to lean over the body. "What happened to the head? Blunt force trauma?"

The forehead and top of the cranium were missing above the startlingly white bone rimming the eye sockets, exposing the mass of charred brain tissue. Below the eye sockets, the fleshy cheeks were burned a deep, leathery black. "Could be, but I doubt it. That's typical fire damage."

"The infamous exploding skull," Bree said.

Leigh glanced from Bree to Matt. "Exploding skull?"

"People think the skull fractures like that because pressure builds up as the brain boils, causing the head to explode," Bree explained. "Somehow they seem to forget that the skull has several natural openings that allow the steam to vent."

"There's actually a very simple explanation," Matt said. "Skin burns first, then the muscle and fat underneath. In areas like the forehead, there is very little fat and muscle below the skin, so the organic components in the bone start to burn quickly. When the organic components are gone, what's left is calcined bone—the mineral scaffold which is extremely brittle and shatters easily under any pressure."

"Like from a water stream or the roof collapsing," Bree supplied.

Leigh leaned closer to the body. Matt reached up to steady her as her eyes locked on the torso where it disappeared under the wardrobe. "See something?" he asked.

"There's something buried in the chest."

Matt stretched upward, trying to peer over the side of the corpse. "I can't see from this angle. What is it?"

"There's a lot of damage and the upper body is curled in on itself, but it looks like a knife." She paused. "It's just . . ."

"What?"

Leigh remained silent for a moment, then she straightened. "Let's wait until the body is out from under all this. We'll see better then."

"Rowe told us to leave the wardrobe in place because he didn't want to risk scattering body parts until you got here," Bree said. "But when you're ready, I'll pull in some guys to move it. Even mostly burned, I'll bet that thing still weighs a few hundred pounds."

"We're going to see fractures from it," Paul said. "That thing could crush a living person, forget about fire-damaged bone."

"I didn't think about that." Leigh eyed its bulk critically. "It looks solid. Are you going to be able to tell trauma injuries from fire injuries?"

"Absolutely. It's all about fracture speed. It's also how I'll be able to tell when the head injury occurred, but we're going to need to find all the pieces of the skull to do that." Matt straightened and Leigh stepped back into the main pathway to give him room. He started to follow and then stopped, his eyes fixed on the corpse, his brows drawn together in confusion. "What's that?"

"What's what?" Leigh asked.

Bracing his hands on his knees, he leaned over. "There's something under the body."

"Debris?" Bree asked.

"No, it's . . . fleshy. Charred flesh, but definitely muscle tissue."

"Disarticulation?" Kiko asked. She moved to the other side of the body for a better view. "You mean partially tucked under the wardrobe?"

"Yeah."

Kiko squinted at it. "I see it. I don't think that's from our vic." She glanced up at Matt, the corners of her eyes creased in concern. "You're thinking a second body."

"Too small for an adult. It could be a child, or, worse, a baby."

Kiko winced and lost a bit more color.

"I guess we'll find out soon enough. When the morgue techs get here, the first thing we'll do is move the wardrobe and transfer the victim to a body bag. That will give us a clear view of what's underneath. And then the real work begins."

"Oh yeah," Paul said. "And that's going to take hours."

"Why will it take hours *after* the body is secured?" Leigh asked.

"Because that's only part of the remains." Matt sidled out of the debris. "I can already see we're missing both hands, one forearm, and some of the skull. We won't know if the feet are intact until we move the wardrobe. Those missing bones didn't burn away, they're simply scattered around the body where they fell when the tissue was incinerated. But before we release the site, we need to find every piece of bone and tissue we can. And that means searching and sifting." Matt turned to Bree. "We're going to need artificial lighting brought in. Otherwise, once we lose the sun, we'll be working blind."

"We have portable lights and generators. I'll make sure you

have what you need."

"Thanks."

"We'll have to do an examination to establish cause of death. Do you have any idea how the fire started?" Leigh asked Bree.

"Not yet." Bree turned to face a large pile of debris. "But this is definitely the point of origin."

Leigh scanned the debris and what was left of the walls around it but didn't see anything in the charred materials that set this area apart from the rest of the store. "You're sure? The back of the building is in even worse shape. You said that the longer the fire burns, the hotter it gets and the more damage is done."

"True, but you're not accounting for the fire load—the amount of flammable material in an area. The showroom was full of wood, fabric, foam cushions, and carpet. But the workroom was full of stain, lacquer, varnish, and paint thinner." Stepping a few feet to her right, she plucked a can from the rubble. The lid was gone and the upper edges of the can blossomed outwards in razor-sharp petals.

Paul whistled sharply. "That can essentially became a bomb. What's it made out of—stainless steel?"

"That would be my guess. The heat of the fire caused the contents to reach their flashpoint—the temperature where a flammable liquid will ignite. But trapped inside the can, the chemicals essentially became explosive from the pressure buildup. Projectiles like this ripped away at the walls in the back area, further weakening the structure. And then there's the dumpster."

Matt peered over Bree's shoulder. Outside, behind what was left of the wall, a large metal dumpster smoldered. "What was in that?"

"Pretty much everything that shouldn't be," Bree said in disgust. "Discarded cans, dirty rags, scraps of wood. When it went up, it just added to the fire load on that back wall."

"So add all that together," Matt said, "and you've got an accelerated fire, but not necessarily the point of origin."

"That's exactly my thinking. You have to realize how flames move in a fire—up and out, just like the smoke and gases that are produced. So a fire on the floor may have a very small ignition point, but from there, the smoke and heat will rise up and out, creating a V pattern."

"And you can see that pattern in this room?" Leigh stood with her hands on her hips, scanning the area around them. "I'm totally missing it."

"That's because the key here is that part of the pattern is missing. When these buildings were built in the nineteenth century, typical construction involved lath and plaster for the inside walls. Look right there—" Bree pointed to a section on the wall, where the plaster had crumbled away to reveal scorched studs and strips of lath. "—and you can see part of the V." She held up her hands, the heels pressed together, palms spread in a V shape and examined the wall through them. She pointed to the outside edge of the shape. "As we move out from the rough centerline of the V, more and more lath remains."

"There's a void on one side," Matt said, studying the area critically. "Could there have been something else there? Something else that deflected the flames, or burned and has now collapsed?" He critically studied the piles of debris in front of that section of wall. "Hold on. The wardrobe. It was standing against that wall."

"That's my guess, and I'll confirm it with the owner, if this isn't him or her. If so, then part of the V pattern is on one side of the wardrobe, but, as it burned, it became unsteady and toppled over, either during the fire, or when we extinguished it."

"Is it definitely arson?" Juka asked.

"It's too soon to be definitive. But I can tell you this from past experience—when a fire starts accidentally, if someone is in the room with it, they either try to put it out or run like hell. They don't usually stand there and let themselves burn to death."

"But when someone is already dead or unconscious and a fire is set to hide the evidence and the identity of the victim, you'd want that victim as close to the fire as possible," Leigh said.

"Right. Once the body's removed, I'll be doing my own investigation of the site looking specifically for an incendiary device. Are you ready for me to send in the crime scene guys? They did initial pictures with Rowe, but they'll want to shoot more while you remove the body and do your search."

Matt glanced at his students—they were ready. "Let's get started."

Sunday, 7:17 p.m.
Wharf Street
Salem, Massachusetts

Matt slammed the door on the coroner's van and gave it two sharp raps with his fist. The van pulled away into the darkening evening and disappeared around the corner as it left the wharf and headed back to Boston.

He made quick work of shedding his Tyvek jumpsuit, rolling it up inside out and jamming it in a nearby trash can. He tugged at the neck of his T-shirt, trying to separate the material from his sweaty skin. The fall breeze felt refreshingly cool against his overheated body after hours inside the steamy fire scene.

He walked over to where his students stood on the green space by the wharf, stripping out of their suits and chugging the water bottles Bree had provided. "Good work today, guys. We'll pick this up again tomorrow at nine. I'll call Rowe tonight when

43

I get home, and we'll decide where to go from here."

"What about starting with an autopsy?" Paul suggested, grinning at Juka.

"Funny," Matt said dryly. "Yes, a standard autopsy will be done, but I have something else in mind first. I'd like to do a 3D autopsy using the MRI facility at Mass Gen. We can reconstruct the body from the inside out before Rowe even picks up a scalpel. It will show bone damage as well as soft tissue damage in layered 3D. It might even show us the cause of death if the fire itself wasn't responsible."

Kiko whistled. "Sounds cool."

"I've never done it myself, but I've seen papers on it. This would be the perfect time to try it out."

"What about the dog?" Juka asked.

Matt thought of the tiny charred body they'd unearthed beneath the victim. He needed to actually examine the bones to confirm, but he was ninety-five percent certain it was a small dog. "Too pricey and time consuming to use on the dog. We'll necropsy it the old-fashioned way. I don't know if it's a clue or collateral damage, but either way, it's evidence."

"Too bad there wasn't a tag," Paul commented. "That might have given us victim ID."

"We're never that lucky," Matt said dryly. "Now, everybody got a ride home?" There were nods all around in response. "Great. I'll see you tomorrow."

He swung his bag onto his shoulder and started down the street, past the last engine still on site and around the corner. Leigh's midnight-blue Crown Victoria sat at the curb halfway down the street. Her car was draped in long shadows between the streetlights, so he didn't see the top half of Leigh's body hidden inside the car until he was almost beside her. He lowered his bag silently to the concrete as she backed out of the passenger side and slammed the door.

She let out a gasp of surprise when his hands landed firmly on her hips, spinning her to press her back against her vehicle. He stepped into her, trapping her between cool metal and warm skin.

"Matt!" Her hands slapped against his chest. "What are you doing?"

"Huddling over charred remains wasn't exactly how I envisioned our date ending. I'm trying to recoup some of our day." He moved closer.

She pushed back against him, and he allowed her an inch of space. "I'm filthy. I'm covered with soot and God knows what else. And I'm sweaty."

He grinned at her, thinking that the dark smear along her cheek was an endearing testament to hours of hot, miserable work. "So what? I am too. It was a hundred degrees inside that scene and a steam bath to boot. Relax. You're not going to make me dirtier than I already am. And my olfactory sense got blown out in there. If we smell sweaty, my nose won't notice for at least another twelve hours."

Ignoring her halfhearted, spluttered protests, he leaned in, using his body to hold her still while he cupped her jaw in his hands, his fingers slipping gently under her hair. He brushed his lips over hers, feeling her still instantly. Her body remained frozen, her hands pressing against his chest for only a moment, then she relaxed into him, one hand sliding over the damp cotton of his T-shirt into the hair at the nape of his neck, pulling him closer as her lips opened under his.

His fingers gripped her hips reflexively, holding her tighter, simultaneously reveling in the length of her pressed fully against him and cursing their lack of privacy on a public street—

"Matt, I forgot to ask. Did you want to meet at the lab or at the ME's office . . ." Suddenly spotlighted in the warm glow of a streetlight, Kiko stammered to a halt as she came close enough to the couple tucked into the shadows to realize she was interrupting a private moment. "Wow. Sorry. Never mind, then. I'll just touch base with you tomorrow morning. As you were." With a wide grin, she spun and jogged off down the sidewalk.

Matt tipped his head down to rest his forehead against Leigh's. A puff of air feathered over his lips as she let out a frustrated laugh. "Foiled again. We're never going to get a moment alone at this rate."

He tipped up her chin with a finger and pressed a soft kiss to her lips before he reluctantly released her and stepped back. "Not that this is the time or the place, but I just couldn't help myself."

"Typical man," Leigh scoffed, but her eyes were smiling as she lightly ran her fingers down his forearm. "When are we going to try to make up that date?"

"When we're on a case? Your guess is as good as mine. But I'll make you a deal. The first evening we both have free, even if it's just to steal a few hours at the end of the day, let's do something, just the two of us."

"Deal. You need a lift to your SUV?"

"Nah, it's just a block away and I'm enjoying the cool air after all that heat and humidity. Give me a call tomorrow morning and I'll let you know what Rowe and I decided. Have a good night."

He gave her a gentle push toward the driver's side door and then stood by as she started the car and waved through the windshield. He watched until her taillights disappeared from view around the corner.

After picking up his bag, he made his way into the deeper shadows of the night.

CHAPTER FOUR:
VENTILATION

Ventilation: the operation of opening or removing windows and doors, and cutting holes in the highest points of the structure to clear smoke from a building.

Monday, 10:55 a.m.
Office of the Chief Medical Examiner
Boston, Massachusetts

Matt pushed through the door of the autopsy suite just as Leigh turned the corner at the end of the hallway. "Good timing. I was just going to call."

Leigh glanced at her watch. "I thought we weren't starting till eleven."

"We aren't. But Rowe's champing at the bit to begin and I want to review the 3D autopsy results first."

"It's already done?"

"Rowe pulled a few strings after I called him last night. He knows someone in the radiology department at Mass Gen who arranged time for us on the scanner at six this morning. I owe the guy a bottle of Glenfiddich for sneaking us in so quickly and then doing the analysis right away."

"Let's take a look, then." Leigh reached for the door handle, but Matt put a hand against the door, holding it closed. "What?"

"I just want to warn you. This is going to be unpleasant."

She frowned. "Autopsies always are."

"I know how much they bother you. But even with full

ventilation, it's bad."

"I smelled the body yesterday."

"You smelled the fire yesterday. This could put you off pork indefinitely. Just be prepared."

Entering the autopsy suite, the smell of charred flesh assaulted Leigh. Her gorge rose and she swallowed hard to keep it down. Across the room, Kiko, Paul and Juka stood clustered together in a tight knot; none of them even glanced in the direction of the body lying on its side on the table. She forced herself to look, struck afresh with horror by the dark, crusty tissue, the contracted, curled limbs, arched spine, and charred, shattered skull. More pieces of the skull lay on a tray on a nearby countertop. The small, charred body of the dog lay on a tray on a second autopsy table.

Already gowned and gloved, Dr. Edward Rowe gave her a nod of greeting. "Good, we're all here. Abbott, did Lowell explain what he's showing us this morning?"

"I think I've got the gist of it—a virtual autopsy in three dimensions done by X-ray."

Matt motioned Leigh and Rowe over to the counter that held his laptop, his students following. "That's right. This procedure gives us the ability to look at a certain part of the body based on its ability to block X-rays. We'll be able to see both soft tissue and bone damage in layered 3D."

"Why did you go to all this trouble?" Leigh asked. "I mean, we're doing a real autopsy anyway."

"This actually provides more information than the real autopsy. Remember, the body is so badly damaged from the fire that simple things like gender and age are completely masked."

"But I've seen you figure out age and sex from just the bones."

"Sure, but these bones are so fragile, they could be destroyed when we strip them. The 3D autopsy gives such detailed information that I can virtually visualize the landmarks I need to make my estimates without ever physically handling the bones."

Matt opened a series of windows and an image of the victim spread across his screen in tones of gray. The external form was clearly visible, depicting the exaggerated positioning and rough texturing of the burned tissue. "As you can see, the 3D recreation is very realistic. But from here we can go inside the body." With a few clicks, Matt brought up the skeletal components of the body and zoomed in on the pelvis. "I had an hour or so with the scans this morning, so I can tell you from the skeletal structure of the pelvis and the intact section of the skull that our victim is female. From the pubic symphysis and the sternal end of the fourth rib, I'd place age between early forties and early fifties."

Rowe whistled. "Now I see why you were pushing for this. I guarantee I'd never be able to get that close. Could you clearly visualize the bone trauma?"

"Yes." Matt opened up a new window, a view of the skeletal torso. The blade of the knife was clearly visible as a solid white lance sliding between two ribs. "The blade enters between the fourth and fifth ribs, just to the left of the sternum piercing the left ventricle of the heart." He pointed out the contact point and everyone leaned in, squinting. "But if you pull back and look at the rib cage, minus the knife—" *Click.* Another window. "—you can see that this wasn't the only knife strike.

"There's a break in the shaft of the third rib, and the ends of ribs two and three show nicks near the sternum. And this furrow?" Matt pointed to a jagged mark on the surface of the sternum, mid-chest. "That's where the knife tip skidded across the surface before penetrating the chest wall. It looks like three knife strikes before the final blow where the knife was planted. Of the four blows, at least three of them pierced the heart." Another view, this time showing the internal tissues. "And if you look here and here, those are tissue infiltrates. Blood clots, basically."

"So the vic was alive when she was stabbed," Leigh stated. "But was she alive when the fire started?"

"That would depend on the lag time between the knifing and the fire," Rowe said. "With the heart pierced, she would have bled out within two minutes, tops. But if the victim was alive and breathing at the time of the fire, the heat would have seared the tissues in the nose and throat, and the smoke will have left visible traces of soot in the airway and lungs. If those tissues are clear, then that knife is your murder weapon."

Leigh walked back to the autopsy table. The dark handle of a knife was clearly visible in the bright examination lights, the hilt protruding from the corpse mid-chest. *God, I hope she was dead long before the fire did this.*

The hilt of the knife was smooth, but just above the pommel was a symbol, mostly obscured by blackened flesh. "Have you taken pictures of the weapon in place?"

"Yes, all external photos are done." Rowe circled the table to join her.

Leigh leaned in to examine the knife more closely, but the strong scent of roasted flesh drove her backward, nearly choking on a gag. She turned her face away in hopes of clearer air, inhaling through clenched teeth. "There's a symbol on the base of the blade." Her words came out half strangled, so she cleared her throat and tried again. "It may help identify who owned it."

"Let me remove it so you can get a better look." Rowe grasped the handle of the knife in one large hand. Carefully and slowly, he pulled it from the corpse; it came loose with a soft sucking sound. He held it flat across both palms for her to see.

Although heavily coated with soot and charred bits of tissue, the hilt of the knife was made of smooth black stone that ended in a pointed, textured silver tip. An upturned crescent moon cradled a five-pointed star enclosed in a circle at the base of the four-inch blade.

Paul leaned in from one side. "Is that a pentagram? We've got a devil worshipper on our hands?"

After pulling on a pair of latex gloves, Leigh took the knife. She held it under the exam lights, turning it back and forth. "It's actually a pentacle. A pentagram is the star if it's missing the circle. I know some Satanists use pentacles pointed down and superimposed with the head of a goat, but those in the Craft would tell you an upside-down pentacle is simply that: upside-down. This is a sacred Witchcraft faith symbol. And the weapon is an athame, a double-bladed ceremonial knife and one of the four elemental tools in the Craft—athame, wand, pentacle and chalice."

There was a moment of stunned silence. "And you know this how?" Matt finally asked.

"Because I was a cop's kid in Salem. Other kids rebelled by smoking, drinking or doing drugs. A cop's kid knows they're basically under surveillance by every other cop in the district 24/7. If I pulled some stunt, my father would have known about it from his cronies before I was even brought down to the station. So my teenage rebellion phase consisted of dabbling in Witchcraft. They don't call us 'The Witch City' for nothing." She looked up to find everyone staring at her with varying expressions of surprise. "What?"

Matt let out a small laugh. "I would have never pegged you for that. The robes and the hat and the spells?"

"See, that's where outsiders have ideas about Witches that are completely wrong. Anyone who's been to Salem has seen Witches. Robes are optional. Most dress just like you do, so I guarantee you've passed them on the street. They live and work and worship, just like anyone else."

"I'm sure they do," Matt clarified. "I'm not making fun. It's just that you seem too down to earth for that."

"And maybe that's why it didn't stick. But I can still do a mean tarot reading to tell you your past, present and possibly your future."

Matt crossed his arms over his chest. *"Really?"*

She gave him a pointed look. "Maybe we could circle back to the evidence now?"

"Do Witches use knives in their ceremonies?" Paul stared at the blackened blade, suspicion darkening his face.

"It's never used as a cutting tool. It represents fire and is used to channel psychic energy."

Matt let out a half laugh he abruptly tried to stifle.

Leigh fixed him with a dark stare that had him coloring slightly. "I know this isn't going to be your thing. You're too grounded and far too based in science to accept their beliefs, but respect them for what they are."

Looking chastened, Matt gave a short nod.

"It's used for casting ritual circles, charging water in the chalice or inscribing candles," she continued. "Another tool—a curved sickle called a boline—is used for cutting twine and herbs. But they're never used as weapons. If any ceremonial blade comes into contact with human blood, even from an accidental cut while handling, its power dissipates and it can't be used in any further rituals. It would be discarded immediately."

"This knife could lead us straight to the murderer," Kiko said. "I've seen these knives in the Witch shops; they come in every design imaginable. If you can find out who owned this specific one, it should be a solid starting point."

"It might not be that simple," Leigh said. "It could be the murderer's, but it could also be the victim's, or someone else's entirely." Leigh carefully sealed the athame in an evidence bag and handed it to Matt to examine. "I'll start surveying Witch shops this afternoon to see if anyone recognizes it. Is there anything else we need to know from the virtual autopsy? What about the skull damage? Could you tell if that injury happened before or after the fire?"

"I can't tell that yet," Matt said. "We'll deflesh and examine any bone if either the virtual or hands-on autopsy shows a traumatic mark. So far, it appears that only the head, thorax and pelvis are affected. At this point, I'd chalk the pelvic injuries up to the wardrobe collapsing, but I need to substantiate that. We'll leave that discussion until we can get the bone under the scanning electron microscope and show you the results. It'll be easier to explain that way."

"And the animal? You're sure it's a dog?"

"Ninety percent of the bones that come into an ME's office are actually animal bones. Forensic anthropologists are trained to identify one from the other as that's a lot of what we do. Once I have the skeleton to work with, I'll know for sure. I won't be able to guarantee a specific breed, but I should be able to ballpark a few that might match."

Leigh indicated the knife in Matt's hands. "What about trauma?"

"There are no signs of a knife wound. But from the X-rays, it looks like someone went to town on that dog. The skull was completely shattered, which I suspect happened before the fire started."

Leigh glanced back toward the dark nightmare huddled on the table. She knew she was stalling but she simply couldn't help herself. "Okay, so for the human victim we've got a start on age and sex. But what about an ID? Are we going to be able to use dental in this case?"

"I had a cursory look while we were doing photos," Rowe said. "There is definitely damage to the teeth, but I got a glimpse of some melted dental work that looks relatively intact. We have X-rays, so once we have a better idea of who we're looking at, I should be able to use dentition to back it up. If not, there's always DNA."

Leigh looked up sharply. "You'd still be able to run DNA on tissue like that? It's not destroyed?"

"A lot of it certainly is, but if we sample far enough into the body, we'll avoid thermal damage. There might be blood left in the cardiac chamber. If not there, then deep quadriceps muscle should do."

Matt touched Leigh's arm. "Same deal as last time? Duplicate samples—one to Boston University and one to the state lab?"

Leigh nodded. "That worked well. I still don't have the state lab results back from the Bradford case, but you guys had it to me inside of a week." She turned back to Rowe. "Any identifying marks on the victim's body you could see that might help in going through missing-person reports?"

"Any dermal markings would be obliterated by now. There was no jewelry found on the body, but both hands were disarticulated around the remains. If there were any rings, they would have been scattered with the bones."

"We went around the victim, thoroughly screening and sieving everything," Matt said. "We recovered all the disarticulated carpals and tarsals and phalanges, but there was no sign of any jewelry."

"Maybe the murderer removed them?" Juka said.

Leigh slowly turned around. As he so often did, Juka stood a step back from the group, always watchful, but often silent. "You're thinking burglary?"

Juka shook his head. "If burglary was the motive, there was jewelry mingled in the debris that was likely more valuable. But if the murderer burned the victim to hide her identity, he wouldn't want to leave any unique pieces, like a ring or a watch, on the body. So perhaps he removed them before setting the fire."

"I agree. Also, this killing says 'premeditated' to me. The design of that knife is modern so it's unlikely it would have been for sale in the antique shop. I'll check that with the owner, but if not, then the murderer brought it to the scene."

"Do Witches carry an athame at all times?" Paul asked. "Could it have been a heat-of-the-moment kind of killing?"

Leigh shook her head. "No, an athame is a ceremonial dagger only. Most Witches leave it on their altar when it's not in use. It's a message. Someone is either telling us something or was telling the victim."

"Are we ready to start, then?" Matt gave her a rueful smile.

Apparently, her stall tactics hadn't fooled him. Leigh stifled a sigh and gave a curt nod. *Let's get this over with.*

Matt pulled a surgical gown from a hook on the wall, slipped it on and tied it closed. He gloved up, and then he and Rowe both donned safety glasses and masks.

Leigh stepped back to stay out of splash range and Matt's students gathered around her. Kiko's lips were pinched together and she was breathing too quickly through her nose. Both Paul and Juka stood stock still, but Paul's gaze occasionally strayed toward the door as if longing for escape.

"You guys are doing great," Leigh said, *sotto voce* so Rowe couldn't hear them. These kids were used to bones, but in the last few weeks they'd dealt with mutilated, bloody and burned corpses. They'd impressed her with their staunch staying power, even through the worst of it all.

Matt and Rowe carefully rolled the victim onto her back, allowing Rowe access to the thoracic cavity. Beside Leigh, Paul made a strangled sound, his eyes locked on the corpse. Lying on its back, the body seemed even more contorted, arms curled in to protect itself, legs frozen in midair, spine arched as if on a scream of agony.

Leigh closed her eyes, but the vision followed her into the

dark. So she opened them and watched Rowe start to cut into the charred flesh, praying her stomach wouldn't betray her distress.

CHAPTER FIVE:
GRIMOIRE

Grimoire: information about rituals and the magical properties of natural objects collected in book form for a Witch's reference. Also called the *Book of Shadows.*

Monday, 3:20 p.m.
Draw Down the Moon Witch Shoppe
Salem, Massachusetts

The moment Leigh stepped into the shop, she felt herself drawn back to earlier times. The complex mixture of smells—incense, scented candles, bags of herbs and oils—and the gentle notes of the pan flute hanging almost motionless in the air evoked a rush of memories from her teen years. Her eyelids slid closed as she drew in a breath full of magic and familiarity, her lips curving in a smile. They'd been good times, and even though she hadn't remained in the coven, she'd never forgotten the lessons about community, tolerance and outward giving.

She opened her eyes, her shifting gaze touching briefly on familiar objects. The shop was filled to overflowing, but didn't seem cluttered. Colorful hand-decorated potion bottles sat under bright lights in a glass display cabinet. Nearby, shelves of tiny vials of golden oils waited to be mixed into custom potions. Pentacles and crystals hung from heavy cords, dangling in a shining row from a long wooden dowel suspended from the ceiling. Baskets of spell kits—containing a candle, mixed herbs, an amulet and instructions—promised help in love, a career, glamour or empowerment.

Leigh spotted the shopkeeper standing behind the counter, deep in conversation with a couple, the only customers in the store. Of the half dozen Witchcraft shops in Salem, this was the oldest and largest. She had high hopes of getting answers here and not having to spend her day running all over town.

"—crystals are conductors of energy," the tall, graceful Witch behind the counter told the couple as Leigh approached. "Or wear them on your body to direct energy and healing to that location. You can plant them in your garden to encourage a fruitful growing season. I keep crystals in the four corners of my house for protection."

The Witch was dressed in a draping black blouse and a long flowing black peasant skirt, the bottom embossed with crescent moons and Celtic knots that fluttered and swayed as she moved.

Leigh stood patiently while the couple purchased a selection of crystals. Then the Witch turned to Leigh. "Can I help you?"

Leigh held up her badge. "I'm Trooper Leigh Abbott of the Massachusetts State Police. I'm looking for some assistance on a case."

The woman cocked her head slightly, her dark hair rolling off her shoulder to tumble down her back. "Elanthia Wakefield. I'm not sure how I can be of assistance in a police investigation."

Leigh glanced back to make sure the shop was now empty. "I have a piece of evidence I'd like you to look at." She laid her messenger bag on the glass counter, under which silver jewelry sparkled.

"Do you mind if I ask what kind of investigation this is?"

"Not at all. It's a murder investigation." Shock flared in Elanthia's eyes for a brief moment before the Witch quickly composed herself. Leigh opened her bag and pulled out the knife, charred and blackened, still sealed in the evidence bag that bore her notes and initials. "This was found at a murder scene. I recognized the symbol of Hecate immediately. I was wondering if you carried an athame like it or recognized the design."

Elanthia took the knife, and studied it closely. "You're familiar with our Craft?" Her gaze flicked to Leigh before dropping back to the blade in her hands.

Leigh's face heated. "I . . . was involved in my teen years. But . . ."

"No need to be embarrassed. If you were once a part of us, then you know that we don't judge. If the Craft is right for you, then you'll return to us when the time is right. We'll still be here." She turned the knife over in her long, slender hands, running the pad of her index finger over the hilt of the knife. "I recognize this blade. It was a beautiful piece."

"We believe it's the murder weapon."

One brow arched gracefully. "I may be able to help you. If it's the athame I think it is, it's one of a kind." She set the knife on the counter. "I need to check my sales book to be sure. I'll be a few minutes. Feel free to browse the shop." Elanthia disappeared into a back room.

Leigh tucked the knife safely back into her bag, then slowly wandered through the store, idly picking up an item here or there and finally stopping in front of the shop altar. It was set up under a lace-draped window, and a beam of dappled sunlight fell over the midnight-blue altar cloth, highlighting the Tree of Life at its center, stitched in gold. She flashed back to the altar that once graced her bedroom—black cauldron, athame, white and black candles, silver chalice, a small brass bell, several quartz crystals, and her wand. She ran her fingertips along the edge of the brass pentacle tile that lay in the middle of the altar. The metal was warm beneath her touch, lit by the beam of sunlight.

"You miss it."

Leigh whirled to find Elanthia beside her, a black book folded against her breasts. "What?"

"You may no longer be a member of the Craft, but a part of you misses it."

"I haven't thought about it for over ten years. But when I look back . . ." She trailed off, frowning. When Elanthia stayed silent, Leigh glanced over, sensing the question in the other woman's patient gaze. "When I look back I realize how much being part of the community helped me through my teen years. I went from being without a mother to having countless mothers to guide and comfort me. It was . . . a family, of sorts, a sisterhood when all I had was my father. Kind of makes me wish I had that now." She laughed uncomfortably. "I have no idea why I'm telling you this."

"The heart knows who it can trust. You picked a difficult career path. There must not be many women in your department."

"I'm it."

"Really. And your father?"

"He died in the line of duty four years ago."

Sympathy shadowed Elanthia's face. "I'm sorry for your loss."

Leigh pulled herself ramrod straight. "That's the way life goes, isn't it?" she said, struggling to contain the dogged grief that never seemed to fully heal. "Did you find something?"

"I did." Elanthia led the way back to the counter, where she opened the book. "That knife is indeed a unique item. It was commissioned by one of my customers nearly a year ago from a local metalsmith who does custom work with gemstone handles."

"Sounds expensive."

"It was. But Moira could afford it."

"A woman ordered it? You're certain?"

"Yes." Elanthia suddenly went absolutely still. "Your victim is

60

a woman." It was a flat statement, not a question.

"I'm afraid I can't reveal that at this point in the investigation."

The Witch considered her for a moment before slowly turning back to the book. She ran an index finger down the ledger until she came to the entry she was looking for. "Moira Simpson commissioned that knife last January. It was delivered to her in March." She picked up the blade again, peering through the plastic. "High-chromium stainless-steel blade with a handle of midnight stone. Personalized with the sign of Hecate."

"High-chromium stainless steel? That seems unusual for such a traditional piece."

"It was unusual and very expensive. A custom piece. But all Moira's orders were custom."

Leigh studied the other woman, noting the disapproving set of her mouth and the restless drum of her fingers against the ledger. "You didn't like her."

"I'm not saying that."

"Your body language is."

Elanthia sighed. "You know we of the Craft believe in 'live and let live.' But I confess to being human and somewhat annoyed at Moira's motives."

"Motives? In what way?"

"Moira approached me last year, just before Yule. She wanted to explore the Craft and asked to join our coven as an initiate."

"Most covens maintain their maximum membership. You had room in yours at the time?"

"Normally we have thirteen members, one for each moon of the year, but we'd lost a few. One from a battle with cancer, one moved out of state with her job. Moira said all the right things and seemed very sincere, so we welcomed her in for a year and a day."

"The initiation period before a member formally joins."

"Yes. But we knew long before that that Moira wasn't going to work out. My first clue should have been orders like this." She tapped an index finger on the sales book.

"Orders?"

"This isn't the only piece this metalsmith made for her. There's a matching boline, made with the same materials. And she commissioned her wand from him as well. It was a lovely design, made out of twisted threads of metal, in silver, to match her athame and boline. She also commissioned ceremonial robes; hired someone in Boston for that work." Her lips pursed, then released. "Only the best would do for Moira."

"She must have been well-off to afford items like that."

"Her husband Stephen was killed in an industrial accident a few months before their only son was born. Moira sued and was awarded a huge settlement. She's never had to work a day since. And now that her son is grown and has moved out on his own, Moira has time to spare for whatever activity catches her eye. Until a few weeks ago, that was us."

"She's not with the coven anymore?"

"No. It became clear almost immediately that Moira was all about the symbols, rather than the substance of our Craft. You know we keep our covens small, and she saw a small group as an easy way to move up the ranks, so to speak."

"But there are no ranks in a coven. Unless things have changed, duties within a coven are all divided up equally. There is no designated leader and all responsibilities are shared."

"That's exactly how things still are. Because of that division of labor, it takes energy and commitment to be a member of a coven. In the end, Moira wasn't willing to do what needed to be done."

Leigh pulled out her notepad and started to make notes. "And your coven is . . ."

"The Circle of the Triple Goddess. It's an all-female coven.

I'd be happy to provide the names of current members."

"That would be very helpful. What happened several weeks ago?"

"Moira got into an argument with one of our members about our activities within the community. We believe in giving back in any way that we can, but she was highly disapproving of some of the community groups we aided. She was all for assisting abused women and orphans, but when it came to AIDS patients or those trying to reintegrate into society after serving time in prison, she thought it looked bad. We believe that anyone who needs help or is genuinely trying to start over and atone for previous wrongdoings is worthy of assistance. When we were unwilling to bend to her 'rules,' she quit the group."

"Saving you the trouble of asking her to leave," Leigh said.

"At that point, I have to admit that I was considering casting a spell for the good of all to change the situation. But in the end, she left us first."

"Have you heard from her since?"

Elanthia closed the sales book with an aggressive *snap*. "Only by way of others."

"Meaning?" Leigh asked.

"I've heard through the grapevine that she's talking badly about the Circle as well as its members to anyone who will listen."

"Angering members of the Circle?"

Elanthia looked at her sharply. "Enough to commit murder? Assuming that's who your victim is, that's simply not our way. Harm to none and good to all. Let me assure you that no one in the Craft would resort to murder. We would have other . . . ways."

"You'd be surprised what people can be pushed to. Could you give me a description of her?"

"I'd place Moira in her early to mid forties. She spent a

fortune on spa treatments and expensive makeup, but a woman knows. About five foot four or five and maybe a hundred and twenty pounds? Salon-streaked shoulder-length blond hair, blue eyes. Wears designer clothes and carries a handbag with a price tag that would feed a family of four for several months." She frowned. "I'm sorry, that was unkind."

"But honest. Did she own a dog?"

Elanthia paused for a few beats too long before answering. "She owned a Pomeranian named Maxie. She doted on that dog like it was her child."

"You didn't like it?"

"I try not to dislike anything or anyone, but that dog was . . . aggressive. Little and yippy and it would take your finger off if you dared touch it."

"Sounds charming."

"Not particularly. But speaking of her actual child, if you really suspect that Moira is your victim, you'll want to talk to her son, Flynn." She slipped a black address book from beneath the counter. "I'll make you that list now." Head down, she started a column of names and telephone numbers.

"Let me start with you, then. Where were you between midnight and four thirty on Sunday morning?"

Elanthia looked up sharply, realization dawning in her eyes. "We're all suspects."

"If the victim is confirmed to be Moira Simpson, then she was killed with a tool of the Craft after breaking from the coven and expressing her negative feelings about it. I have to consider the possibility."

The Witch remained motionless, except for the steady *tap tap tap* of her pen tip against the paper. "Of course you do. I have no alibi. I was in bed, alone." She frowned. "But I can assure you that I didn't kill her. That would go against everything we stand for."

Leigh said nothing and simply nodded.

Elanthia finished the list of twelve names and handed it to Leigh.

"Thank you," Leigh said, offering a business card to Elanthia. "If anything else occurs to you, anything at all, no matter how small, please feel free to give me a call. Thank you again." She started down the long aisle, but turned at the sound of her name.

Elanthia stood before a tiered display holding wooden bowls of tumbled gemstones. She ran her hand over the edges of several carved wooden bowls before selecting a flat moss-green stone, banded with patches of gray and gold. "This stone reminds me of your eyes. I'd like you to have it." Coming closer, she held out the stone to Leigh.

Leigh took the flat oval stone, running her thumb over the smooth, polished surface. "It's lovely. What is it?"

"Jasper. It's carried for protection and courage. I suspect your vocation takes you into some dangerous situations."

"It can. I'm sorry, I can't accept gifts. What do I owe—"

"You owe nothing. Think of it as a token from one member of the Craft to another, to ensure your safety." She stepped back and tipped her head gracefully. "Blessed be, Trooper."

The words Leigh hadn't spoken for over ten years rose to her lips as if it had been only yesterday. "Merry meet again." She stepped from the shop and out into the weakening late-afternoon sun. She stopped on the front step, her eyes fixed on the stone in her hand as she continued to stroke it with her thumb. Then she slid the jasper into her pocket for safekeeping and headed for her car.

Chapter Six:
Flash Back

Flash Back: the tendency of fires fueled by flammable liquids to reignite after being extinguished. Vapors boiling off from flammable liquids can conduct flame from a distant ignition source back to the originating container. Also called backflash.

Monday, 4:32 p.m.
Essex Detective Unit
Salem, Massachusetts

"Hey, Abbott. I hear you caught a new one."

Leigh paused in the aisle that bisected the double row of cubicles in the bullpen. "I did."

Brad Riley, the squad rookie, sat in his cubicle, a disorganized jigsaw puzzle of paperwork spread out before him, a pen clutched in his shaking hand. His neatly trimmed strawberry-blond hair was unusually disheveled and his sport coat hung drunkenly off his chair, one arm dragging on the worn carpet.

"You okay?" she asked.

"Sure." The single word was jagged as broken glass. His Adam's apple bobbed as he swallowed, and then his pen dropped to his desk to roll unnoticed to the floor as his hands fell limply into his lap. He slumped forward, his elbows on his thighs. "No, I'm not."

Leigh glanced around the bullpen; it was deserted. After setting her messenger bag against the half wall, she rolled a chair from the opposite cubicle into Riley's doorway. "What's going on?" He raised his head and Leigh instantly recognized the haunted look in his eyes and her stomach sank.

"I got called out to Haverhill this morning. A neighbor reported hearing a knock-down-drag-out going on in the apartment next door, followed by gunfire. The Haverhill boys took one look and called us." He hung his head. "Jesus, Abbott. A guy took out his family. Shot his wife in the head multiple times—there was so much damage, I actually couldn't tell how many times—and then he went through the house hunting down his five-year-old son and two-year-old daughter." A shudder rippled through him. "Then he turned the gun on himself. It was a massacre. Blood and brain matter everywhere. The wife will have to be identified by DNA or fingerprints because there's nothing left of her face. But . . . that wasn't the worst part."

Leigh didn't make him say it out loud. She'd been there herself, and knew the gut-wrenching horror of those tiny corpses. She rubbed a comforting hand on Riley's shoulder. "Child victims are the worst."

"I haven't had that many cases and they've all been adults, most of them junkies. You know a violent end was always in their future. But kids . . ."

"They never had a chance to live."

Riley sat back slowly, letting his head tip against the back of his chair. "Yeah. And one of the people they trusted the most betrayed them in the worst possible way." He paused for several seconds, his fingers clenching around the padded armrests of the chair. "The neighbor said the parents had been having trouble for months and the wife wanted to leave. I guess he felt if he couldn't have her, no one could. The kids either." His eyelids clenched shut. "And now they're all gone."

"This is the kind of case that really hits you hard," Leigh said. "Don't forget that you can talk to the department counselor, if you need to."

A harsh laugh broke from Riley with an explosive crack as his eyes shot open. "The counselor? Do you know the hell I'd catch from the guys if I went to the *counselor*? Real cops don't need a fucking counselor."

Leigh's temper flared. "That's bullshit," she snapped. "Worse than that, it's Morrison talking." Riley sat up, flushing, but Leigh cut him off before he could speak. "If you're going to survive working this job, you need to learn when it's time to think for yourself. I know they consider me the token department female, but use your head. There's no shame in admitting that you need a little help with a nightmare situation. You don't have to tell them you're going. *Just go.* You think today was bad, wait until you have to stand in on those autopsies. That'll be worse. If you need help, get it."

Silence hung heavy for several seconds as Riley stared at her, taken aback by her unusual burst of temper. "You're right," he mumbled. "Thanks."

"You're welcome. You're new on the force, Riley, but you have a good head on your shoulders. Don't let them push you around. It's not worth it just to be one of the guys."

Riley sat back in his chair, looking drained and spent. "I hear you and the scientist are back in the saddle."

Leigh's jaw sagged in shock. "Back in the . . . what?" *They can't know.*

"You're on a case together." Riley fixed her with a cockeyed stare. "What did you think I meant?"

"Uh . . . that. Yes, there was a burn victim down at the wharf. Matt and his team are good; they've already given me age and sex just from a virtual bone analysis. And we have some other leads. We may already have a connection to either the killer or the victim."

"Sounds good. I just wanted to let you know that I was serious about my offer. If there's anything you need, just ask." He looked down at the blizzard of paperwork on his desk. "It's not like this one's going to court."

Leigh patted his knee. "Why don't you take a break, get some coffee and some air, and then come back and finish up."

"Good idea." When he pushed back from his desk, Leigh stood and rolled the spare chair back into its cubicle. "You want anything?"

"No, thanks. I'm good."

"Okay. I'll be back in fifteen."

Leigh picked up her bag and quickly walked to the back of the bullpen. She sat down at her own neat desk, setting the messenger bag on the floor. Her gaze flicked over the silver frame in the corner, a smile touching her lips at the man in his dress blues who gazed back at her. *Hi, Dad. Miss you.*

She turned her attention to the stack of mail by her keyboard. She flipped through it, recognizing results from the state lab and court documents. She hesitated at an unmarked manila envelope with no return address. Her name and the department address were neatly printed on the front in black magic marker. Opening the envelope, she pulled out a color photo.

Shock sluiced over her in an icy wave as all the blood drained from her head. A dull buzz hummed in her ears as tiny green and black spots bloomed in front of her eyes. The photo slid from her numb fingers and drifted to the floor. She pressed her palms against the edge of her desk, her eyes fixed unseeingly on her blank computer monitor as she simply concentrated on sucking air into her lungs.

She closed her eyes as she fought for control. She was seeing things. This wasn't real.

She dragged in a ragged breath, steeling herself to look at the photo again.

Look, damn it. Don't be a coward.

She picked up the photo with clumsy fingers. She felt the

force of the blow once again, but held on tightly this time, crumpling the edges of the snapshot with the force of her grip.

The man in the photo lay sprawled face down in a snowy alley, his arms thrown wide over his head, a handgun flung a foot away from his right hand. His heavy winter coat was covered with a light dusting of snow as if he'd lain there for a while. But the most striking feature was the puddle of blood that spread out in a gruesome halo around his ruined head—thick dark blood against snow sparkling brilliantly white under stark police lights.

Her gaze darted desperately back to the photo tucked into the corner of her desk.

She'd been there in the flesh four years ago, thirty feet away, kept at bay by crime scene tape, several officers, and Kepler's direct order to keep her out of his scene. She'd ranted and struggled desperately, but they'd been relentless.

One of their own had gone down and they'd do anything to see justice served. Even if it meant holding back a fellow officer, the daughter of the fallen man. They all knew she'd show up. The call of *officer down* was broadcast while she'd been out on patrol. Against Kepler's wishes, word had filtered quickly through back channels and as soon as Leigh heard, she'd roared down the highway toward Salem, lights and sirens flashing, holding out hope to the last moment there'd been a mistake.

There was no mistake.

Instead, Leigh watched helplessly as her greatest nightmare became reality and the man she loved more than anyone, her only remaining parent, was pronounced dead. As crime scene pictures, just like the one she held in her hand, were taken. As evidence was gathered and pictures were taken of a second body, a drug addict well known to Vice. As both lifeless bodies were loaded into a van and driven to the morgue.

A shiver ran through Leigh as she remembered those moments from four years ago. She looked down at the photo, feeling chilled to the bone, as if she stood once again in that snowy dark, staring down at her father's body.

Pull yourself together. You're a cop. Think like one. She took a deep breath and forced herself to step back and consider what she held. Someone had sent her a photo of her slain father. Who would do such a thing? And why? She flipped over the envelope on her desk. There was no return address, but it was postmarked Boston. The handwriting was unfamiliar.

Leigh tried to turn off all emotion and consider the photo as just a piece of evidence. This was a crime scene photo, she was sure of it. No other photos could have been taken this close up except by people involved in the investigation. So the question was not only who mailed the photo, but also how did they get access to it? The case never went to trial and the pictures were never made public. *Did someone inside her own department send the package?*

Leigh turned the photo over, looking for any other information pointing to its origin, only to be hit by a new shock wave.

Several sentences were scrawled in black magic marker on the back on the photo: *Your father wasn't the hero you think he was. He was a dirty cop. Soon the world will know it. And you'll be the one to pay for his crimes.*

She jumped when her cell phone rang, her heart hammering sharply against her ribs as she nearly dropped the photo again. She fumbled for the phone, not taking the time to check the caller ID. "Abbott." Her voice came out as a rough croak, her tongue leaden in her mouth.

"Hey, it's me." Matt's voice sounded foreign in her ear, as if from another life. "How did it go this afternoon?"

She struggled to force her brain to connect with what she was hearing. "Go?"

"You know, at the Witch shop."

71

The Witch shop? How could he expect her to concentrate on work at a time like this? "Fine."

Silence.

"Can you be a little more specific than that?" Matt finally asked. "Did you find out who owned that knife? Or who—"

"Matt, I have to go. Kepler's here." The lie rolled off her tongue too easily for her own comfort. "I'll call you later."

"Sure. Leigh . . . is everything okay?"

"Why wouldn't it be?"

"You sound funny. Are you upset about something?"

She squeezed her eyes shut, cursing herself. Of course he would know something was wrong. Too often he could see inside her so clearly, but she'd lose the last of her control if he was gentle with her right now. She needed to end this call before he sensed she was completely falling apart.

Before he knew what a coward she was.

"I'm fine. But I have to go. I'll talk to you later."

She set the phone on her desk, her head dropping as she worked to pull herself together.

Her phone rang again immediately. She didn't even look up, letting Matt's call go to voice mail. *I'm sorry. I just can't. Not right now.*

Her phone finally stopped ringing, the silence in the bullpen suddenly oppressive.

As if by magic, Elanthia's lyrical voice burst in her mind—*Jasper. It's carried for protection and courage.* Leigh slid her hand into her pocket, pulling out the polished gemstone. She turned it over in her hand a few times, the smooth slide of the stone warm against her skin.

She took a deep breath, centering herself and closed her fingers around the stone. *Courage.*

She needed to get out so she could clear away the panic and think. Sitting up straight, she surveyed the bullpen over the top of the dividers. Still alone. In a sudden flurry of activity, she jerkily jammed the photo back into the envelope and then into her bag.

She didn't know what the photo meant yet, but she was going to get to the bottom of it. And for now, she'd do it on her own.

At least until she knew what the hell was going on.

Chapter Seven:
Controlled Burn

Controlled Burn: a planned fire tended by a qualified crew ignited under specific conditions of fuel and weather. Prescribed fires are set in specific areas to manage vegetation, reduce wildfire hazards, or enhance wildlife habitats.

Monday, 9:12 p.m.
Lowell Residence
Brookline, Massachusetts

Taking a deep breath, Leigh knocked on the door, and then forced herself to stand still. When her fingers worried the hem of her blazer, she clenched her hand into a fist, cursing her fit of nerves.

The door opened and Matt stood in the entranceway. His brows rose in surprise at the sight of her.

"Hi."

"Ah, there's your voice. I thought you'd lost it." She stared at him, baffled, and he must have read her confusion. "Since I called you this afternoon, the only way you'd talk to me was by text. I was beginning to think you had laryngitis."

She drew breath to speak, but there were no words. Her shoulders drooped and she found herself staring at her shoes.

"Be a gentleman, Matt. Let her in."

Leigh's head snapped up at the sound of Matt's father. Matt stepped back, pulling the door wide to reveal Mike sitting in his wheelchair a few feet behind his son. Teak, Mike's Belgian Malinois service dog, stood patiently beside the chair. As always, Mike looked well groomed, from his neatly trimmed gray beard to his stylish clothes. It struck Leigh afresh that Matt's father always looked strong and capable; she half expected him to climb out of his wheelchair and start striding around the house. But his withered legs would never allow that.

He smiled up at her, his green eyes warm and welcoming. "Leigh, it's good to see you. Come in. It's getting cool out there." The older man's gaze darted to his son's clouded expression and then back to Leigh as she stepped into the hall. "You two must have some case details to discuss. If you need me, I'll be in the family room with Teak. With the TV on. Loud." With a pointed look at his son, he deftly swiveled his chair and rolled down the hallway, Teak following close behind.

When Leigh turned to him, Matt only shrugged. "I didn't tell him anything. It drives me crazy the way he just knows things."

"He's an intuitive man. Look, Matt—"

Matt held up a hand. "Why don't you come in first? You look like you've been run over by a truck and need to sit down."

"I admit that's kind of how I feel." Leigh followed Matt into the adjacent living room. The wide trio of windows looking out onto the street was dark, but a tall brass lamp threw warm light over a comfortable armchair and a well-padded sofa grouped around a cheerfully crackling fire. A hardcover book lay on the table beside the chair, partially covered by an edition of *The Journal of Forensic Sciences,* spread open, lying face down. Leigh stopped just inside the doorway, shifting her weight awkwardly, her eyes on the homey scene. "I've interrupted your evening."

"No problem." He sat down on the sofa, patting the open space at his side. Leigh dropped down beside him, setting her bag down on the floor by her feet. "So . . . what's going on?" he prompted. When she hesitated, he pushed harder. "I know something's happened. I could hear it in your voice. And in the

75

silence afterward."

Leigh sat back, letting her head fall back against the cushions. "Something came in the mail today that . . . shook me up."

"What do you mean?"

Leigh was silent for a minute before forcing herself to reach for her bag. She withdrew the photo, now sealed in an evidence bag, and held it tightly against her body. "This came just before you called." She looked up, her face heating as she met his concerned gaze. "I'm sorry I lied to you. Kepler wasn't there. I just didn't know what to do. It was a shock and I was struggling to process it, let alone talk to you and—" His hand came down over hers and she stopped the tumbling flow of words. The breath she pulled in felt jagged and ice-cold.

"Can I see it?" he asked gently, his fingers closing over the bag.

She nodded, letting the photo slide from her grasp.

He frowned, his brow furrowed in confusion as he took in the death scene. "I don't understand. Why would anyone send this to you?"

"Because that's my father." Her voice cracked on the last word. Suddenly he was too close, and the concern in his hazel eyes threatened her tenuous control. She surged to her feet, walking to the dark windows, looking out to the nightscape beyond the glass, lit only by streetlight filtering through the half-denuded fall foliage.

She never heard him move, but suddenly he was behind her, his arms sliding around her waist to pull her back against him. His head dropped forward, his cheek pressed against her ear and his breath feathering lightly over her throat. She hadn't realized she was cold, but he felt wonderfully warm wrapped around her. Her hands came up to interlace with his, holding on tight.

"I'm sorry," he whispered. "It's no wonder you were upset."

For a few minutes, they simply stood in silence as Leigh calmed herself. Then, blowing out a long breath, she stepped from his arms, instantly missing his warmth as she stood on her own again, but somehow feeling better for the independence. "That's not the worst of it."

"How can it get worse than that?"

She circled back to the couch, sat down and picked up the photo from where Matt had dropped it on the cushion. For the space of several heartbeats, she simply stared at the image. She hardly needed to study it; it was burned into her memory now. "I was at the scene." She pushed on, ignoring Matt's murmur of sympathy. "I was out on patrol that day. Back then, I was still part of Field Troop A. I'm sure they didn't want me to know, didn't want me there, but word like that filters through the ranks. I made it to the scene as fast as I could . . . but it was already too late. He was gone."

Matt pulled the photo from her fingers and laid it on the table so he could take both of her hands in his. "What happened?"

"The story I got from Harper that night was that Dad was participating in a joint investigation between the detective unit and the Salem PD's Criminal Investigation Division. Heroin is a big problem in the area. Within the city, that's Salem PD's jurisdiction. But there were a couple of associated homicides that brought us into it. Some local dealers had been found dead, so a joint investigation was launched. Dad was out with Detective Oakes that night. Oakes had a CI—a confidential informant—he wanted to question and Dad went along. Oakes wasn't there when it all went down. According to Oakes, the CI wasn't at the designated meeting place, so they split up to look for him. Ten or fifteen minutes later, he heard gunshots and went to investigate." Leigh's gaze skittered to the photo. "That's how he found Dad, lying dead in an alley. The CI was dead too, about twenty feet away. They'd killed each other. Dad must have shot first because the CI was hit in the chest, but Dad . . . he . . ."

"His was a head shot," Matt finished for her when words finally failed her.

"Yes." A strangled whisper. "And just like that, my family was gone."

Matt clasped her hands a little tighter, but let her keep some of the distance she maintained. "Why would someone send this to you?"

"Because of what's on the back." She pulled one hand free and picked up the photo. Turning it over, she handed it back to Matt.

He quickly scanned the message, his expression hardening. "Someone's trying to sully his reputation. And yours at the same time. Does this have anything to do with the Bradford case? You've been a household name since then."

"I have to admit the thought occurred to me. Someone out there might resent my recent celebrity status. *Our* status, really. Every article on me has included something about Dad, about the hero who died in the line of duty. Maybe that pissed somebody off? Someone already holding a grudge?"

"Possibly," Matt said cautiously. "Is there any way to trace this?"

"Maybe. When I first got it, I was so shocked I didn't handle it properly." She shook her head and frowned at her own misstep. "As soon as I realized what it was, I should have used gloves to preserve any fingerprints. But I wasn't thinking clearly."

"Leigh, give yourself a break. You were understandably shaken."

"Maybe, but that doesn't change the fact that I may have destroyed my own evidence. As soon as I started to think, I bagged the photo and the envelope. It's a standard envelope with no defining features, postmarked Boston. We could narrow it down to the individual postal station but in a city the size of Boston, I'm not sure it's going to tell us anything."

"What about DNA?"

Leigh nodded thoughtfully. "I wondered about that. The envelope is sealed, but I can't tell if it was licked shut or is one of those self-sealing types. So that leaves me with a choice—do I bring this to the attention of the department and have the lab run it for DNA and prints? Or do I go it alone?"

"Go it alone? Why on earth would you—" Matt abruptly cut off as his gaze flicked back to the photo. "You're worried someone in the department is involved." Color suffused his face. "You think someone in your own department did this?" His voice rose, the words edged with anger.

"I'd be stupid to ignore the possibility."

Matt examined the photo with a critical eye. "It's a crime scene photo," he said flatly. "No one else could take a picture like this. If the media got there, they'd have been blocked outside the scene. Look at the angle. This was taken by someone practically standing over your father."

"Exactly. But it's more complicated than that. Anyone in the department could have access to this file without even needing to sign it out. So could members of the DA's staff. There are electronic copies of the photos, so the computer system could have been hacked. And because it's a closed case, it's now officially public record and anyone can request access to the file. It's primarily up to the DA to grant access. But if he won't, an application can still be made via the Freedom of Information Act."

"So anyone can have access?"

"Not fully. If the DA allows a civilian access to the file, they won't be allowed all the information. They'll get a sanitized version without witness names or personal information like addresses and phone numbers."

"The photos could still be there?"

"Yes. But if someone outside the department requested access, that would leave a paper trail. I'll look into it."

Matt was silent for a long time, with only the crackle of burning wood to break the silence as ruddy firelight flickered over them. Leigh finally tapped his knee. "What are you thinking?"

He glanced at her sideways. "What about Morrison? He's pretty pissed at you right now."

"He's always pretty pissed at me; he just has a real reason right now." Exhaustion washed over her in a rush and she slumped forward, bracing her arms on her thighs. "But I get your point. I've thought of him myself. He'd love to see me discredited."

"But . . ."

"But it doesn't feel right to me. For all his heavy-handed behavior, he's actually a solid cop and he respects the badge. And when he talks to me about my father, there's a reverence in his tone. And disgust for me. He thinks Dad would be horrified to see the kind of cop I've become and thinks I smear his good name. But he respects Dad's memory."

"Or at least appears to."

"Or appears to," Leigh conceded. "I can't discount him, but in some ways Morrison almost seems too obvious. Especially coming on the heels of the case being flipped to me, it makes me wonder if someone is setting us both up. Someone is aware of the animosity and is hoping I'll leap to a conclusion and blame Morrison because of our history."

"I don't like him, or trust him," Matt said stubbornly.

"Me neither. But I'm not about to point fingers too easily. If I'm going to accuse anyone, I need to know they really did it. But with suspicions that this could have come from inside the department, I'm not confident about going public. At least not right now, with just this."

"You're expecting more."

"It doesn't make any sense that this is all they're going to send me."

"What about if we do the DNA? We can run it at BU and that keeps it out of the detective unit altogether. You don't know if there even is any DNA, so that would be a good place to start. Then if there is and you need to run a comparison, you can worry about how to work that later. Maybe take it to Rowe for help. Surely he couldn't be involved in this."

"No way, no how." Leigh leaned back against the sofa, turning the possibility over in her mind. "That works. If I come to the lab tomorrow, can you take a sample from the envelope?"

"Sure. You know we'll help in any way we can."

"Thanks. Just talking this over with you makes me feel a little better. It really knocked me off balance."

"Of course it would. Especially when you're up to your ears in a new case."

"Speaking of which, I haven't updated you yet."

"You don't need to do that right now while you're worried about this other stuff. That can wait until tomorrow, when you're up to it."

"No, I'd like to talk it out with you. It'll help me clear my head."

The range of expressions that flitted over his face told her clearly of his internal struggle to both take care of her and let her stand on her own two feet. "If you're sure."

"I am." Leigh quickly outlined her trip to Draw Down the Moon. "We're obtaining dental records for Moira Simpson. The description I got this afternoon certainly makes it sound like she's our victim. I also can't reach Ms. Simpson by phone, and no one is at her home. It's the logical next step. Rowe will be able to tell us for certain at some point tomorrow, depending on when the records arrive."

"And if it's her?"

"Then I go tell next of kin."

"I want to come with you."

Leigh met his eyes, surprised. "To inform next of kin?"

"Yes. I know it's a lousy job, but it has to be done. And I remember how hard it was to break the news to Tracy Kingston's parents. I'm not an official representative of the force, but it's my case too, and maybe I can answer some of their questions."

Leigh stared at him in silence for a moment, then acquiesced. "Okay. But you let me do the talking unless I open up the floor for you."

"Deal. Now, can we put this away for the night? How about a glass of wine?"

"You have no idea how much I'd like that." When Matt stood, she placed her hand in his and let him draw her from the sofa. Together they left the room, leaving the photo face down on the table, temporarily forgotten.

CHAPTER EIGHT:
IMMUREMENT

Immurement: a form of execution where a person is walled up within a building and left to die from starvation or dehydration.

Wednesday, 4:43 p.m.
Simpson Residence
Salem, Massachusetts

"Ready?" Leigh asked.

"Yes." Matt took a step backward on the shallow front step of the single-story colonial, letting Leigh take the lead.

She rapped sharply on the door. Then there was only silence.

"Maybe he's not home?" Matt suggested. He leaned forward, squinting through one of the long, narrow windows that flanked the front door. The front hallway was empty.

"Car's in the driveway," Leigh said. "Give it a minute."

Finally, from inside the house, a floorboard creaked. The dead bolt shot back and the door opened to reveal a slight man with hunched shoulders and buzz-cut brown hair. "Yes?"

"Flynn Simpson?" When the man nodded, Leigh extended her badge. "I'm Trooper Leigh Abbott of the Massachusetts State Police. This is Dr. Matt Lowell from Boston University. Can we come in?"

Confusion flashed across the young man's face but he pulled open the door, allowing them to step inside. The house was tiny, the entire front taken up by an open concept living and dining area. The furniture looked comfortable, but there were few decorative elements.

"Please, have a seat."

Matt and Leigh sat on a small sofa. The young man circled the coffee table to sit in a well-worn recliner opposite a flat-screen TV.

Alarm bells sounded in Matt's head. There was something peculiar about the way the young man moved—something unnatural and stiff, but, at the same time, vaguely familiar. Eyes narrowing in concentration, Matt studied the man across from him. He sat very still, his left shoulder tilted slightly higher than the right, his left arm pulled tight against his torso, the elbow in an odd locked position, even as his left hand hung loose.

"—I'm sorry to inform you—"

Matt dimly heard Leigh's words of condolences as his gaze continued to skim over the other man. And then he saw it—an odd bump under the man's sleeve, just visible where it protruded from the back of his left arm. An involuntary thrill coursed along his nerve endings. What were the chances? Actually, he knew exactly what the chances were—approximately one in two million. But to be able to see this in person, in an actual clinical patient—

When Leigh turned to stare at him quizzically, he realized he must have made some small sound at the discovery. He grimaced in apology and forced his attention back to what Leigh was saying.

"—and I'm sorry for your loss, Mr. Simpson."

"There's no mistake?" Simpson asked, his face pale and his eyes glassy with shock.

"I'm afraid not," Leigh said. "Dental records confirm her identity."

"But I don't understand. Mom was supposed to be in Boston for the week. She had some sort of getaway planned." The corners of his lips trembled. "She loved her spa getaways. She told me she was going to be massaged and mud wrapped and polished, and she'd come back next weekend looking like a twenty-year-old."

Leigh pulled her notepad from the pocket of her blazer. "Where was she supposed to go?"

"I don't remember the name, but she said it was on Newberry Street."

"Fancy," Matt commented.

"Only the best for Mom." Simpson gave an uneven laugh that ended as a croak before dropping his face into his right hand. Matt noted that his left hand lay in his lap. If he was correct, Simpson wouldn't be able to raise that hand to his face.

Silence reigned for a moment, only broken by Simpson's harsh and ragged breathing. Matt glanced at Leigh, but she raised an index finger, telling him to wait.

Finally, Simpson broke the silence. "You said her body was found in an antique store fire. Was it an accident?"

"We don't have the report back from the fire marshal yet. But we do know the fire wasn't responsible for your mother's death."

The young man's body jerked as if struck. "What do you mean?"

"Your mother was stabbed to death with a weapon that was found at the scene. In fact, she was killed with her own knife."

"Her own knife . . . Hold on, do you mean her athame?"

"You're familiar with the tools of her Craft?"

"Craft? I wouldn't call it that. More of a hobby. Mom gets . . ." He swallowed hard. "Got bored easily. It came from not having a job. My dad died in an industrial accident before I was born. The money from the lawsuit set Mom up for life. In the end, that worked well because I've had health problems since childhood and that allowed Mom to spend her time caring for me."

"Because of the FOP," Matt stated.

The younger man froze. Then he slowly turned to stare at Matt. "How could you possibly know that?"

"Wait," Leigh interrupted, grasping Matt's forearm. "What's 'FOP'?"

"Fibrodysplasia ossificans progressiva." When Leigh stared at him in confusion, he explained. "It's a progressive bone disorder in which soft tissue is genetically misprogrammed to turn into bone following an injury."

"Soft tissue . . . meaning . . . ?"

"Connective tissue, ligaments or skeletal muscle." Matt turned back to Simpson. "I'm a forensic anthropologist. I was called in to consult on this case because of the nature of your mother's remains. But as a trained osteologist, I recognized your symptoms from the way you move and hold yourself. When were you diagnosed?"

"When I was seven. The doctors thought I had a soft tissue sarcoma and tried to surgically remove it."

Matt winced.

"What?" Leigh asked. "Is that bad?"

"Any soft tissue trauma will trigger the process to turn that tissue into bone. In attempting to cure his 'cancer,' the doctors inadvertently furthered his real disease. Unfortunately, it's a fairly common misdiagnosis of FOP. A mass is found, often in the abdomen, and cancer is suspected. It's only when they go in that they realize the mass is actually normal bone, but, by then, the damage is done."

"Mom was horrified," Simpson said. "She blamed herself for not finding the right specialists."

"It wasn't her fault," Matt said. "Because it's such a rare disorder, most doctors wouldn't even consider it."

"No, but that's the kind of woman she is . . . I mean, was. She was very involved in my health care. There is no treatment for this disease, but she learned everything she could and made sure that I saw all the right specialists. And if she didn't like the answers she heard from one, she took me to another. She spared no expense or effort." He looked up and met Leigh's eyes. "I don't understand why anyone would do this to her."

"We're looking into her connections to the Witchcraft community. Mr. Simpson, I'd like to go back to your earlier comment. You called her Craft a 'hobby.' Why would you say that?"

"Mom's whole world was wrapped up in me for the longest time. I was a clumsy child, and FOP only made it worse. We were constantly in doctors' offices or at the hospital for treatment or as she tried to find someone with a different opinion on how to manage the disease. But when I graduated from college, and got a job and moved out, suddenly she was at loose ends. So she got a dog to spoil and she tried a bunch of new things—yoga, Pilates, sailing, tennis lessons, Witchcraft. She's been at that for a while now. Maybe she's finally found the right thing for her." With a sharp intake of breath, he caught himself, his eyes closing briefly as his head drooped. "I'm still talking about her in the present tense. I'm sorry, I just need a little time to—"

"It's all right, Mr. Simpson. We understand you've had a shock. Can we get you anything?"

"No, thank you. My partner will be home soon. He's what I need."

"Good." Leigh glanced sideways at Matt before continuing. "You mentioned a dog."

"Yes, Maxie, my mother's Pomeranian." A hand flew to his mouth. "She'll be all alone now. I have to go get her." His eyes darted around the house as if sizing up its suitability for an animal. "We don't have any pets because I can't risk having something underfoot, but we'll have to take her. She can't go to a shelter. My mother loved that dog." His voice cracked on the last word.

"Unfortunately, the body of a small animal was also found at the scene. Did Maxie wear a collar with a tag?"

"Maxie didn't like anything around her neck and since my mother carried her whenever they went out, she didn't see the need for a collar." Simpson seemed to curl in on himself, but only his right side obeyed, leaving him twisted awkwardly.

"Are you well enough for us to ask you a few more questions?" At his nod, Leigh continued. "Your mother actually quit the coven a few weeks ago. You weren't aware of this?"

"She never mentioned it to me." His gaze shifted between cop and scientist, only to return to Leigh. "Which is surprising because we talked every few days or so."

"Maybe she felt uncomfortable about the falling out?"

"Maybe. That might also be why she wanted to get away for a week." Simpson's expression suddenly sharpened. "You said she was killed with an athame. Do you think someone inside the community did it?"

"We're looking into it. Many things don't connect for us yet. Do you know if she was familiar with the antique shop where she was found? Is she a regular customer?"

"Not that I know of, but that would be right up her alley."

"I understand she had expensive tastes," Leigh said.

"Don't get me wrong, I loved my mother and she was my guardian angel for many years. She always put my needs ahead of her own. But she was used to having money and spending it on the very best. It was her reward to herself for her other losses in life—a husband and a normal child. Then she became used to a certain standard and worked to maintain it."

"Did she ever give you the idea that the Witchcraft community didn't like her spending habits? Was anyone jealous of her wealth?" Matt asked.

"Not that she ever mentioned. I thought Mom was very happy there." Simpson sighed. "I really hoped she was. She deserved to be happy."

"One more question, Mr. Simpson. You understand this is all part of regular procedure. Can you tell me your whereabouts between midnight and four thirty on Sunday morning?"

Simpson drew back as sharply as his damaged body would allow. "You think *I* did it?"

"I'm not saying that, Mr. Simpson. But most murders are committed by people known to the victim. I just want to remove you from any potential suspect list right away."

Simpson fixed her with a prolonged stare. "I was home, in bed asleep with Aaron. You can talk to him if you need corroboration. He works from home here as a realtor."

Matt went on alert as Leigh stiffened. "Your partner's not Aaron Dodsworth, is he?"

Simpson's brows crinkled in surprise. "That's him. Do you know him?"

"No, but his name came up in a conversation yesterday with the owner of the shop your mother died in. He'd listed his shop for sale with your partner as his realtor."

"I had no idea. Aaron handles a lot of properties. He discusses some of them with me, but he never mentioned that one. What a strange coincidence."

"It is," Leigh said lightly as she flipped her notepad closed and pulled a card from her pocket. "All my contact information is listed here. If you think of anything else, please don't hesitate to contact me. With your permission, there's one other thing we'd like to do. We'd like to go through your mother's residence. There might be some information relevant to the case there."

"Of course." Simpson rose, carefully balancing his weight on both feet before removing his hand from the arm of the chair. "I have a key to her house."

"I'll get a warrant, but your permission to enter her residence will go a long way to speeding up that process."

"Then you have it. Hold on, I'll get you the key." He shuffled off down the hallway.

Matt watched him go, noting the care with which he placed each foot. When a misstep could cause irrevocable pain and suffering, caution was well-founded.

He jerked when Leigh smacked his arm. "Stop staring at him like he's a specimen under your microscope," she hissed. "He's a human being and he just lost his mother."

"I know that. But do you know how rare this condition is?" he whispered back. "I've never seen a real FO—" Matt cut off abruptly as Simpson reappeared, a silver key on a large ring extended in his hand.

"Please keep it for as long as you need it. And here's one of Aaron's cards. He'll probably be home in an hour or so."

Leigh took the key and card. "Thank you for your help. I'll let you know when we're done at your mother's and you can have access to her things."

"Thank you."

Matt and Leigh said their good-byes and walked silently to their cars, both parked in front of Simpson's house. Matt paused with his hand on the driver's door, looking back up toward the house.

Simpson still stood in the doorway, hunched and frail, a man trapped in the shell of his own body.

It was a picture of imminent death.

CHAPTER NINE:
CONCEALED SPACE

Concealed Space: enclosed or hidden areas between walls, ceilings and roofs or attic floors, soffits, etc., where fire can spread unobserved.

Wednesday, 5:57 p.m.
Boston University, School of Medicine
Boston, Massachusetts

Leigh slammed through the door of the lab and immediately stalked toward Matt, who stood near a gurney surrounded by his students. "What was that at the Simpson house?" she demanded, punctuating her words with a stiff index finger to his chest.

"What?"

She glared at him. "You wanted to come along to be supportive and to supply information, and the moment you saw him, you mentally checked out."

"I didn't 'check out' " Matt protested. "I just got . . . distracted. Professional hazard."

"You can hardly blame him," Paul interjected. "I'm mean, we're talking about FOP. Do you know how . . ." He stuttered into silence when Leigh nailed him with her laser-sharp green eyes.

Leigh turned on Matt again, her irritation rising when he simply regarded her calmly. "I see you filled your students in."

"This is an opportunity to teach them something they'd likely

91

never see in practice."

She balled her hands into fists to thwart the desire to grab Matt by both shoulders and shake some compassion into him. She knew it was there, but currently the scientist was winning out over the human being. "Would you turn off the teaching for once? You were there to comfort the next of kin. You weren't even listening when I talked to him, were you?"

"Of course I was."

"What did I say when we first sat down?" Crossing her arms over her chest, Leigh fixed him with a pointed stare.

"You expressed your condolences and . . . uh . . ." Matt shrugged and gave up. "Okay, I wasn't listening. I knew I was looking at something I should have been able to recognize, and I was trying to put the puzzle pieces together. Do you know how rare this disorder is? Only about one in two million babies are born with FOP."

"Thank God for that," Kiko murmured.

Leigh stopped glaring at Matt and turned to Kiko. "Why?"

"You saw him. Wasn't it obvious?"

"It wouldn't have been to her. Hold on, I can explain better with pictures." Matt selected a heavy volume from the bookcase by his desk, and then returned to the group, flipping rapidly through the pages. "You have to understand that this disease is a horror, an absolute nightmare. It's being locked in your own body, knowing all that finally awaits you is death. There's no treatment. No hope." When he looked up to meet Leigh's eyes, his were serious, the sparkle of excitement quenched. "I'm sorry if I seemed more interested in him than in his mother, but coming across this was a bit of a surprise and I automatically switched to professional mode. Did you notice that he couldn't bend his left arm?"

Leigh closed her eyes, picturing Flynn Simpson's stiff posture. "Yes. I didn't really take note at the time, but now that you mention it . . ."

"That's because his elbow has likely fused. Remember what I said about FOP causing soft tissue to turn into bone. Let's say an injury occurred to a muscle in his upper arm. In a normal person, you'd have some pain, possibly some swelling, but in the course of a few days or weeks, the muscle would heal. When an injury like that happens to someone with FOP, it sets off a chain reaction that replaces the damaged muscle with totally normal bone. But the replacement essentially immobilizes that part of the body. Now, imagine that happening with every bump, bruise, vaccination, and influenza-type infection. Or, in the case of Mr. Simpson, the surgery to remove his 'cancer,' which wasn't cancer at all, but would have been a new bony growth.

"There's no treatment, and life expectancy is rarely more than forty years. Over time, mobility is lost, and your untouched brain is trapped in the shell of your ossified body. The disease spares several muscles—the heart, the diaphragm, the tongue and the muscles around the eyes. So your heart continues to beat and you continue to live, if you could call it that, but you've turned to stone."

Leigh realized her mouth was sagging open in horror and hurriedly snapped her teeth together with an audible click.

"Mr. Simpson appears to be in his late twenties," Matt continued, "but I don't think he'll see forty, not with his disease so far progressed. Death in most FOP patients tends to result from one or more common factors—catastrophic head injuries from falls due to lack of mobility, pneumonia, or cardiorespiratory failure when the muscles of the chest and back harden and the ribs don't permit the lungs to expand. So the patient suffocates."

"They're literally trapped inside their own skeleton," Leigh breathed.

Matt nodded and turned the book around so everyone could

see it. "After a lifetime of injury, this is what he can expect."

Leigh stepped forward to examine the double black-and-white photograph. One side of the photo was a man, his back to the camera, his emaciated body held stiffly and his head at an awkward angle. Ribbons of bone ran down his back: hard, unnaturally protruding twists under pale skin.

Matt tapped the photo with an index finger. "This is Mr. Harry Eastlack. He died in nineteen seventy-three at the age of thirty-nine from pneumonia. By the time he died, all his joints had fused and the only things he could move were his lips, but he could barely talk because his jaw was fused." He tapped the other side of the photo. "Mr. Eastlack was kind enough to donate his skeleton to research. When the skeleton was defleshed, this was what they found."

The photo was reminiscent of a normal skeleton from the rear, but with flowing cascades of extra bone where muscle would normally lie in an adult. Bone dripped down the spine and between the ribs, and joint locations were obscured by sheets of abnormal skeletal growth. The vertebrae in the neck were fused into a solid column. "My God . . . ," Leigh murmured.

Kiko gave a little shiver. "The whole idea freaks me out. I understand the genetics of it and the pathways that cause the tissue replacement, but I can't mentally disconnect from the damage done. It would be a nightmare to know that you're slowly dying of such a horrific disease."

"Think about it from his mother's point of view," Juka pointed out. "What would it be like to know that you were going to watch your child suffer and die, and you were helpless to stop it?"

"And it sounds like she was a good mother," Matt said. "As he said, no effort or expense was spared to try to cure him. And that was twenty odd years ago when they didn't even know what caused the disease. They've identified the mutation now, but there's still no cure."

Leigh blew out a breath. "Okay, I guess I can see why he caught your eye. But how did you know it was FOP?"

"It was an educated guess—the bony outgrowths on his left arm gave it away. He's got good motion in his right arm, but the left is nearly frozen. I suspect a fall as a child to do one-sided damage like that. Either way, he's not in good shape. He's not steady on his feet either. He'll be in a wheelchair soon." He closed the book and set it on a nearby benchtop. "Are we good now?"

"Yes." Leigh glanced over her shoulder. The gurney on the other side of the lab held a single set of human remains. All that was left was the skeleton; the flesh had been stripped away. "Is that our vic?"

"Yes." Matt slid his fingers around the curve of her elbow and guided her toward the gurney.

"You worked fast."

"We started on Monday just as soon as Rowe finished the autopsy. Even with all three of us, it still took a day and a half to strip the bones by hand, both the human victim and what I can now confirm was a dog." He indicated the metal tray on a nearby counter that held the small canine skeleton. "We moved the remains here late last night once all the tissue was removed and we didn't need full ventilation anymore."

"Have you had a chance to examine the remains?"

"That's what we were doing this morning." He glanced at his watch. "We've got information for you, but are you sure you want to do it now?"

"I'm here now, so let's do it."

"Then get out your notepad. You're going to want to write this down."

CHAPTER TEN:
CHAR BLISTERING

Char Blistering: bubbles or raised, cracked segments of carbonized material formed on the surface of charred or burned wood.

Wednesday, 6:08 p.m.
Boston University, School of Medicine
Boston, Massachusetts

Matt and Leigh joined the students grouped around the gurney. Leigh stood at the foot, taking in the neat skeletal arrangement, laid out in anatomical formation. This wasn't her first experience with skeletal remains—after their first case, she'd seen enough for a lifetime—but this was her first burn victim. Instead of the uniform, smooth ivory she was used to, these bones were a charred and shattered jigsaw puzzle. Seemingly random areas of bone were smudged with char, and long bones were spider-webbed with lengthy stretches of cracks and chips.

"How do you know where to start?" she asked. "It looks to me like she was beaten to death, but I know a lot of this must be fire damage. How can you tell which injuries happened before the fire?" Matt opened his mouth to speak, but Leigh interrupted him. "I know how much you'd love to turn this into a detailed three-hour lecture, but try to just hit the highlights for me, okay? Put the extra detail in the—"

"Written report, I know," Matt said, resignedly. "We'll need more time to complete the analysis, but we have some solid preliminary data on fracture and char patterns. First, we know death occurred due to sharp force trauma."

"Finding the knife in the victim was kind of a giveaway," Paul quipped.

"Just a bit," Matt agreed. "But you need to know more than what the murder weapon was, you need to know *how* she died. All that information is here. First of all, look at the angle of entry. Here are the kerf marks left by the knife strikes." He pointed out the four defects in the ribs and sternum. "Paul, grab a probe and show Leigh."

"Sure." Paul picked up a straight, stainless steel probe from a nearby tray. "It's easiest to show on the sternum." He slid the probe carefully into the nick in the heavy bone, holding it almost vertically. Leigh leaned in for a closer look. "Do you see this slight angle? This means the knife strike came from slightly below the contact point."

Leigh straightened in surprise. "From below? DMV records report her height as five foot five. That's kind of short for the blow to have come from below."

"And the angle's wrong for an upward thrust. Here, let me show you. Kiko." Matt crooked his fingers in a "come here" gesture, then he clapped a hand down over her shoulder to hold her in place. "If I was going to stab Kiko from below, the angle would be more like this." Matt mimed driving a knife into Kiko's ribs from below at a steep upward angle. "That would work, but it's not what we're seeing here. The angle is more like this." He mimed a second blow, holding the invisible knife palm down and coming across in an awkward attack, almost parallel to the floor. "That doesn't make any sense, especially when you're looking at multiple strikes in an area where there's a lot of bone resistance so additional force would be required."

Leigh circled Matt and Kiko, her eyes locked on Kiko's midsection as she ran through the demonstration in her head. "Wait, I've got it. She was on the floor." Squatting down on the balls of her feet, she mimed driving a knife straight down into the torso of a supine victim. "She was stabbed while on her back. That would allow multiple strikes from the same angle with the required amount of force."

"Bingo." Matt held out a hand and pulled Leigh to her feet.

"But then the question is—why was she on the floor?"

"We think we know. But first, you need to understand the difference between fractures in wet and dry bone so you can tell perimortem fractures from postmortem fractures. I know you're familiar with kerf marks and how a solid object passing through bone leaves an imprint behind. In the same way, heat-induced fractures leave their own microscopic and macroscopic signatures. Using these signatures, we can reconstruct both what happened and the order in which the injuries occurred. The challenge in this case is the conformational changes that occur in bone exposed to extreme heat—it changes shape so you can't simply fit the pieces back together cleanly. But the crucial point is that once there is an existing first fracture in a bone, a second break can't cross it. That's how you can map the order of injury."

"Handy," Leigh said. "But can you tell if a break was there before the fire?"

"Yes. Heat fractures are only formed under specific circumstances—the bone dehydrates causing it to warp and shrink. When that stress becomes excessive, it results in an abrupt break similar to a sharp force trauma fracture."

"Doesn't that cause problems, then? How can you tell between fire damage and sharp force trauma?"

"It's a challenge," Matt agreed. "But wet bone behaves differently. First, heat-induced fractures only happen in dry bone—bone that's charred black or calcined. Normal bone doesn't fracture from heat stress because the moisture content gives it too much resilience."

Leigh swiveled to stare at the bones on the gurney. "So if

there's a fracture in uncharred bone, it happened before the fire."

"Exactly. Now, what you really need are some answers. These guys were busy while we were gone today. Kiko was working on the skull, and the guys spent time on the electron microscope looking at fracture patterns. I don't even know the results yet." He eyed the boys. "Let's start with you two. How'd you do on the EM?"

"Good," Paul said. "Our biggest concern was the location of the knife strikes and fractures caused by the wardrobe." He circled the table and pointed to the right femur. The head of the femur was cleanly separated from the shaft of the bone. "This intertrochanteric fracture is from the wardrobe falling. The victim was on her left side, so when the wardrobe burned and collapsed on the body, the force of the blow landed on the victim's right side. This break, as well as the fractures in ribs seven, eight and nine, are all a combination of heat-induced and blunt force trauma."

"Postmortem versus perimortem?" Matt asked.

"Yes," Juka said. "I went back and looked at the 3D scans to confirm. There was no tissue infiltration at those locations—the victim was already dead. Put it in context of the wardrobe collapse and everything lines up. Except for the four sharp force trauma kerf marks we've already identified from the knife, all bone injury below the neck is postmortem and mostly fire-related."

"Good work." Matt turned to Kiko. "But I bet things will get more interesting with the skull. Am I right?"

"I haven't started the reconstruction yet, but I spent a lot of time studying the fragments." Kiko donned a pair of gloves and walked to the head of the table. "The skull is in pretty poor shape, but we were lucky that we were able to recover all of it." She picked up the skull, the top ragged, a gaping chasm where the forehead should have been. The jagged edges were ashen gray, but charcoal black outlined the empty eye sockets and crept down to smudge the midsections of bone. "We've got these pieces here." Kiko pointed to a metal tray that held a dozen or so shards of varying size. "They make up the top of the cranial vault. All of those fractures are clearly heat-induced. However . . ." Kiko turned the skull sideways, extending it toward Leigh. "There are several fractures here, in the squama just above the supermastoid crest—above and behind the ear. As you can see, this is unburned bone and the fracture pattern clearly suggests blunt force trauma."

"Someone bashed her in the head and knocked her to the floor," Leigh stated. "She was incapacitated and then stabbed. Would she have been conscious?"

Matt moved to Kiko, carefully slipping the skull from her hands to study it himself. "Hmmm . . . maybe. She took a good hit, but she may have only been stunned. I guess the other question is would the murderer have waited for her to regain consciousness? Did the murderer simply want her dead or did he want her to suffer through that death?"

"You say 'he,' " Paul commented. "What if it was a woman?" He turned to Leigh. "You said that the victim broke from her coven. Aren't they usually mostly women?"

"Not always, but this was an all-female coven. You've got a good point though. A woman might not have the strength to hold someone still while she stabbed them. She'd need them to be restrained or incapacitated somehow." Leigh patted Paul on the shoulder. "Nice catch."

He grinned in return, warmth at her praise coloring his pale cheeks.

Leigh turned back to Matt. "Was there any sign that the victim was restrained? Any trace of rope or cloth? Chains? Wire?"

Matt shook his head. "Nothing. And we went through the

area under the body with a fine-toothed comb looking for bone fragments and the disarticulated hand bones. If there had been something, we would have found it. Now, rope or cloth could have burned away when the hands fell apart. You can sometimes find traces of something like that in a fire if it's in a protected area of the body. The wrists weren't. But because of final body positioning, I don't think she was restrained. The head injury was likely all the advantage the killer needed."

Leigh made a few notes. "I've gone through the list of coven members Elanthia Wakefield—the owner of Draw Down the Moon—provided. So far, I've got nothing. Moira left the coven because of an argument with another Witch about their charitable work in the community. I tracked her down—she's out on the West Coast on a business trip. She's been away for the past two weeks and won't be home for another week. I confirmed her alibi with the hotel management, so she's in the clear. Of the other members, all but three have alibis for the time of the murder. Several commented that they knew Moira was badmouthing the Circle of the Triple Goddess to anyone who would listen, but they brushed it off as simple spite because she didn't get her way."

"That's what they say, but would they actually act on it?" Kiko said.

"That's where the alibis are important and most of them alibi out. Of the three that didn't, one joined the coven after Moira left and never met her. Another is old enough to be my grandmother and wouldn't have the strength needed to overpower a woman forty years her junior. If she did it, then she needed someone else's help. The third is Elanthia Wakefield herself."

Matt cocked his head, watching her. "And you don't think she did it?"

"I don't. She's a true member of the Craft and strikes me as holding very firmly to the rule to harm none. I can't definitively take her off the suspect list, but I have no evidence linking her to the crime, and I don't feel it in my gut. Now, as far as physical evidence goes, I checked with the owner of the antique shop and he confirmed he'd never seen the athame before and it wasn't part of his inventory."

"Hang on a second," Matt said. "Mentioning the shop owner reminded me—what do you think about the fact that Flynn Simpson's partner had access to the shop where his mother died?"

Leigh's lips flattened into a tight line. "I don't like coincidences. Or believe in them."

"Wait," said Kiko. "You've lost us. How did the victim's son's partner have access to that shop?"

"When I spoke to the shop owner yesterday, he mentioned the store had been up for sale for a few weeks."

"The store," Juka repeated. "Meaning the contents?"

"Both the physical space and the inventory. The owner was aiming to retire within six months. That deadline has moved forward now that he has no stock. Aaron Dodsworth, Flynn Simpson's partner, was the realtor."

"In alibiing himself," Matt said, "Simpson alibied his partner too. They were in bed together on Saturday night when the murder occurred."

"And so far, there's no motive or evidence pointing at Dodsworth."

"What about money?" Paul asked. "The greatest of all motivators. Moira Simpson was *rich*."

Leigh tapped her notepad against her palm, deep in thought. "Normally, family members are the first people we look at, especially when there is a lot of money at stake. If money's the issue, we should be looking at Flynn."

"I'm not sure you fully understand the extent of his disease,"

Matt cut in. "Imagine someone like him during a struggle. If anything happened, he wouldn't just be bruised and battered, he'd be seriously injured with life-threatening or, at the very least, life-changing consequences. He'd be crazy to take that chance. And we saw him. I certainly didn't spot any fresh injuries."

"Good point. Simpson also speaks about his mother as if the woman was a saint. She gave him all her time—and he needed a lot with his disorder—and no expense was spared. So if you look at it that way, if Dodsworth killed his partner's mother for her money, he'd risk losing that partner forever if he found out. He'd be wiser to keep the golden goose happy and keep her purse strings loose if money was what he was after."

"But what if that partner was dying?" Kiko said. "That greatly decreases the likelihood that he could benefit."

Leigh rounded on Matt. "How long has Simpson got?"

Matt shrugged. "In his current condition, assuming no catastrophic accidents to dramatically shorten his lifespan, maybe another ten to fifteen years? And I'm not sure why Dodsworth would commit murder this far in advance. Who knows what might have happened to Moira Simpson in the next decade."

"Dodsworth runs his own business," said Juka. "Maybe he needs money right now."

"Yeah." Paul drew the word out slowly. "Maybe he wanted to speed up the timeline, so he killed the mother and then once the son inherits, he planned to push him down the stairs and then watch him calcify and die."

"That's not a very convenient timeline if part of the plan is waiting for Flynn Simpson to die. Besides, while gay marriage is legal in this state, they haven't taken that step, so there's no automatic inheritance for Dodsworth at this point," Leigh said. "On top of that, he's been alibied. So he's on my list to interview tomorrow because I don't like the connection, but so far we have nothing concrete pointing toward him, whereas we have a lot of evidence pointing toward the Witchcraft community. And back to that. I followed up with the metalsmith who designed Moira's athame. He confirmed that he designed and made that knife as part of a set—the athame, a boline and a wand."

"A wand?" Paul asked. "Aren't those usually made out of wood?"

"Usually. But the point of a wand is to conduct energy, so both wood and metal are used. Many in the Craft have more than one wand of different materials and styles."

"And once again, Moira went for the best with an original art piece," Matt said.

"Unique and showy, yes. Her wand was custom-crafted of interwoven threads of metal so it looked like it was made out of an intertwined web. The metalsmith said he'd send me a picture as he photographs all his original art to post on his website. Also, he said they were unique pieces and he's made nothing else like it, so the murder weapon is definitely her knife."

"Speaking of showy, there's the dog." Matt turned to the small bones laid out of the tray. "We found the remains of a microchip, but it was so close to the surface that it was fried by the fire, so no help in ID there. We tried to confirm that it might be a Pomeranian, since we know that was what Moira owned. Size and skeletal structure certainly matches and we've also got the X-rays, which showed a partially collapsed trachea."

"A collapsed trachea? From the fire?"

"No. Apparently it's a common problem with Pomeranians. Makes them cough like a two-pack-a-day smoker. But knowing Moira and her love of expensive accessories, I'd guess that the dog was a purebred, which means that DNA would probably be able to confirm the breed, if you need to go that far."

"I don't think we will since victim ID is wrapped up at this point, but you took samples in case we need to run it later?"

"We did."

"Then I think that will do for now." Leigh was interrupted by the strident ring of her cell phone. After a brief conversation, she turned back to Matt. "That was Bree. She wants to meet tomorrow. Because it's a murder investigation, she pulled in some favors and will have the lab results first thing in the morning. She also said there was something recovered at the scene we need to see. She can make time at eleven. You interested in tagging along?"

"Absolutely. Where do you want to meet?"

"Bree lives in Salem, so rather than having us drive out to the Department of Fire Services in Stow, she's arranged for us to meet at the fire department headquarters in town. Do you know it?"

"No, but I'll find it. I'll meet you there at five to eleven." Matt scanned the remains. "You guys can keep going here?"

"That's the plan," Kiko said. "I'm going to start the skull reconstruction."

"And we'll keep cataloging the bone injuries," Paul said. "We're off to a good start, but we still have a long way to go with this much damage."

Matt rubbed his hands together in apparent satisfaction and grinned. "Great. Sounds like tomorrow could be a big day."

CHAPTER ELEVEN:
CLEAN BURN

Clean Burn: a burn pattern seen on noncombustible surfaces like metal, brick or cinder block where direct flame contact or intense radiated heat burns away soot and smoke condensate.

Thursday, 10:53 a.m.
Chief James F. Brennen Memorial Fire Headquarters
Salem, Massachusetts

Leigh waited in front of the corner diner while Matt parked behind her Crown Vic. Shading her eyes against the sun's bright glare, she studied the huge Federal-style red brick building across the street. Located on the corner of a busy intersection, it was just a few blocks from the site of the wharf fire. Two of the four garage doors were open, bright red trucks facing outwards.

"How did it go at the Simpson house this morning?" Matt asked from behind her.

She started slightly at the sound of his voice. She hadn't heard him approach—the man could be stealthy as a cat. She looked over her shoulder to see herself reflected in his sunglasses. "Not bad. I was lucky to catch Judge Connor this morning in chambers before he went into session. Riley had some time, so he came along and gave me a hand."

"You know I would have helped if you'd asked."

"I know. But when it comes to things like legal searches, it's better to leave the first sweep to the cops. It didn't take us very long. She lived in an exclusive condo downtown. High security, very luxurious, very elite. But not too big, so we were in and out fairly quickly. Her condo was everything you'd expect from what we've heard of her so far—expensive furniture, fine crystal, spectacular jewelry, tasteful art. No surprises until we found the box in her guest-room closet that contained her supplies from her time in the coven. Everything carelessly tossed together in a jumble: cauldron, candles, chalice, herbs, crystals, potion bottles, oils, books on the Craft. But most telling of all, her grimoire was also there."

"What's that?"

"It's also called a Book of Shadows and is one of a Witch's most precious possessions. It's essentially a journal of her experiences in the Craft: dreams, rituals, spells, potion recipes, coven members, daily practices. So, to carelessly toss it away . . . Well, let's just say that Elanthia would be horrified."

"Do you still have yours?"

Caught off guard, Leigh jerked slightly. "Actually, yes. I fell out of touch with the Craft but, even then, it didn't seem right to throw it away. It was an important part of my youth."

"So a good memory for you."

Leigh smiled. "That's a nice way to describe it. Anyway, there were a number of things that should have been in the box, but weren't."

"The athame."

"Actually, the entire matched set from the metalsmith was missing. Riley and I took the place apart, specially looking for any trace of them." She glanced at the streetlight that was about to turn yellow. "Come on, let's catch the light."

They started across the street.

"So the question is, what happened to them," Matt said. "Did the killer steal them or did she give them away?"

"Or did she sell them on eBay or at a pawnshop? We need to

107

follow up where they went. eBay will be trickier to track, but Riley is calling local pawnshops and those in and around Boston, since we know she liked to visit Newberry Street. We also recovered her laptop, which I've already dropped off with Tucker." Rob Tucker, the detective unit's computer hotshot, had been instrumental in helping solve their first case. "He's going to go through her email and files and see if there's anything there that might shed some light. And I'm going to call the other Witchcraft shops to see if they take secondhand items."

"You know," Matt said, "when you think about it, you keep a grimoire."

Leigh glanced over at him. "I know. I told you I put that away years ago."

"No, I mean you *still* keep one. Your notepad." He tapped his knuckles against her blazer pocket where she always kept her notepad and pen. "It contains your experiences and tricks of the trade."

They walked together up the wide sunlit driveway that ran the width of the building and entered the dim quiet of the garage. To their right was a shiny red engine, a large panel of dials and gauges and draping loops of yellow hose peeking out from just behind the cab. To their left, a huge ladder truck filled the bay from garage door to the rear wall, the massive ladder stretched along the length of the truck roof from windshield almost to the back bumper. The front doors of the cab were open, and a heavy black turnout coat hung from the hand bar installed beside the open door. Below the coat was a pair of boots, toes neatly pointing toward the truck, with a pair of bunkers puddled limply around them. Inside the truck, a helmet lay on each seat.

"Set up for a fast getaway?" Matt suggested.

"Looks like it. If all your stuff is right here, you can just step into it and go." The sound of something metallic striking the concrete floor echoed through the garage, and Leigh peered toward the back of the building. "Come on. Sounds like someone's here."

Emerging between the two vehicles, they approached two young firefighters, busily folding hose and loading it onto the back of the engine, who directed them up a wide set of stairs to the administrative offices.

They found Bree inside the main control room, a huge open space with a long L-shaped console that ran along one side and the back of the room. Two uniformed men sat at the console, surrounded by blinking lights, monitors constantly scrolling information and maps lining the walls, listing every street and fire hydrant in Salem. The low murmur of the radio was a constant background noise as the fire alarm operator at the desk routed calls to stations all over the city while staying abreast of ongoing incidents.

Bree nodded as they entered the room, and quickly finished her conversation with one of the men. She crossed the room toward them, a file folder tucked under her arm. "Thanks for coming. I've had time to look over the reports. We definitely have something unusual."

Bree led them down the hallway, past bulletin boards overflowing with newspaper clippings of local fires, and open doors leading into neat, sparse sleeping quarters.

They turned into a small conference room near the end of the hallway. Once seated, Bree opened the file folder. Lying on top of a stack of papers was a piece of scorched metal sealed in a plastic evidence bag. "Let's start with this." She passed the bag to Leigh. Inside was a pentacle, approximately two inches in diameter. "This was found at the scene. I asked around and one of the guys who was in the initial attack said he'd seen it nailed to the front door. As the fire progressed and the door burned, it got lost in the debris near the entranceway. I know this is Salem, but it seemed unusual to me that it would be on the door. People tend to wear pentacles as charms, or have them woven into cloth or inscribed onto chalices, but you don't normally find one nailed to a door. I happened to catch the shop owner that day; he'd never seen it before, which made me think it was related to the fire itself. Or the murder."

Leigh passed the bag to Matt, who took a moment to study the design. "I'm betting this isn't a coincidence considering the knife."

"The murder weapon?" Bree leaned forward over the desk, her eyes alive with interest. "There's a connection?"

"The knife was a ceremonial athame adorned with a crescent moon and pentacle," said Leigh.

Bree cocked an eyebrow. "Interesting. I didn't get the impression the shop owner is a practicing Witch. Then why so many symbols left there?"

"I talked to him earlier this week," Leigh said. "He doesn't have any ties to the Craft, and his only link to the crime is that the victim used to shop there occasionally. While he recognized her face, he didn't remember her coming into the store in the last six or eight months. But the pentacle adds another layer to the theory that the killing was related to the victim's involvement with the Craft."

"You think someone inside her coven killed her?" Bree asked. "Wouldn't that be a little obvious, leaving a pentacle like that and using a ceremonial knife?"

"There's also the fact that a Witch considers the pentacle to be the symbol of creation, not of death."

"Unless that juxtaposition is exactly what they were aiming for," Matt suggested. "She quit the Craft, so it no longer applied to her. Her own athame was used against her so maybe turning the pentacle symbol around metaphorically is all part of the message."

"That's hardly a message for the victim," Bree said dryly. "It might, however, be a warning to others. 'Don't mess with us' . . . that kind of thing?"

Leigh plucked the pentacle from Matt's hands to study it again. "It just doesn't seem right. The Craft is all about 'live and let live.' "

"What about black magic? There must be some Witches in the area that practice the black arts."

Leigh nodded slowly. "It's worth looking into."

Bree flipped through papers in the folder. "Let me give you something else to look into. The lab results are back. Once you removed the body from the scene, we went back in to take samples from our suspected point of origin. That's when I saw it—a *very* minor difference in a roughly one-foot-square section of flooring."

"What does that mean?" Leigh asked. "Something else was there?"

"That's right. Something was on the floor that initially protected it from the fire. There was even variation within that section because part of it was under the body, which sheltered it even longer. We took scrapings from a number of spots, and that's where we hit pay dirt." Bree referred to a lab report. "When the mass spec results came back, they were positive for cellulose, lignin, hydrocarbons, red phosphorus and a mixture of protein, sugars, resin . . ." She slapped the report back down on the desk. "And a list of other things that I won't bore you with. And likely couldn't pronounce anyway."

"What on earth is all that?" Leigh asked.

"The lab guys love to make it more complicated than it needs to be," Bree said. "Scientists. Ask for a straight answer and get gobbledygook." She rolled her eyes.

"Hey!" Matt protested.

Bree stabbed an index finger in Matt's direction. "Present company excluded of course. As for your question, basically, it's wood, canola oil, red phosphorus and latex rubber. That combination had me stymied at first so I bounced it off the guys when I caught them sitting down to dinner last night. I used to work with these men, so they're always extra willing to help out, and their combined experience is priceless. Doc finally hit on it when he remembered that red phosphorus reacts violently with latex. Add to that that it wasn't the wood from the floor we picked up but newspaper and it all comes together.

"This is how we think your killer set up his time-delay incendiary device," Bree explained. "Take a latex rubber balloon, and half fill it with canola oil. Add one small piece of solid red phosphorus, maybe about the size of a pea, being very careful not to contact the balloon in the process or it's game over then and there as suddenly you're stuck in the middle of your own fire. Tie a string around the end of the balloon and suspend it. Spread a loose stack of newspaper on the ground beneath the balloon. Then simply poke a hole in the bottom of the balloon with a pin and sit back and wait. Or, if you're smart, run like hell."

"The oil drips onto the paper," Matt said. "Then as the level drops, the red phosphorus—I'm guessing it floats in the oil—finally contacts the latex of the balloon. I assume there's an exothermic reaction at that point?"

"English, please," Leigh said in a resigned tone. "Remember, we're not all science majors."

A small smile curved Bree's lips as she translated. "The latex reacts with the red phosphorus producing a sudden burst of heat. The heat melts the balloon, causing it to burst into flames. Then those flaming bits of latex fall to the floor."

"Onto the oil-soaked paper," Matt finished. *"Whoosh!"*

"Whoosh indeed. The oil would have splattered the floor and

the victim's clothing and it all would've ignited. The oil also would have accelerated damage to the body by ensuring that her clothing was well engulfed. But something was nagging at me, so I went back through the scene photos. We took really extensive shots of the point of origin. One of the items we found in the debris was a long armed hook. I didn't think anything of it at the time because of all the other odd junk in the store, so we didn't take it into evidence, but it's there in the pictures. Keeping this scenario in mind, I think the hook was jammed into the door of the wardrobe in order to hang the balloon."

"I don't understand something," Leigh said. "How would a pile of newspaper protect the floor? Surely it would have burned in the fire."

"Think about the last time you tried to start a fire with newspaper. You have to let air in between the sheets or it won't burn due to lack of oxygen. The killer may have thought that a bigger pile was better for getting the fire going, but in actuality, he could have snuffed his own fire that way. A thick pile of paper would have insulated the floor temporarily, giving us that slight gradation in burn patterns. Luckily for the killer, he had enough oil soaked into the edges and top layer to get the fire started. And with the size of the fuel load in there, once it was going, he didn't need the paper anymore. Eventually, even the thick layer of paper burned."

"Ingenious," Leigh said. "This certainly tells us something about our killer."

"It tells us that he knows at least a little chemistry," Bree agreed. "But there's something more intriguing about the red phosphorus. It's so pure that it's basically a controlled substance."

"Why would a chemical like that be a controlled substance?" Matt asked.

Bree leaned back in her chair, casually crossing her arms over her chest. "Because it can be used in the production of meth-amphetamine."

Matt's eyebrows shot skyward. "Meth? I had no idea."

"Guess you haven't been cooking anything up in the lab, then."

"My students keep me on a short leash," Matt shot back.

"If the red phosphorus is controlled, that actually gives us a leg up," Leigh observed, ignoring their banter and quelling the urge to roll her eyes. "Chemical houses will be required to document all buyers. That could significantly narrow our search. At the very least, it will give us a paper trail to start with."

"God knows, we love a good paper trail." Matt's tone clearly said otherwise. "But I guess it's a good thing because I bet there'll be no way to trace the latex or the oil. Too common and—"

Matt was interrupted by the ringing of Leigh's cell phone. She pulled it out of her pocket, glanced at the caller ID, and froze. "I need to get this. Sorry." She accepted the call. "Abbott." She automatically straightened in her chair. "Yes, sir. I'm meeting with the representative from the state fire marshal's office at FD headquarters, but I can be back at the unit inside of an hour. Yes, sir. I'll see you then." She ended the call.

"Was that Kepler?" Matt asked.

"No, Detective Lieutenant Harper. He needs to see me ASAP."

Concern flashed over Matt's face. "About what?"

"I have no idea. But there was something in his tone I really didn't like."

"When the chief needs to see you right away, it's never a good thing," Bree said.

Leigh gnawed on her bottom lip. "No, it isn't. But I guess I'll find out soon enough. Now, where were we?"

"We were talking about the incendiary device," Matt said.

"How much lead time did this give the killer? From the time the device was set, how long did he or she have to get out of there?"

"Depending on the size of the hole in the balloon, I'd estimate as much as six or seven minutes. Plenty of time to be long gone by the time the fire really got rolling." Bree pulled several sheets of paper from the folder and passed them to Leigh. "These are your copies of the lab reports. I haven't had time to finish my scene report yet, but I'll email it to you later this week."

Leigh stood and they shook hands. "Thank you. You've given us a great lead."

"I hope so. I hate firebugs. Find this guy and let's put an end to it."

"We'll do our best."

"I'll walk you guys out."

They were halfway down the stairs when an ear-piercing alarm went off—a long, deafening beep, followed by a series of beeps and whoops. Bree crowded them against the stair railing. "Stay to the side," she snapped.

A voice came over the loudspeaker. "Attention Engine One, Engine Four, Ladder One and C-Five, a telephone alarm for a reported structure fire at one-four-five Linden Street."

Pounding feet came behind them as men in dark-blue uniforms streamed down the stairs. Across the garage bay, several men and one woman shot through the hole in the ceiling, sliding down the fire pole into the garage below. From a hallway at the foot of the stairs, a man wearing a white uniform shirt sprinted toward the trucks. "There goes the deputy chief," Bree said. "Should be clear now. If you lean over the railing, you can watch them leave."

It was organized chaos below: Men shouted at each other while stepping into boots and pulling up bunkers and suspend-

Jen J. Danna

ers. They tugged on turnout coats and jammed helmets on their heads as they climbed into the cabs. Trucks roared to life. The smaller engine pulled out first, flipping on lights and sirens as soon as it cleared the bay door. The ladder trucks rumbled out next, with the deputy chief's Tahoe right behind. In seconds they were gone, headed south down Lafayette Street, sirens screaming into the distance.

Leigh turned around to lean against the banister in the now-quiet garage. "Is it always that fast?"

"We aim for no more than sixty seconds on average. With that location, the first unit should be on scene in about three minutes. The faster they get out the door, the better. Might just be the difference between a simple contents fire versus a full-blown structure fire." Bree glanced at her watch. "I have to head back to Stow. Let me know when you have something new. Talk to you later." She took the stairs two at a time and disappeared around the corner in the direction of the control room.

"Are you going to start on the chemical supply houses right away?" Matt asked as they crossed the now-empty garage.

"That'll be later today if I'm lucky, but more likely tomorrow. I need to head back to the unit and then I'm going back to the Witchcraft shop. I want to ask Elanthia Wakefield about the pentacle and the possibility of the black arts being involved. And I have a few more questions about coven membership now that we're leaning toward a female killer. You?"

"Heading back to BU." His eyes took on a speculative gleam. "You free tonight?"

She cast him a long sideways glance as they broke back out into the sunlight. "I should be. What have you got in mind?"

"My dad's playing poker with his cronies. Four of them around the kitchen table playing cards and drinking beer all

116

night. How about I pick up a pizza and we do dinner at your place?"

"Sounds good. Seven work for you?"

"Great. See you then." With a grin, he jogged toward his SUV.

Leigh turned toward her own vehicle, her mind already spinning around new possibilities from the morning's discoveries. *We're on to you, firebug. Just you wait . . .*

Chapter Twelve:
Extension

Extension: spread of a fire to unburned areas or adjacent buildings through open doors or unprotected openings in the attic.

Thursday, 11: 54 a.m.
Essex Detective Unit
Salem, Massachusetts

Leigh tapped lightly on the door frame of Detective Lieutenant Harper's office. "You wanted to see me, sir?"

Harper looked up, scowling. "Yes. Come in and shut the door."

Leigh's stomach dropped with a sickening lurch. She couldn't think of anything she'd done to displease the unit chief that would require a closed-door meeting. *What if he knows about the photo?* Shock abruptly shot through her, setting her fingertips tingling. But she pushed that thought away. How could he know about it already? She'd barely learned of it herself.

She closed the door, entering the big corner office, lit by a spread of windows that ran the length of two full walls, overlooking Washington Street and the bright waters of the cove beyond. She took a chair opposite the wide cluttered desk. "Is there something wrong, sir?"

Harper picked up a folded newspaper and slapped it down on the edge of his desk in front of her. "Read the *Salem Times* today?"

"No, sir. I . . ." Leigh's gaze landed on the headline and her breath caught. PENTACLE KILLER ON THE LOOSE. And then below it in smaller type, A RETURN TO THE BURN-ING TIMES? "What the hell is this?" she asked, knowing the press wasn't privy to this information yet.

"That's exactly what I wanted to know," Harper snapped. "We're just days away from Halloween. Already the city is swarming with tourists. This isn't exactly the publicity we need right now." He scowled. "I got a call from the mayor first thing this morning. I hadn't even had my coffee and he's on the phone ranting about the morning edition."

Leigh found the byline—Jason Wells—but she didn't recognize the name. She quickly scanned the article, wincing at the details revealed—an athame as the murder weapon, a pentacle found on the door, a rampant fire, Witches as the hunters or the hunted? She sagged back in her chair, the newspaper still clutched in her hands. "This is alarmist BS."

"Of course it is. I know that and you know that, but Joe Citizen out there is going to be afraid that there's another out-of-control killer out there. We're only weeks out from the Bradford case. That's still damned fresh in everyone's mind."

"I'm aware of that, sir. What I want to know is how did he get his details? They certainly weren't from me."

"I figured that. You're too smart to play that game. But there are others that might not be, who would get a thrill from spill-ing those details just to be the 'unnamed source.' "

Leigh rapidly reviewed everyone who was involved in the case. "Some of this information could have come from the morgue techs, although Rowe would have the head of anyone who talked to the media. I bet it was one of the firefighters. They were all over that scene and saw everything. They were the ones who found the pentacle. Which I just learned about myself from Trooper Gilson."

"Which explains why that information was new to me," Harper said. "I'm going to talk to Sharon about this."

Leigh silently agreed. Sharon Collins, the DA's press officer, had an especially deft hand with reporters.

"She may have a connection with this reporter and can get him under control," Harper continued. "He's covered all the bases in this article in terms of alarming everyone. Are the Witches the killers or the victims? Who's safe in this town? Who's next?" He leaned over the desk, his gaze drilling into hers. "There isn't going to be a next. I don't want another serial case. Find out who's leaking this information. I also don't want any acts of retribution going on against the Witches. They're an established part of this community and are a part of the tourist trade that keeps the local economy running. I don't want to see anyone going off the deep end and taking it out on them. The population in this town is going to triple in the next few days. I won't have chaos endangering more lives."

"Yes, sir."

Harper sat back in his chair, yanking on his tie to loosen it. "Damned reporters. Everything's a story and everything has to be blown out of proportion. I don't like getting hysterical calls from the mayor." His voice was calmer now. "You know what he's like at this time of year. His office is overwhelmed and it all runs downhill from him."

Leigh heard the roundabout apology in his tone and some of the tightness in her shoulders relaxed. "And you got caught in it. I'm sorry."

One eyebrow quirked with a touch of Harper's normal humor when he wasn't getting pounded by both the media and the mayor. "No need to apologize, Abbott. Just get this sewed up. How's the case coming?"

"We have victim ID and the cause of the fire. The victim's son has been informed and his partner is on my list to talk to this afternoon as he was the realtor handling the sale of the antique store. I also have a lead I'm going to be running down this afternoon on someone with potential motive. Considering that practically all the evidence from the crime scene was destroyed, we're doing pretty well."

"Good." Harper's curt nod told her the interview was over.

"Thank you, sir."

Leigh left the office and strode down the hallway toward the bullpen, her hands clenched at her sides. *Bloody reporters. Who gave him that damned information? If this doesn't stay quiet—*

"The 'Pentacle Killer,' Abbott? Nice moniker."

Leigh froze in mid-step, her jaw clenching. She recognized that voice and the way the words dripped with malice. "I didn't come up with it," she said, turning to glare at Morrison.

"I doubt you could come up with something so clever." Morrison leaned coolly against a doorjamb. "Was the attention from the Bradford case dwindling, so you felt you needed to pump it up with something else?"

"Screw you, Morrison. I didn't talk to the reporters." She took a step back, forcing her hands to uncurl. "But if I find out you're behind it, let me assure you, there'll be hell to pay."

She stalked down the hallway, anger burning white-hot in her chest.

Best way to wipe the smirk off his face is to solve this case.

And to do that, she needed to go back to the source, back to the heart of this case.

Back to the Witches.

CHAPTER THIRTEEN:
BURNING TIMES

Burning Times: a historical period from approximately 1000 CE until the end of the seventeenth century when Christian churches used torture and death to stamp out heretical religious practices and Witchcraft. The wealth and property of convicted individuals was seized by the church or distributed to reward the accuser. The majority of victims were women and children, although some pets were also killed as "familiars." In point of fact, Witches were only burned in Scotland and continental Europe; they were hanged, drowned or crushed in England and the US.

Thursday, 1:13 p.m.
Draw Down the Moon Witch Shoppe
Salem, Massachusetts
Leigh was escorted to a small back room by a young Witch. There she found Elanthia Wakefield, standing at a worn wooden workbench, its surface stained with drops of oil and scattered with herbs. She paused to inhale the fragrances of heather and cinnamon before she rapped lightly on the open door.

Elanthia smiled when she saw Leigh. "Come in, please. I'm sorry I couldn't join you out front, but I'm in the middle of a potion for a customer."

A single element gas burner flamed under an enamel pot; it steamed as Elanthia stirred the contents with a stained wooden spoon. A one-hundred-dollar bill sat on the bench next to the burner. Scattered around the table were tiny glass vials of golden oil, bottles of spring water, a pile of cinnamon sticks, small bags of herbs and a larger sack of coarse sea salt. "What are you making?"

"A money perfume to bring prosperity. What can I do for you, Trooper?"

"First of all, I wanted to let you know that it was Moira Simpson's body that was discovered following the fire."

Elanthia's brows knit, sympathy deep in her eyes. She raised both open hands skyward. "Goddess protect her soul." She resumed slowly stirring the contents of the pot. "I had hoped it wouldn't be Moira. Which makes no sense because we wish harm to no one and some other poor soul would have been lost in that fire if it wasn't Moira. Were you able to contact everyone on the coven list?"

"That's why I stopped by. Everyone on that list was a current member. I was wondering if there were any members who left the coven while Moira Simpson was with you."

Elanthia's hand jerked and her spoon rapped lightly against the side of the pot. "We lost two members during that time. They never pointed fingers. In fact they gave a very good reason to transfer to a new coven, but I always wondered."

"About what?"

"They're lesbians. All are welcome in our coven, but some Witches of different sexual orientations prefer to be in all-lesbian or all-gay groups. Sherry and Jocelyn joined the coven about three months before Moira. Then eight or nine months later, Jocelyn told me they'd found an all-lesbian coven to transfer to. I blessed them on their faith journey, of course, but I have to admit I did wonder why they didn't stay when they initially seemed happy with us."

"You think Moira made them uncomfortable?"

"Never within my hearing, but members of the coven

sometimes interact individually or in smaller groups, so I was not privy to all their conversations. However, I noticed something in circle casting. Since there is no hierarchy within the group, all members mix freely. But Sherry and Jocelyn always seemed to keep their distance from Moira. As Moira often tried to be near me, I noticed their distance."

"Moira considered you the leader of the group."

Irritation flashed in Elanthia's eyes. The reaction surprised Leigh as the other woman always seemed so cool, but perhaps that was only the face she showed the outside world. Perhaps her control was starting to waver.

Elanthia turned back to her pot. "Excuse me for a moment." She turned off the gas and moved the pot to a metal trivet on the table. Holding her hands over the steaming liquid, she murmured, "I ask that this be correct and for the good of all people. So mote it be."

So be it. It struck Leigh afresh how long it had been since she'd heard those words.

Elanthia turned back to Leigh. "It was an old argument with Moira. She wanted there to be a hierarchy when I told her time and again the coven was all about equality."

"You said before that Moira was all about flash rather than substance. I assume that by the time Moira left the coven, Sherry and Jocelyn were gone?"

"Long gone."

"And in criticizing of the group afterward, did she focus on those two particular members?"

"Not that I know of, but I never heard directly. Word filtered back to me, but she would never dare to speak that way in front of me." She closed her eyes for a moment. "I'm sorry, it disturbs me to speak ill of the dead."

"It disturbs me not to find justice for them."

Elanthia sat down on the tall oak stool in the corner of the room, looking limp and tired. "This just isn't something I deal with every day. The thought that one of our members might be responsible for this . . ." She looked up, her spirit suddenly renewed and her eyes bright. "I just don't believe it. I've shared my life with these women, some of them for years. I can't believe it of any of them."

"But you understand that I can't leave any stone unturned. If anyone has a connection to Moira, to the store where she died, or to any of the evidence we found there, I will pursue them. To start, I need Sherry and Jocelyn's full names and addresses."

"They married last year and live together under their shared last name of Haws-Chase. I see them on occasion as they're still customers. Their address is in the sales book up front." She met Leigh's eyes. "They aren't responsible for this. I know you have to follow through, but they had no part in it."

"Then they have nothing to worry about. Now, there's one other thing I wanted to ask you about. The concept of the black arts came up in this morning's discussion." When Elanthia made a snorting sound, Leigh raised a puzzled brow. "You don't give any credence to black magic?"

"There is no black magic. You should know that from your time with us."

Leigh ran her fingers over the bits of dried herbs on the table as she thought back to her days in the coven. The scent of lavender filtered into the air as the delicate purple blooms crumbled under her touch. "You mean because of the threefold law of return?"

" 'Do as ye will and harm ye none.' Our actions, both good and bad, will be returned to us threefold. Do harm to others and it will be revisited upon you threefold. But do good, and good will come to you three times over. There is no black magic or white magic. Only the magic that helps us align with the forces of the universe. You thought to blame this on the black arts?"

"It was suggested. We found a pentacle at the scene of the first fire. Dr. Lowell, my scientist partner, wondered if the killer might be someone practicing the black arts and using the pentacle in contradiction of the Craft's sacred regard for it."

Elanthia elegantly slid off her stool and shook out her long skirt. "That wouldn't be done by anyone genuinely within the Craft unless it was put there separately as part of a protection spell. Someone wishing to point fingers at the Salem Witches could, however, have placed it there. For all the good we do in the community, there are still some who do not accept us."

Elanthia's sharp tone clicked the puzzle pieces into place for Leigh. "You saw this morning's *Salem Times.*"

"Yes. And if I hadn't, I would have found out shortly thereafter when coven members started to call, concerned about their safety. The 'burning times'? Do you know what mention of that does to a Witch?" She turned back to the bench, organizing the bottles scattered haphazardly over the surface. Her voice was steady, but the jerky movements of her hands gave away her agitation.

"I didn't talk to that reporter," Leigh said. "I don't know where he's getting his information. Truthfully, most of that article was speculation and hysteria. He's got the Witchcraft community concerned that they're targets and the general population worried that the Witches are on a rampage. It's ludicrous."

"But it sells papers," Elanthia said flatly.

"I'm sure his editor is very happy. But I'd like ten minutes with him in interrogation to find out who his source is and to ensure that he leaves this case alone."

Elanthia gave her a dark look. "Work fast, Trooper Abbott, before someone else gets caught in the crossfire of this man's thirst for headlines. Now, if you'll come out to the front desk, I'll find that address for you." Elanthia swept past her and out the door.

Leigh cast a long look at the oils and herbs on the table. *Was someone threatened by the Witches and their beliefs and traditions? And would they go to these lengths to show them as evil?* Filing that thought away, she followed Elanthia out into the shop.

Thursday, 4:36 p.m.
Simpson Residence
Salem, Massachusetts

The door opened to reveal a tall, muscular man, neatly dressed in pressed slacks and a button-down shirt. When he saw Leigh standing on the doorstep, he pointed to the Bluetooth headset in his left ear and waved her into the house. "I think it's going to go fast. I can show you tonight if you're interested. Wonderful. I'll pick you up at seven. See you soon." He pulled off the earpiece. "Sorry about that. Realtors—we're constantly on the phone. Can I help you?"

Leigh flashed her badge. "I'm Trooper Leigh Abbott of the Massachusetts State Police."

"Flynn told me about you," he said, extending his hand. "Aaron Dodsworth, Flynn's partner. I'm sorry, but Flynn isn't in. He's at the funeral home making plans for his mother's funeral."

"I'm actually here to see you."

Aaron froze for a moment, as if startled, and then relaxed. "Please come in."

He led the way to the living room and Leigh took the same seat as the day before, pulling out her notepad. "I have a few brief questions. I understand that you had the real-estate listing for Uniquely You Antiques."

"I did."

127

"As the realtor, you had access to the property?"

"I have a copy of the key."

"Do you usually have copies of all keys for all buildings you sell?"

"No. Houses have a single key available to all realtors in a timer-controlled lockbox. We all have the combination to that box. But I always have keys or keycards for the commercial buildings."

Leigh made a note. "When was the last time you were in the store?"

"I showed it to a client last Wednesday. It's in a great location, right by the water in a busy tourist area, so I expected it to sell quickly. The client was still deciding when the store burned down."

"You still have your copy of the key?"

"Of course. But there's not much point in keeping it."

"Please hold onto it for now. Mr. Dodsworth, how would you describe your relationship with your partner's mother?"

"We had a very good relationship. Moira absolutely doted on Flynn, and he on her. Their relationship sort of transferred sideways to me." He leaned forward in the manner of someone about to share a confidence. "Flynn's had some . . . medical issues and his mother has been nothing but supportive. And very generous financially. Flynn never truly wanted for anything."

"How did she feel about her son's same-sex relationship?"

"As I said, she was nothing but supportive."

Leigh leaned her elbow on the arm of the couch, trying to keep the tone of the conversation casual. "Really? I understood she disapproved of a same-sex couple in her coven."

Dodsworth jerked backwards, as if driven away by an unpleasant odor. "I find that hard to believe. She never expressed any such views to us."

"Perhaps I misunderstood," Leigh said. "Can you tell me

where you were on Sunday morning between midnight and four thirty?"

"I was here with Flynn."

"Thank you. That was what he said as well, but you understand that we need to corroborate alibis." Leigh stood and held out her card. "Thank you for your time, Mr. Dodsworth. If you can think of any detail concerning Moira or the store, please don't hesitate to contact me."

"And thank you, Trooper. Both Flynn and I are grateful for all you're doing for us. Moira never deserved this, so it gives Flynn comfort to know you're trying to find her killer."

As Leigh pulled away from the house, she thought about the different descriptions of her victim—the loving, supportive mother versus the shallow, flashy social climber. Was this simply a matter of perspective, or did Moira Simpson really show her family one face, and the rest of the world another?

Thursday, 6:17 p.m.
Haws-Chase Residence
Salem, Massachusetts

"Thank you." Leigh accepted the steaming cup of tea and settled back into the high-backed leather barstool pulled up to the kitchen island. The room was an eclectic mix of late-nineteenth-century charm and twenty-first-century luxury. The rustic brick walls were from the historic structure's original design, as were the heavy beams that crossed the ceiling. But the rest of the kitchen was all modern convenience, from the glossy maple cupboards to the gleaming stainless-steel appliances and granite countertops. The timelessness of a historic downtown Salem location combined with all the comforts of modern life.

"You're welcome." Jocelyn sat down next to Leigh, while Sherry took the stool at the end of the short island. Both women busied themselves fixing their own tea. "Elanthia said we should expect you."

Leigh set her cup down on the granite with a sharp *crack*. "She shouldn't have called you."

"Elanthia has a good heart and I think she feels responsible for our leaving the Circle of the Triple Goddess," Sherry interjected softly.

"Is she responsible?" Leigh asked.

"No," Jocelyn said firmly, flicking a cautious glance at Sherry.

"Did she explain the situation?"

"Look, you can ask around and you'll find that Moira didn't much care for our lifestyle." Jocelyn air quoted the word "life-style," her tone derisive and edgy. "She believed sexuality is a choice. People like that always think it's a choice."

"Jocelyn!" Sherry laid a hand over her partner's arm. "Trooper Abbott doesn't deserve your anger."

With an oath, Jocelyn focused on the ceiling overhead as she appeared to struggle for calm. "I'm sorry," she said finally. "Moira always could piss me off. I guess some old grudges die hard."

"You held a grudge against her?" Leigh asked.

Her chin shot up. "Damn straight. She was never overt, but if she didn't approve, she'd pick at you constantly. Little digs, little slights. All. The. Time. But she was all sweetness and light with the others—constant compliments, small tokens. *I saw this and thought of you.* Sherry was always better at turning the other cheek, but it got to the point in the coven where I couldn't take it anymore. We loved it there, but she ruined the experience for us."

"Elanthia told me she suspected some ill will between you."

Jocelyn said nothing, just stared at her, eyes flat, jaw locked.

Leigh focused on Sherry. "So you joined a new coven."

Sherry beamed. "And we found a wonderful new place to

belong. As much as we regretted leaving the Circle of the Triple Goddess, our new coven is perfect for us."

"It's an all-female group?"

"All female, all lesbian. We are free to explore and live our Craft there, with no questions about our lifestyle or our habits. It's a wonderfully freeing experience." She gave Jocelyn's arm a little shake. "Isn't it?"

Jocelyn turned to face her partner, all anger sliding away as a smile curved her lips. "Yes, it is." She turned back to Leigh. "I guess in many ways, we should be thanking Moira. We're in a really good place right now, and if she hadn't been a such a bitch—"

"Jocelyn!" But Sherry's scold came out on a half laugh.

"—we wouldn't be there." She relaxed her fist, turning her hand over and intertwining her fingers with her partner's. "We're happy now, so we'd have no reason to wish her dead. Besides, it's not our way." She reached to the back of her neck with her free hand and touched the small dark pentacle tattooed just below her short-cropped hair. "Above all else, do no harm."

"So mote it be," murmured Sherry.

"For the record, can you tell me where you were between midnight and four thirty on Sunday morning?"

Sherry looked startled. "We were here. Asleep."

"Together?"

Jocelyn frowned. "Of course."

"When was the last time you saw Moira Simpson?"

"It must have been at Beltane, on May first," Sherry said. "That was our last sabbat with the coven. By Midsummer Night, we were with our new group."

"I haven't even bumped into her on the street since then," Jocelyn said. "I expected to see her this Samhain; you see everyone on Samhain." She looked at Leigh. "That's what you'd know as Halloween night."

"That's the night of the memorial walk?" asked Leigh.

"You've heard of the Samhain candlelight vigil?"

"I've seen it mentioned in the paper."

"Everyone within and without the Witchcraft community is invited to join that night. It begins with a gathering on Gallows Hill, followed by a candlelight walk through town to the Salem Witch Trials Memorial down by the Old Burying Point on Charter Street. Then the Witches cast a circle and light the way for all that we have loved and lost. It's the one time we allow those outside the Craft to witness our rituals."

"It sounds like a lovely way to give back to the community."

"Thank you." Sherry beamed at her. "You should join us this year."

Leigh considered the invitation. "You know, I just might. Assuming this case is solved, of course." She pushed back her chair.

"I'm sorry we couldn't be of more help. And I'm sorry that Moira lost her life in such a horrible way. No one deserves to die in a fire."

Leigh didn't enlighten her as to the real cause of death. She left her card on the glossy counter. "Please let me know if you think of anything else. I'll see myself out."

"Good luck," Sherry said. "We'll keep you in our thoughts."

We can use all the help we can get, Leigh thought as she closed the door behind her.

CHAPTER FOURTEEN:
CHURCH RAISE

Church Raise: a method of erecting a ladder and keeping it upright using guy ropes extending from the top of the ladder to four opposite points of the compass. It allows a team to use a ladder in an open space when there is nothing to brace the top against.

Thursday, 7:02 p.m.
Abbott Residence
Salem, Massachusetts
Struggling to maintain his tenuous hold on both wine bottle and pizza box, Matt rapped on Leigh's front door.

A muffled *"Coming!"* drifted from behind the autumn wreath of twisted grapevine accented with russet leaves and wheat sheaves. Then Leigh stood in the doorway, dressed casually in low-slung jeans and a long flowing top with tiny buttons and a high waist tucked in under her breasts.

He grinned at her.

"What?" She looked down at herself. "Too casual?"

"Just right. And you left your hair down. You should wear it loose more often. Here." He handed her the dark-green bottle as he entered the house.

She read the label, her eyebrows arching. "Cabernet Sauvignon. My favorite. Excellent label too. What's the occasion?"

Matt toed off his shoes, and then nudged them neatly against the wall beside the door. "Dinner alone with you? That's enough for me."

"I can go with that. Come on. Let's eat in the living room where we can be comfortable."

She led the way. The lights were already low and cracking flames danced in the fireplace. "Make yourself at home. I'll be right back."

Matt set the pizza box down on the coffee table and settled into the deep cushions of the couch. Firelight flickered across the antique oak floor and over the seascape oil painting above the mantel. His gaze fell on a picture on the end table. He picked it up, a smile tugging his lips at the image of Leigh, fresh-faced and smiling at the camera. Her similarity to the older man beside her was striking. Judging from the shared eyes and zygomatic bones, he had to be her father.

He glanced up as she came into the room, a tray in her hands loaded with plates, napkins, two wineglasses, and a wide-based decanter that held the red wine. "Nice photo."

She set the tray down on the coffee table, her gaze flicking to the photo, an easy smile of affection curving her lips. "That's my favorite photo of Dad and me."

"Graduation day?"

"What gave it away, our dress uniforms?" She took the photo from him and stared down at it for a long moment. "He was so proud that day. He'd been preparing me for the academy all through my undergrad years. He was so happy when I was accepted. His little girl was finally following in his footsteps." Her eyes took on a pensive gleam and the smile fell away. "If only he'd been able to enjoy it longer. He had hopes that I'd come join him in the detective unit."

"How long were you on the force before you lost him?"

"Two years." She returned the photo back to the table, fussing until it was at the perfect angle. "I joined the unit the year after he died. By that time, Kepler had taken Dad's position as Sergeant. I think Kepler felt a little awkward when I first came on board, because he knew that Dad should have been there. And Kepler had big shoes to fill because after Dad's death, his reputation approached heroic proportions. But we all settled in and made it work. Kepler tends to be a little brusque, but he's a good man." She picked up the decanter and handed it to Matt. "Do the honors?"

"Sure." Matt poured wine into the deep goblets, while Leigh opened the box and served pizza slices onto the heavy stoneware plates. Then they settled back onto the couch.

Conversation over dinner naturally drifted to the case. Matt updated Leigh on the day's progress in the lab—Kiko almost had the skull reconstructed despite the challenges of working with badly damaged and warped bone, and Paul and Juka were almost finished cataloging the injuries—and then Leigh filled Matt in on all her interviews.

"So, did you believe the Witches? They alibi each other, but if they were involved, they could have pulled it off together."

Leigh took a long sip of her wine, then set her glass down next to her empty plate. "They could have, but I believe them. When you work this job, you have to be able to read people. They rang true for me."

"Who's next on the list, then?"

"I'm going to interview the other Witches in the coven, but I also want to look into Moira's life more. That may mean going back to her son. She joined the coven in the last nine or ten months, but her life before then is still sort of a closed book. Her son may shed some light on her other friendships."

"Or lack thereof. It sounds like she was a my-way-or-the-highway kind of gal. Kind of makes you wonder how controlling she was?"

Leigh cocked her head. "In what way?"

Matt drained his wineglass, then idly rolled the stem between his fingertips, watching the firelight waver through the cut glass. "She raised a child who was totally dependent on her assistance. She was used to calling the shots. Maybe that was reflected in her desire to work her way up the ranks in the coven."

"Except there aren't any ranks."

"Maybe she didn't know that when she joined."

Leigh leaned forward, peering into the nearly empty pizza box. "Do you want any more?"

"I think I ate over half of it." He set down his glass and relaxed back into the cushions, rubbing one hand over his stomach. "I couldn't eat another bite."

"Not even carrot cake?"

His hand froze and he glanced up at her. "You made carrot cake?"

"Sure I did, in my copious free time." Leigh lightly batted him on the arm. "I bought it. But at a fabulous little-hole-in-the-wall bakery downtown. It'll blow your mind."

"Give me fifteen minutes, and I'm there." He picked up her hand and tugged her over to curl against his side. "There's one other thing that occurred to me. Simpson is clearly gay."

"You *were* paying attention. I could have sworn you were too busy dissecting his bone structure."

"You're hilarious." He gave her a mock glare. "It just makes me wonder if Moira's disapproval of a committed monogamous lesbian pair is really rooted in her son's sexual orientation. Perhaps she felt that he was too delicate, so she opted to direct her displeasure at someone else instead."

Leigh was silent for a moment. "You may have a point. She seems to have been rooted in 'traditional' values and anything she saw as contradictory to that earned her disapproval—gays, prisoners, AIDS patients, *et cetera*. Elanthia did say that Moira tried to force her community priorities on the group and that's what led up to the final split."

"She also may have upset more than one coven. And if she's been out of the coven for the last three weeks, what's she been up to in the meantime? The son can't help you there—he didn't even know she'd left the Craft—but it merits looking into. But enough shoptalk. We can do that when my students are around. We can't do this . . ." He slipped his fingers under her chin, tilting her head up as his lips dropped over hers.

Leigh made a low humming noise in the back of her throat, and one hand reached around to clasp the back of his neck. Her lips opened under his, parting easily at the stroke of his tongue; she tasted rich, like the wine they'd shared. When the angle proved slightly awkward, Matt slid his lips from hers and down her neck. He'd learned that the spot where her throat met her collarbone was particularly sensitive. Pushing aside her collar, he laid a line of slow kisses from the hollow of her throat across her shoulder, smiling against her skin at her breathy exhalation.

Her hands ran over the muscles of his arms and she practically purred in approval. But she quickly grew restless under his touch and her hands dropped to his waistband. Grasping handfuls of his T-shirt, she yanked at it, nearly hard enough to pull his mouth from her skin. His T-shirt finally slid free and her hands dove underneath.

Matt froze momentarily, his mouth hovering over her collarbone, his breath washing over her damp skin. His fingers twitched where they clasped her hips. *Any second now, she was going to touch his scars. Then she'd pull away and the moment would be lost.* Dread and embarrassment coiled in a tangled mass in his belly.

"More." Her voice was husky as she freed one hand long enough to drag his mouth back to hers. But while she kissed him, his mind was firmly fixed on her hands, back under his shirt, as one wandered toward his right side. He stiffened, preparing for the coming blow, knowing that he'd never really be ready for it—

She went still, and then leaned back far enough to look into his eyes. "You okay? You were with me, and suddenly it's like you're not there."

"Sure. I'm great." He laughed, but the sound had a sharp edge to it. He cursed himself silently as she considered him, then nearly swore under his breath when she pulled out of his arms to stand beside the couch.

She stood for a moment, staring down at him, her eyes sharply assessing. "Lie down."

"What?"

"Lie down," she repeated more slowly.

Cautiously, he stretched out on the couch.

She sat down beside him on the edge of the cushion, her hip pressing against his. "How long has it been since you slept with a woman?"

A shiver of shock ran through him at her question, the hot burn of embarrassment following close behind. "How long has it been since you slept with someone," he retorted, then grimaced. "Sorry."

"It's a question you have a right to ask. Not since my last long-term relationship ended over a year ago. Now, your turn."

"It's been . . . a while." When she simply raised her eyebrows and the silence dragged on, he finally said, "Like since before coming to Boston kind of a while. Okay?" He heard the defensiveness in his own voice and could have kicked himself. *Smooth, Matt.*

She leaned down over him, laying one hand flat against his chest, her face so close that her breath whispered across his lips. "There's nothing wrong with being selective. I'll take it as a compliment that I'm the one you've chosen after all that time." She sank into a long slow kiss with him before pulling back.

"But we have a problem."

He had a bad feeling that he knew what she was referring to, but he played dumb, hoping he was wrong. "Problem?"

"Whenever it looks like we might be getting physically intimate, you pull back. Just like you did in your bedroom after the Hershey house. But then you not only pulled back, you shut me out." He drew breath to speak, but she cut him off. "I'll make you a deal. I'll show you mine, and then you show me yours." She gave a small laugh when his eyes shot wide in shock. "That wasn't exactly what I meant, at least not quite yet. But you're not comfortable in your own skin with me, even though I've told you I don't have any problems with your scars."

He felt hot color flood his cheeks, but she laid one palm gently against his jaw, not letting him turn away. "There's nothing to be embarrassed about. But from where I'm sitting it looks to me like maybe the reason you haven't dated in so long is because you put up roadblocks so no one ever has a chance to see your scars."

He stared at her, not sure what to say.

"I'm not interested in unnecessary roadblocks." She pulled her hand from his jaw, her fingers whispering over his skin. To his shock they went to the tiny buttons that ran up the front of her blouse, slowly undoing them. "I told you, I'll show you mine first." She locked gazes with him. "My scar."

He bolted upright and shifted his hips backward on the couch cushions. "You have a scar? What happened? Were you . . ." His voice trailed off as his gaze fixed on the delicate midnight-blue lace revealed by the parted material.

Silence lay heavy as she undid the rest of the buttons. Then she spread the blouse wide and let it fall off her shoulders.

"And to think I had you pegged as the sensible cotton type." His voice was hoarse as his mouth had suddenly gone dry. Her skin, drenched in firelight, was almost luminous. Stunned, he took in the delicate lace intertwining of leaves and petals overlaying a scant amount of matching dark silk, perfectly framing her breasts. "Was I ever wrong."

"This is my concession to me. I work with a bunch of men who expect me to conform to their dictates of dress and behavior. They don't need to know that those tailored suits hide some spectacular lingerie." She hooked two fingers under the twin satin straps laying over her left shoulder and slid them down to rest against her arm, baring the upper curve of her left breast.

The hunger building in Matt at the sight of her gorgeous body dissolved as his gaze fixed on the small circle of scar tissue. He raised his hand to touch it, and then checked the motion, his hand frozen in midair.

"It's all right." She took his hand in hers, and pressed it to her skin. "You can touch me."

With exquisite care, he ran the pads of his fingers over her skin, feeling the lump of hardened tissue under his touch. "How did—"

She cut him off, the steel in her tone a surprise. "Gunshot wound. Let's just leave it at that."

His gaze jumped to her eyes. There was a banked misery there that he understood on a visceral level. *Deep waters here. Something she's not ready to share yet.*

He knew exactly how that felt.

He turned his attention back to her breast. "You could have been killed." He felt some of the stiffness ease from her body as he focused on the injury itself.

"The doctors said I was very lucky. Apparently it just missed a major blood vessel."

"One of the pulmonary vessels, from the location," Matt said, without pausing to think. "Or maybe the subclavian, depending on the angle."

"Sometimes I forget that you know as much about soft tissue as you do about bones from your time as a medic. Now . . . your turn."

His hand froze over her skin before slowly dropping away to lie limply against his thigh. "My turn?"

"I showed you my scar. Now it's your turn." Their eyes met, held. "Show me yours."

His jaw clenched as his gaze dropped.

"Do you trust me?"

He gave a reluctant nod.

"Then trust me with this."

With a quiet sigh, he sat up. He tugged his T-shirt up and over his head to drop it carelessly on the floor. He lay back against the arm of the couch, his right arm thrown over his head, clearly exposing his damaged side to the firelight. He turned his face away from her to stare sightlessly over the back of the couch.

But she cupped his chin, turning his face back to her. "Don't look away," she said quietly. "We're doing this together." She pulled his upraised arm back down, and took his hand in hers, interlinking their fingers to bring them together to the twisted mass of tissue marring his skin.

He forced himself to look down, seeing it as she did for the first time.

The scar stretched over his side, a full six inches in width and disappearing out of sight below the waistband of his jeans. The skin was a mottled red-brown, a continuous mass of melting, twisted knots of flesh.

Their hands still intertwined, Leigh ran their fingertips over his skin, following a long line of raised, uneven tissue.

Instead of watching their joint exploration of his flesh, he focused on her face, waiting for the reaction he expected from every woman: Horror. Distaste. Worst of all, pity.

But it never came.

She simply took him in, her eyes closely examining every ridge and discoloration. But there was no disgust in her expression.

It was a revelation to him.

The silence stretched until she finally looked up. "Do you know what I see when I look at you?" she asked him softly.

He mutely shook his head.

She released his hand to lay it on her thigh, then pressed both her hands against the defined muscles of his abdomen. "I see a man who works himself hard at the oars—your body clearly shows that." She ran her hands up his stomach and chest, sliding them over his pectorals and wide shoulders, then stroking down over his biceps. Her left hand slowed to trace the fresh scar on his right biceps—a new addition following a narrow escape during the Bradford case. "It's sexy. You didn't look like this three years ago. It's a definite improvement." She laid her hands against his sides, smooth skin under one, and thick, ridged skin under the other. "I also see a man who bears the marks of his time in service to his country. Do you remember what I called your scar before?" She lifted her hand to lightly touch the line of twisted skin running into his hairline at his right temple.

"A badge of honor."

"Yes." Her hand came back to rest against the ruined skin. "Be proud of it." She looked down at the injury. "Can I ask how it happened?"

The blackness threatened to pull him under, but this time Matt fought back. He'd spent too much time during their first case at its mercy. He roughly cleared his throat. "I was with the Fifteenth Marine Expeditionary Unit that established the first land base in Afghanistan—Camp Rhino—and then proceeded into Kandahar to take the airport. But after that, we were tasked with raids in southern Afghanistan. We were trying to take command of a Taliban stronghold when we were ambushed. They were above us in the hills and we were pinned down. It was bad." He closed his eyes, once again feeling the earth shake from explosions, and hearing the whine of bullets flying and the screams of his comrades. "Guys were dropping like flies around me. I was trying to get to those closest to me to patch them up when I got hit." He touched the scar at his temple. "The bullet grazed me, but still cracked against my skull hard enough that I went down. I probably passed out for a few seconds. I came to and managed to get up again to stagger over to one of the men. He was bleeding out fast and I was trying to stabilize him when an RPG—a rocket-propelled grenade—exploded nearby. We were both thrown from the force of the fireball. I had enough left to crawl across the sand and turn him over to see if I could help, but he was gone. The last thing I remember was pain like I'd never felt before—like my body was burning from the inside out. And then it all went dark."

Leigh remained silent, but stroked his skin soothingly as he talked.

"When I woke up, I was back in Camp Rhino. One of the other medics had done his best to patch me up, but out there in the field, all you try to do is keep the guys alive; you don't aim for pretty. If I'd been stateside with a plastic surgeon on call, I'd look different, but I was in a field hospital and this is how I turned out." He looked thoughtful for a moment. "I've thought about plastic surgery and having it reshaped—"

"No!" Leigh's eyes widened at her own outburst.

"You'd leave it?"

"Yes. You know how I feel about it. I just don't think it's worth the pain of surgery to remove something so meaningful."

His gaze dropped to her own scar and he considered it carefully. "You've never thought about having your scar done?"

143

Pain streaked across her face. "Some marks deserve to be worn," she said bitterly.

She startled him when she abruptly rose up, swung one leg over his hips and settled over his pelvis. His hands involuntarily came to clutch at her hips, holding her down firmly, increasing the pressure for both of them for a moment before he forced himself to let go.

Any thoughts of scars vanished from his mind.

"Now," Leigh said smoothly, leaning down to run her tongue over his lower lip. "Where were we?"

She gave a little gasp of surprise when he suddenly reared up, one arm banding around her back and pressing them skin to skin. His free hand came up to brush the straps off her right shoulder, only to replace them with the heat of his open mouth on her skin. "Right about here, I think."

Leigh gave a low groan, her fingers threading through his hair, holding him closer. With a gentle nudge of his head, he pushed hers back, exposing her throat to his explorations. Her head fell back and she leaned back into his hands as they spread wide behind her shoulder blades, supporting her weight.

She slid one hand from the back of his head, sliding down the smooth skin of his back to slip lightly under the waistband of his jeans—

The sharp peal of Leigh's cell phone split the air and they both froze. Sitting up, Leigh dropped her head down onto his shoulder, gently rapping it a few times in frustration. "No, no, *no*!"

"You have to take that?"

"Yes." She practically growled it. She pulled her phone off her belt. "Abbott." She sat up straighter, but stayed sprawled over his hips.

Alarm jolted through him when she went still in his arms. He pulled back to see her face.

Her expression had gone from soft and aroused to composed and alert. "Where?" Pause. "Got it. I'll inform Dr. Lowell. We can be on scene within ten minutes." She ended the call.

"What's happened?"

Leigh was already sliding off him and shrugging into her blouse. "We have to go. That was Bree. There's a fire in progress at a Catholic church. One of the firefighters from last Sunday's scene is there and reported a pentacle nailed to the front door. We need to hurry. They're fighting the fire right now and she wants us on scene."

Matt rolled to his feet, reaching for his own shirt. For one brief moment they made eye contact, but no words were needed. They both knew what had happened.

Their killer had struck again.

CHAPTER FIFTEEN:
MALTESE CROSS

Maltese Cross: firefighters borrow the symbol of the Maltese Cross from the Knights of Saint John the Baptist of Jerusalem, an organization that traces its origins back to the eleventh-century group of Benedictine monks—*Frères Hospitaliers de Saint Jean de Jerusalem.* When the Saracens used glass bombs containing naphtha to repel Crusaders advancing on their fortresses, hundreds of knights were burned alive. The Hospitallers risked their lives to save their brothers-in-arms from painful fiery deaths. These men were the first organized paramedics group; and the first in a long line of courageous firefighters and first responders.

Thursday, 7:53 p.m.
Saint Patrick's Catholic Church
Salem, Massachusetts
Leigh sprinted down the street, her eyes locked on the otherworldly glow reflected off the low hanging clouds while the rest of the neighborhood was steeped in darkness. Matt's footfalls followed closely behind.

They ran past an engine on the outskirts of the scene. The name on the side of the door caught Leigh's eye—Marblehead Fire Department.

"That can't be good," Leigh threw over her shoulder as she leapt over a length of hose. "They've called in other departments."

They both poured on the speed. The street was awash with the strobe of red, white and blue emergency lights, and the air vibrated with the roar of running engines. Leigh counted as she wove through the jigsaw puzzle of vehicles parked on the street—five engines and two ladder trucks. *A damned big fire.*

Matt cleared the cluster of engines and hit the sidewalk surrounding the church first, but Leigh was right on his heels. They slid to a halt, getting their first good look at the fire.

Saint Patrick's was once the largest Roman Catholic church in Salem, but for the past few months it had been locked and dark. It sat astride a large corner lot, set back from the street by at least fifty feet of lawn, a spiked wrought-iron fence separating the property from the sidewalk. The church itself was built of heavy granite blocks, the front of the building dominated by a towering square steeple flanked by twin towers. The pointed wooden roof of the steeple was ablaze, fiery red outlining the cross on its spire. At ground level, the three sets of heavy double front doors were thrown open. Roiling smoke poured from the doorways and, above them, flames could be seen through the tall stretches of stained glass inset in the towers and steeple. The doors at the back of the vestibule opened into the sanctuary beyond, where flames danced over white-hot piles of rubble. Inside was an inferno, a maelstrom worthy of hell itself.

The fat hoses leading through the doors implied crews inside the building. Leigh counted the hoses—three—but movement at the back of the church made her think they were fighting the fire from both ends of the building. Her heart stuttered at the thought of men alive in those flames. The heat rolling off the fire almost pushed her back, even at this distance.

And the pentacle. Was there someone trapped in there? Or was it already too late?

Suddenly, one of the windows on the side of the building shattered, raining shards of colored glass down over the grass.

The men moving hoses below ducked and protected their faces with their helmets.

Leigh turned away from the fire's fury. "We need to find Bree. She's probably with whoever's running this show." She pointed to a red Salem Fire Department SUV parked on the far side of the street, the back hatch open. "That's the deputy chief's vehicle we saw yesterday, right? Let's start there."

They found an older man in a white turnout coat and helmet standing under the open hatch of the SUV and barking orders into a walkie-talkie. This was clearly the operations center for the fire. Inside, a white board with a chart and hooks was propped against a heavy case. Notes in wax pencil on the board listed the location of each firefighter.

"Message received." He turned, irritation flashing in his eyes at civilians at his scene.

Before he could speak, Leigh palmed her badge. "Trooper Leigh Abbott, Essex Detective Unit. We're looking for Trooper Gilson."

The man jerked a thumb over his shoulder. "Over there. Stay out of the way."

"Thanks."

They strode down the street, checking every vehicle until they found Bree near the back of an ambulance. A firefighter sat on the bumper, his mask and helmet at his hip, his turnout coat unfastened. Soot coated the ends of his hair and smeared his face in a circle where his mask once sat. A medic crouched beside him, fitting an oxygen mask over his mouth and nose.

Matt and Leigh jogged up behind Bree and Leigh tapped her arm. "We came as fast as we could."

Bree glanced over her shoulder. "You made good time."

"He going to be okay?" Leigh asked, pointing at the firefighter.

"He's probably just overheated and needs a little extra

oxygen. But they'll send him to the hospital to get checked out."

"What's the status here?" Matt asked.

"Two alarms called so far, but it's about to go to three. Come on, walk and talk." Bree started back toward the command center. "According to the neighbor who phoned it in, this church has been closed for months. Normally, I'd think that we'd be looking at the homeless using it for shelter and accidentally starting the fire, but the pentacle on the door has me leaning toward arson to match the first pentacle fire."

"When was it called in?"

"Seven thirty-five. Trucks were on scene within four minutes, but these structures are problematic. Masonry like this really holds in the heat and promotes flashover. It tends to hide the fire until it gets big enough to show significantly through the windows. In this case, the fire was spotted by someone driving home and seeing lights in the windows when there shouldn't be any. Right now, we're just trying to contain it until we can guarantee no one's inside. Then we'll pull everyone out and go defensive."

Leigh studied the two trucks pulled up close to the curb, their massive ladders extended, a man perched at the top of each, but no water coming from their hoses. "Is that why there are guys with hoses on the lawn and up the ladders who aren't doing anything yet?"

"Yes. You can't fight the fire from the outside and inside simultaneously because you could bring the building down on the crews inside."

"What about them?" Matt pointed at the team of men, in black turnout gear instead of Salem's beige, axes in hand and wearing air packs, poised at the front door. "Are they waiting for something?"

"That's the RIT—Rapid Intervention Team—Marblehead

sent to help out. They're there in case anyone goes down inside while they're searching the structure."

"Those guys inside better move fast. From the way the flames are spurting out at the roofline, you may lose the roof."

"That's what I'm afraid of. These walls aren't buttressed. The compression of the roof is what's keeping the building standing and with this fire load, the roof is going to start coming down."

Leigh turned to watch fountains of flame pour out of holes in the roof, mixing with thick, choking black smoke. Red and orange light shifted behind the windows and flames licked around stained glass, greedy fingers reaching for fresh air and life-giving oxygen. "You're worried the whole thing will collapse."

"Yes. There are four teams in there right now. It collapses around them, and we could lose men." She pointed upwards. "That's the real problem."

Leigh stared up at the steeple. The wooden slats that originally covered the twin arches on each wall of the tower had burned away and the glow of the fire outlined the heavy bell. Her gaze tracked downward. Inside the front doors, she could see men backlit against the flames as they sprayed water in a futile attempt to control the chaos while searching for any signs of life.

"That bell is probably a ton of solid bronze," Bree continued. "It's a matter of whether we can save the internal wooden supports."

"It must be hard to have to stand back here and watch."

Bree's gaze flicked to Leigh. "After all those years being in the fire? Yeah. I'm not usually at an active fire anymore, I come in after the fact, but one of the guys gave me a heads-up after they found the pentacle." Her hands balled into fists. "I haven't felt the need to get in there in years, but I'm feeling it now. In spades."

An SUV pulled up near the scene, its lights flashing brilliantly, and a tall man in a Salem Fire Department uniform climbed out. "Chief's arrived," Bree said.

"Does he always come out to fires?"

"Anything two alarm and higher."

They arrived at the command center just as the chief joined them. He and Bree nodded to each other in greeting. Then the deputy chief's walkie-talkie screeched to life. "Engine Two to Deputy Joseph."

"Command answering."

"One victim found. Request standby crew."

"Affirmative. Give current location."

"Bravo Charlie corner."

Leigh flicked a look at Bree who read her silent question. "The walls are labeled alphabetically as Alpha, Bravo, Charlie, Delta starting with the front wall and going clockwise around. They found someone in the back left corner of the sanctuary and are asking for help getting them out."

"Engine Five from command," the deputy chief said into the walkie-talkie.

The radio crackled as a new voice came on. "Engine Five."

"Single victim found, Bravo Charlie corner. Proceed to the rear entrance of the church to assist Engine Two."

"Okay on the message."

"Someone's alive in there?" Matt asked.

"No way to know. If we find a body during an active fire, we bring it out. It's too smoky in there to see and you don't have the time to take a pulse or check for respiration. You just get them out. Once they're in the clear, we'll know more."

The radio squawked again. "Engine Two to Deputy Joseph."

"Command answering."

"We're bringing the victim out."

"Message received. Bring the victim to the front lawn."

"Come on," Bree said. "We'll meet them over there."

Matt, Leigh and Bree jogged across the street and through the gate, skirting the edge of the property to stand waiting against the fence, looking toward the back of the church. Several paramedics carrying heavy packs joined them in case the victim needed medical attention. Finally a team of four men came around the back corner of the church, two of them carrying a limp body. They laid the body down in the grass and several paramedics knelt as Matt and Leigh crouched closer for a better look.

The body was badly burned, the skin singed and blistered. The clothing was mostly burned away and the body was partially curled into a fetal position. The hair on the head was gone, as were the eyebrows. Leigh's lips curled in distaste as she realized the ears were also missing. The smell of freshly burned flesh was almost unbearable.

One of the paramedics looked up to find Bree. He silently shook his head and repacked his bag.

Bree pulled her radio off her belt. "Trooper Gilson to Deputy Joseph."

Static over the radio, then, "Command answering."

"We have a confirmed fatality."

"Message received."

Once the paramedics moved away, Matt dropped to his knees beside the corpse. He leaned in to take a good look before glancing up at Leigh. "You need to see this. Come around to the other side."

Leigh circled the body and several firefighters to kneel opposite Matt.

"Anyone got a flashlight?" he asked.

At least half a dozen flashlights were pulled from turnouts by the firefighters around them. Matt accepted Bree's.

"Thanks." He looked at Leigh. "Ready?" When she nodded,

he slipped gloved fingers under the chin of the victim, gently tipping it up. He flipped on the flashlight shining it directly down on the neck.

The slash across the throat nearly went from ear to ear. The heat had pulled back muscle tissue, exposing the ridged windpipe beneath. The tissue was charred, but the damage was unmistakable.

Leigh sat back on her heels. "Dead before the fire started, then."

"Autopsy will tell us that."

Around them, firefighters dispersed, heading back to the fire as the victim was beyond their help.

Leigh looked up at Bree, still crouched over the body. "Are they still looking for more victims?"

"They'll finish the search, but I think they've covered almost all the interior. At this point, I want them out ASAP." Her gaze trailed back to the steeple.

"You need to call Rowe," Matt said to Leigh. "I don't think we need him here tonight, but he needs to send some techs for the body."

"Agreed." Leigh pushed up from the ground, already reaching for her phone.

"Wait."

She froze. "What?"

Matt leaned over the body and swore softly. "Come in closer." He waited as Leigh drew in a breath of fresh air before leaning in. He pointed to metal burned into blackened tissue. "This doesn't say 'homeless person' to me."

It was a blackened cross with blunt knobs on three of the four arms.

She met his gaze over the ruined remains. "A priest?"

"That would be my guess with a cross this large. I'd assume this is something you'd wear over your clothes, not under them, or as a charm on a necklace."

"Guys, we need to move this body." Bree whistled, and motioned two firefighters over. "Let's move the vic near the fence so the body is out of the way before we go defensive." She pointed a finger at the younger of the two men. "Joe, find a tarp to cover it. Then I need you to stay with it until someone from the ME's office arrives. No one touches this body unless Trooper Abbott or I give permission."

Leigh stood. "I'll call Rowe." She walked a few feet away to make the call.

When she returned a few minutes later, the body lay near the fence, its lower half covered with a bright yellow tarp. Bree squatted down next to Matt, her head bent low as he indicated something on the victim. "Rowe's sending up a van and a couple of techs," Leigh told them. "He agrees that he doesn't need to be here, but he'll make time tomorrow for the autopsy." She turned to Matt as he unfolded the rest of the tarp to cover the body and then stood. "Do you need to be there? Would this body be considered a forensic anthropology case?"

"No, it's not burned badly enough. But I'd like to be there if Rowe doesn't mind. It's definitely connected to our case."

"I'll clear it with him. You're already a part of this case so—"

A huge section of roof near the middle of the building suddenly collapsed in a cyclone of spinning flames, swirling black smoke and an explosion of sparks. As flames billowed toward them, the team of firefighters in the foyer hurriedly backed out to stand in the ruined doorway, dragging the heavy hose with them. An explosion of orders and responses burst from Bree's radio.

"That's it. Everyone needs to get out *now*. Screw standing on the sidelines. I'm headed to the operations center. The DC will need help accounting for everyone." Bree took off like a shot, sprinting over the grass toward the road.

As if on cue, a bellowed shout somehow managed to rise above the cacophony of flame, radio chatter, engine roar and water stream. "It's coming down. Get clear!"

Leigh's breath seemed to freeze in her lungs as the steeple swayed drunkenly, fire framed in every broken window. It hung there, almost motionless for a moment before the tower crumpled with a terrible grinding noise, collapsing into the gaping flames below with a crash that vibrated the ground under their feet. The remaining sections of the roof shuddered and began to fall inwards. With the loud grating of stones being ripped apart, one the side walls of the church began to buckle outwards in a thick cloud of dust and debris. Several firemen on the grass leapt clear as the heavy stones thundered to the ground, then quickly got back into position, careful to leave a good distance between themselves and any other potentially unstable walls.

Matt pulled Leigh back several paces even though they were well clear of the collapse, his crushing grip on her arm belying his outward calm. "He's killing more than just his victims. If we lose any firefighters . . ." Matt turned his gaze back to the fire.

"Come on. Maybe we can do something to help." Leigh looked at the fireman still kneeling beside the body. "Stay with the victim." He gave a quick nod and she and Matt sprinted after Bree.

The operations center was a frantic hive of activity. The chief, deputy chief and Bree were clustered around the accountability board, checking off men as they were located. Several senior firefighters clustered around them.

Bree glanced at them as they ran up, stress and worry carving deep grooves around her mouth. "We can't raise one of the crews," she said curtly before turning back to her radio, trying to contact the missing men.

Leigh turned back to the blaze. The RIT team was gone, disappeared into the flames, their path marked by the new hose leading through the central door. Firemen fled the building, some under their own power, others with help. But when a firefighter staggered out the front door, face mask askew and half carrying, half dragging the limp body of a comrade, Matt grabbed Leigh's arm. "I'm going over. They're shorthanded now and I can help."

She nodded, wishing she had the skills to join him. "Go. Be careful and stay well clear of the building."

He bolted off toward the injured men, sprinting through the gate and toward the far side of the property where men were collapsing against the bars of the wrought-iron fence.

"Hey! Where is he going?" Bree took a half step after him, but Leigh jumped forward, catching her arm.

"Let him go. He was a battlefield medic with the Marines in Afghanistan after 9/11. He probably knows more about emergency triage than anyone else here. Let him help."

Bree shook off Leigh's hand, but gave a quick nod of her head as the radio in her hand squawked and she turned back to the accountability board.

Across the grass, Matt quickly joined the impromptu medical station. He immediately bent over to assess an injured firefighter sprawled on the grass, weakly trying to pull off his face mask with a gloved hand. Several medics ran up, carrying loaded packs. After a brief discussion, one of them opened his pack, handed some supplies to Matt and they both got to work over the firefighter.

"HELP! I need help!" A firefighter staggered out the center door of the church. Her face shield was smashed and she was trying to support the body of another firefighter. She made it to the top of the steps before collapsing, both of them tumbling down the steps like limp rag dolls.

Bree and Leigh took off at a run, beating several firefighters to the bottom of the steps. Bree easily kept up with Leigh, moving amazingly fast for someone wearing so much equipment. Matt met them at the bottom of the steps, where the heat rolled off the fire in blistering waves. The female firefighter was trying to sit up, pushing off her ruined mask. "Cody needs help. I found him under a pile of rubble at the back of the sanctuary." She coughed raggedly, spraying blood over the sleeve of her turnout coat. Turning her head to the side, she spit out some blood and then wiped her mouth with her glove. "He got caught when the steeple collapsed."

"Move them away from there. You're too close." Bree looked directly at Matt and Leigh. "Especially you two. Help Eccles."

Firefighters picked up the body of their fallen comrade, carrying him across the grass to the temporary medical station, several medics meeting them partway. Matt and Leigh each looped one of the woman's arms over their shoulders, slowly walking her across the grass. They lowered her down to sit with her back against the fence. Two paramedics joined them, but she batted away their hands. "It's not that bad. I ate a little smoke and put my teeth through my lip. Go help Cody. He needs you more than I do."

"There's three medics working on him now," one of the young men said, pushing her hands out of his way and dabbing the blood at her lip. "You need oxygen and that lip's going to need stitches. Now sit!" He slid an oxygen mask over her mouth and nose, ignoring her protests.

"Charging to two hundred."

The words penetrated the surrounding noise. Leigh whipped around to the man still on the grass. He was surrounded by paramedics and she could only see parts of his body, but it was enough to make her stomach clutch painfully. Blood painted his face, and his eyes were glassy and staring. His coat and shirt were open, exposing his bare chest. One of the paramedics applied paddles to his chest and then his body arched off the grass. The paramedic checked his carotid. "V-fib, no pulse, charging to three hundred."

Leigh felt Matt move up behind her, his chest at her back as he watched the scene over her shoulder. As the injured man was shocked a second time.

"Still no pulse. Charging to three sixty."

Two men ran up, pushing a gurney over the grass.

"Let's move him. Start CPR."

The still body of the downed man was quickly lifted to the gurney and they started to run with it across the grass, one of the paramedics doing chest compressions as they went.

"They're moving him." Relief loosened some of the tension in her body. "He's got a chance, then."

"No."

Leigh turned to find Matt still close behind her. The resigned look on his face made her blood run cold. "What do you mean? They're taking him in."

Matt's gaze stayed on the gurney as it was lifted into the back of one of the ambulances on the far side of the road. "It's no good. He's gone. I've seen that look before. His eyes . . ."

Leigh stared in horror as the ambulance doors were slammed shut and a paramedic pounded on the doors twice. "They lost him?"

"They never had him. That's a major head injury. Paired with smoke inhalation . . . They can't declare death here, they have to take him in for that. But it's too late."

Lights flashing and siren wailing, the ambulance sped off down the street, carrying its futile burden.

Fury tightened Leigh's chest and vibrated through her frame—they'd lost one of their own in the fight.

"NO!" The bellow from across the grass had them both spinning toward the sound. A burly firefighter was struggling against one of his comrades, his face a twisted mask of pain. Another firefighter jogged up to them yelling instructions accompanied with jerky hand motions. The other man's head bent as he stood stiffly on the grass, a dark, miserable figure backlit by the raging fire. The man yelling instructions clapped a hand on the firefighter's shoulder before his head rose to give a curt nod. The group broke up, returning to work with heavy feet and even heavier hearts.

Leigh touched Matt's arm. When he turned to face her, she saw her own distress mirrored in his eyes. "Go back to the medics. I'm going to see if I can help Bree. I might just be in the way, but I won't know until I ask. It's killing me to stand here, doing nothing."

Leigh's gaze stayed on Matt as he jogged back to the temporary medical station on the grass, then she turned away in search of Bree. She hated feeling useless, but for now she had a victim she couldn't touch until the ME examined him, and her scene was burning up before her eyes. If only—

She had just cleared the gate and stepped onto the sidewalk when someone moved directly into her path. She took an involuntary step backward, one hand clutching at the nearest iron fence rail to keep her balance.

"Trooper Abbott, Jason Wells for the *Salem Times.* Can you confirm that tonight's fire is related to Sunday morning's blaze?"

Leigh's eyes narrowed on the man crowding into her personal space. He was young, probably only in his mid-twenties, with perfectly coiffed blond hair. He looked like he'd just stepped out of a fashion catalog, complete with cable-knit cashmere V-neck sweater. He held a shiny silver pen and a small pad of paper in an expensive leather cover.

"You. I saw your article today. You've caused enough trouble. I have nothing to say to you."

The young man doggedly continued on as if she hadn't

spoken, falling into step with Leigh when she turned away and stalked down the sidewalk. "Aren't you concerned about a serial killer, Trooper Abbott? Especially considering the pentacle found on the—"

Leigh rounded on him. "Who told you that?"

"A reliable source."

She leaned in closer. The man's expensive cologne nearly made her head swim, which was saying something when the air was already thick with smoke and the smell of burning wood. "Who?"

"A reliable source," Wells repeated, slowly, as if she didn't understand him the first time.

It might have been the stress of a second victim coupled with the loss of a firefighter, but anger exploded in Leigh. She struggled to keep it locked down and was still biting back the caustic comment that sprang to her lips when Wells launched into his next line of attack. "Do you plan to inform the public, Trooper Abbott? It's in their best interest to know that another serial killer is on the loose. And isn't it convenient you're on the case again."

Leigh jammed her hands in her pockets to keep from spoiling his pretty face with a broken nose or a black eye. She was too tired, too emotional, and too short of temper for this, and Harper would have her head if she went after the reporter. "Are you implying something, Mr. Wells?"

Wells's face took on a wide-eyed expression of feigned innocence, but his dramatics weren't lost on Leigh. *Slimy son of a bitch.*

"Of course not," he protested. "It's just . . . you were so successful during the Bradford case, we're looking for a similar result here. If you're not willing to comment on the serial killings, can you at least shed light on the source of the fires? Was Trooper Gilson able to pinpoint the cause of Sunday's blaze?"

"No comment," Leigh snapped.

"Sunday's victim has been identified as Moira Simpson. Until recently, she was a member of a local coven. I understand she was killed with an athame. Should the Witches of Salem be worried for their own safety? Or do you think the Witches are responsible for her death?"

"You should watch what you put into print, Mr. Wells. Your unfounded theories could cause a panic. If that happens, rest assured, we'll make sure the blame for it rests on you. If you want a quote for your paper, talk to Sharon Collins. She'll be happy to feed you the party line. Now get the hell away from this scene before I have you arrested for interfering in a police investigation."

With that, Leigh turned away to stalk down the sidewalk. When she looked back moments later, Wells was gone.

She stopped then, wrapping her fingers around the tops of the wrought-iron rails and letting the temper thrum through her as her gaze was drawn back to the blaze. The men and women of the Salem Fire Department continued to fight the fire, but they were no longer trying to save the building; they were simply trying to extinguish the blaze. Water cascaded down from massive ladders above, streaming directly into the gaping hole where the roof once rose. Huge clouds of gray steam billowed up, mixing with heavy plumes of black smoke, temporarily obscuring the men on top of the ladders. On the ground, water streamed from hoses through shattered windows and the front doors. Several men were taking advantage of the collapsed side wall, using the large gap to stream water directly inside. But the pall of death hung over the scene. Firefighters moved around the site, shouting at each other as they fought the flames, but the scene was somehow quieter than before, more subdued, grief radiating from the men even from behind face masks and through choking smoke.

Leigh felt their anguish like a punch to the gut. She knew the feeling of having a fellow cop go down in the line of duty, knew how razor-sharp the pain felt. Knew the overwhelming despair when the one who fell was a loved one.

She also knew the agony of having to continue to do the job despite the gaping hole in your heart and the desire to simply curl into a ball and weep.

Leigh shut out the rawness of the grief around her, and let her anger burn bright and feed her.

Now there were two more victims who needed justice.

CHAPTER SIXTEEN:
BACKDRAFT

Backdraft: rapid burning and the explosion of superheated gases in a confined space after an oxygen-starved fire is suddenly ventilated.

Friday, 1:53 p.m.
Office of the Chief Medical Examiner
Boston, Massachusetts

Matt looked up from the dissected throat of the victim when the door of the autopsy suite slammed open and Leigh burst through at a breathless half run. "Sorry I'm late. I was called to a fatal stabbing downtown this morning. I just got free."

Matt straightened. "Nothing related to this case, I assume."

"No." Leigh slid the strap of her messenger bag off her shoulder and set it on the counter, well away from any possible splashes. "It's less than a week until Halloween and the tourists are already swarming. Put that many people and alcohol together and this kind of stuff always happens. We always see an uptick in crime at this time of year, although usually it's not murder. Salem PD deals with most of it, but things got out of hand last night and I was on call. Thankfully, there were several eyewitnesses to the killing, and it didn't take long to discover where the suspect was staying. He's in lockup now. Maybe that will give Jason Wells something else to write about so he'll leave us alone."

Matt's gaze dropped to the fist Leigh unconsciously clenched and unclenched at her side. "That's the reporter who was in your face last night?"

"Yes. He gave the *Salem Times* another above-the-fold screaming headline about last night's fire." Using both hands, Leigh sketched out the title in the air as if it were a billboard. " 'PENTACLE KILLER STRIKES AGAIN!' He's purposely stoking the fires of hysteria to sell papers. I'm waiting for Harper to call me into his office again." She drew in a deep breath. "But enough about that little weasel." She came to stand at the end of the table, her lips tightening as she took in the scene. "Where are we with the autopsy?"

"We're almost finished," Rowe said.

Leigh's face went a shade paler when her gaze landed on Rowe standing near the open chest cavity, cradling the bloody heart in his gloved hands.

"Sorry I missed it," she said flatly.

Rowe laughed as he laid the heart on the weigh scale. "No, you're not. You're always game, Abbott, but you can't hide it. You hate autopsies."

"And here I thought I had you all fooled," Leigh deadpanned. "So, what have we got so far?"

"Male victim, approximately fifty to sixty years of age," Rowe recited. "Death was due to exsanguination."

"Not fire?"

"No. No soot in either the lungs or the trachea."

"So the same set up as last time. The throat slash was responsible, I assume?"

"Yes." Matt motioned her over to where he stood. "Take a look at the wound." He glanced at the students clustered around him. "Guys, give us some room here."

Matt's students stepped out of the way, letting Leigh move in closer. She hesitated for a moment, then firmed her jaw and stepped up to the table.

"You saw this last night, but Rowe dissected back the tissues so we could really see it." Careful not to touch the body, Matt pointed out the salient landmarks. "It's a little hard to see because of the heat damage and the charring, but this center tube leading straight down from under the chin is the trachea or windpipe. On either side is the carotid sheath enclosing the carotid artery, jugular vein and the vagus nerve. As you can see, both the carotid and jugular are completely severed on the left side and the carotid is partially severed on the right."

Leigh looked over at Rowe, who was stripping off a pair of bloody gloves and replacing them with fresh. "How fast did he die?"

"He would have been unconscious in about five seconds and dead a few minutes after that. Blood loss would have quickly resulted in hypovolemic shock."

"So dead before the fire was set," Leigh mused. "What's the point of the arson, then? Clearly, it's not to kill. The victim is already dead. Unless the sick bastard was aiming to take out a firefighter or two, in which case, he struck pay dirt."

"To cleanse?" Kiko suggested. "Especially in a religious setting like this. All sins wiped clean by the fire?"

"It makes more sense that it's a practical exercise," Paul said. "The killer simply wants to destroy any trace evidence. If he sets the fire and gets out, then the worst-case scenario is that it doesn't take and the body is found as is. But the victim's already dead. The fire is just icing on the cake in terms of him getting away scot-free."

"But then why leave the knife the first time?" Juka said. "Your theory of evidence destruction doesn't work when he leaves the murder weapon on scene. Or, worse than that, in the body."

"But the knife didn't point directly to the killer because it belonged to the victim," Leigh said.

"That also negates the likelihood that the fire was set to hide the identity of the victim, seeing as the knife led directly to her," Rowe stated.

"We were lucky there because it was a custom piece," Leigh said. "If it hadn't been, we might still be struggling to identify her."

"Has a murder weapon been found at the second fire yet?" Matt asked.

Leigh shook her head. "Not that I know of. I asked Bree to concentrate on that area and I'm hoping to hear from her soon."

"How's she doing?" Kiko asked quietly.

"None of them are in good shape," Leigh said sharply. "It hurts when you lose one of your own."

Not able to touch her with his bloodied gloves, Matt leaned sideways, pressing his shoulder to hers. The eyes that met his shone with banked anger. But simmering behind the anger was more pain than simply the loss of an unknown firefighter.

She gave him a wan smile before turning to Kiko. "I'm sorry. You're concerned for them and I'm snapping at you. I haven't talked to Bree personally this morning. All I could get was her voice mail so I left a message. I assume they were back in there first thing once the site cooled enough to really go through it."

"The church is likely unstable," Matt said. "They'll be slowed down because they'll have to ensure the remaining walls don't collapse. They won't take any risks, not after last night."

"No, they won't." Leigh reached into her blazer pocket for her notepad and pen. "Okay, back to the throat wound. Are we looking at another athame?"

"Not sure yet." Matt pulled back some of the charred tissue. "The wound here on the left looks like it's gone right down to the bone, striking the fifth cervical vertebra. If we're lucky, once the tissue is dissected away, we'll be able to identify kerf marks on the bone. It missed the hyoid altogether, so that won't help us."

"What about a head wound?" Leigh moved to the top of the table, and studied the skull. The scalp had been retracted and the top part of the skull removed with a Stryker saw. The spongy gray brain lay in an open container on the counter. "Any signs of a blow like we saw with Moira Simpson?"

"No skull injuries, no signs of cerebral hemorrhage. But we did find another sign of incapacitation." Matt circled the table to stand down by the right knee. "Squat down here, on the floor. We can't roll the body over right now, so you need to get low to see this."

Leigh threw him a questioning look, but crouched down.

"I noticed the asymmetry in the body yesterday. The left leg was starting to pull into the typical curled formation, but the right leg wasn't. And that's because of this." Slipping a hand under the right calf, Matt lifted the leg into the air, exposing a deep slash just above the crook of the knee.

Leigh hooked her hands over the edge of the table, pulling herself up a few inches higher to see better. "He was hamstrung?" she asked in amazement.

"Yes." Matt pointed out a mass of bunched muscle under the blistered and charred surface of the back of the thigh. "See this bump? When the muscle started to contract from the heat nothing was holding it down at one end, so it formed this mass above the knee." He slowly lowered the limb to the table. "The killer slashed the back of the knee with a blade, right down to the distal femur. That cut the tendons holding the hamstrings in place. With no muscles to flex the knee, the leg remained straight despite the heat of the fire. A wound like this would bleed badly as the slash cut the popliteal artery. The victim would have been bleeding out even before the fatal blow."

Leigh surged to her feet, her gaze darting from Matt to Rowe. "The victim couldn't run?"

"The victim couldn't *walk*," Rowe clarified. "In my opinion, the victim was on his knees at the time of death."

"Why do you say that?"

"The trachea." Rowe pointed to the slash in the neck with a freshly gloved finger. "The cartilaginous rings are sliced on an upward angle."

"So the killer disabled the victim by hamstringing him. The victim fell to his knees, the killer yanked his head back and slashed his throat."

"I wonder if there's some significance in the method of death." Matt came to stand at the end of the table, his gaze fixed on the body. The scene played over in his head, killer and victim in a final dance of death.

"What do you mean?"

"Well, assuming from the cross we saw that this is indeed a priest, that's a man who spends a lot of time on his knees in prayer. And they found the body at the front of sanctuary near the altar. The throat wound, the exsanguination . . . the blood of Christ spilled for all sinners."

Leigh crossed her arms over her chest, looking up at him in surprise. "I had no idea you were religious."

"I'm not. But you pick things up as you go through life and I was friendly with the chaplain in my unit when I was overseas. Anyway, it's just a thought. Nothing in the first death indicated anything like that."

"No, but maybe the method of death is more suited to the individual victim than the killer. Maybe—"

With a whoosh, the autopsy suite door swung open and Bree marched in, an evidence bag clutched in one hand. Her face looked drawn, and there were dark circles under her dull eyes and deep brackets around her mouth. She nodded curtly to the medical examiner. "Rowe. Sorry to barge in on you."

"Gilson. What can we do for you?"

Bree's gaze ran over the body on the table, and some of the

tightness in her face eased.

She was expecting the body of the fallen firefighter.

She marched briskly across the room. When she reached Leigh, she held out the bag. "You need this. We found it in the church near where the body was found."

Matt stared at the blade in surprise. Instead of the expected straight bladed implement, the bag contained a knife with a long curved blade and a soot-covered white stone handle. He stripped off his gloves and stepped forward for a closer look. "Is that . . . a sickle? Like you'd use to harvest crops?"

"Close. I mentioned this to you before. It's one of the ritual knives of the Craft—a boline." Leigh ran her fingers over it, feeling the metalwork on the grip of the knife. "It's the same design as the athame and it matches the pictures the metalsmith emailed me."

"The handle's a different color," said Paul. "You're sure it's from the same set?"

"The white handle is typical. Athame handles are usually black; boline handles are usually white. But the metal and stonework are clearly from the same metalsmith as the athame used in the first killing. I can also tell you this piece didn't come into the killer's hands through any local pawn or Witch shops. Both Riley and I struck out there."

"What's a boline used for?" Kiko asked.

"It's a work knife, not a ceremonial knife like the athame. Witches cut herbs, flowers, or cord with it, or use it to carve candles or wands with runes or symbols."

"Let me see that." Without waiting for Leigh's response, Matt took the knife from her, ignoring her glare. He studied it for a moment, turning it over in his hands.

"You're looking at the curve," Kiko said. "And the length of the blade."

"Oh, man." Paul leaned in closer. "That would be . . ." He

winced and left the rest of the sentence unuttered.

"What?" Leigh demanded.

Matt held the bag up so everyone could see the knife. "Look at the shape of the blade. This wouldn't require a slash. Just slide the curve of the blade around the leg or throat and rotate it sideways."

Leigh's expression wrinkled in distaste.

"That's why the left carotid is severed, but not the right."

Matt's gaze landed on Paul, who immediately threw up his hands. "No way. Just the thought of this is grossing me out."

Matt fixed him with a flat stare and waited.

"Fine," Paul muttered. "Standing or kneeling?"

"Standing to start." Matt handed Leigh the blade, then grasped Paul's shoulders and turned him so they were both facing the same direction. He held up his right hand, his fingers and thumb curved into a rough approximation of the blade, and slipped his hand around the back of Paul's right knee. "The first strike was like this." He rotated his hand toward the outside of the leg. "That takes the victim down."

He pressed on Paul's left shoulder, pushing him down to his knees on the tiles, ignoring the muttered *I hope this floor is clean.* Standing behind his student, he lightly grasped his hair to tip his head back before cupping his hand around the front of his throat, the edge of his hand tipped toward the floor. "See how the 'knife' angles down? And assuming the killer is right-handed, he or she would likely keep the knife rotated to the left to give more leverage to the slice." He jerked his hand to the right, imitating the fatal blow. Paul melodramatically fell forward onto his hands and knees.

Kiko leaned over to tap him on the shoulder. "You can get up now," she said dryly.

Paul climbed to his feet, wiping his hands off on his jeans.

"That gives us the upward cut to the throat," Leigh said.

"And it explains the slashes and why they don't just go straight across but seem to bend around the leg and throat." She held up the bag, peering intently at the blade. "Scorching notwithstanding, this blade looks pretty sharp."

"It would have to be," Rowe said. "It cut through cartilage like it was butter. It also allowed the killer to be fast. The victim could be down and bleeding out within fifteen seconds."

Kiko gave a little shudder. "Then he could have still been bleeding out when the fire was set."

"Not for long though," Rowe said. "And he certainly wouldn't have been aware of what was going on around him." He turned to Bree. "I attended to the firefighter first thing this morning."

Bree stood stiffly, as if braced for impact. "And?"

"Death was nearly instantaneous. When the steeple collapsed, he sustained a significant blow to the head. He had a comminuted fracture of the parietal and temporal bones."

"Meaning . . ." Bree made an impatient gesture with her hand.

"Bone fragments were driven into the brain. He never knew what happened. There was no smoke inhalation. I'm sorry."

Bree turned away for a moment, her head bowed and her hands balling at her sides. Then she whirled on Leigh, a pointed index finger stabbing the air. "You catch this son of a bitch, do you hear me?"

Leigh jerked back at the unexpected attack. "I hear you just fine. We're working as fast as we can."

"Funny, it doesn't look like it. Salem FD is putting the fires out and I'm giving you all the data you need. Why aren't you moving on it? A firefighter is dead and more are at risk."

"We *are* moving on it. We need time to build the case or it will all fall apart and the arsonist will walk."

"We know the risks." Bree went on as if she wasn't listening, and Matt noticed that she'd subconsciously identified herself

171

as a firefighter. "Our eyes are open every time we walk into a scene. Accidents happen—faulty wiring, lightning strikes, smoking in bed." Her eyes blazed and she leaned in, nearly spitting her words. "But this is murder. He's killing my men just as much as his victims."

"There's a team of us working this case. We're doing everything we can."

"I'll bet you went to bed last night. I spent a good part of last night with the DC, consoling a widow who's wondering how she's going to raise two little girls by herself. How she's going to explain to them that Daddy isn't coming home after shift. Is never coming home."

"Look, I understand what you're feeling. I've—"

Bree's fist crashed down on a countertop, rattling instruments on stainless-steel trays. "There's no fucking way you understand! I worked side by side with Cody when he was a probie. Before I became the fire marshal, I was his lieutenant and I taught him the ropes. I put my life in his hands, just like he put his in mine. And then, just like that, he's gone? Do your job and fix this. I won't lose another one, not on my watch."

She spun on her heel and marched from the autopsy suite, the door swinging back and forth in her wake.

Face deathly pale, Leigh started after her, but Matt caught her arm. She vibrated under his touch and tried to yank her arm out from under his grip.

"Leigh. Leigh!" When she continued to struggle, he jerked her arm, swinging her around to face him. Her right hand curled into a fist, and for a moment Matt thought she was going to hit him. He braced for the punch . . . but it didn't come. Instead, she stood stiffly under his hand, her breath sawing through gritted teeth. He loosened his hold on her, but didn't let go. "She's angry and hurting and sleep-deprived. She's striking out at the only person who can actually do any good here because she's feeling helpless. She's not yelling at you, she's yelling at the first available punching bag. And that just happened to be you."

"Lowell's right, Abbott." Rowe stepped forward to clap a hand over her shoulder and give it a squeeze. "I've known Gilson for years. I've never seen her react like that. She was a damned good firefighter and now she's a damned good fire marshal. But it's killing her that she's relegated to the sidelines on this one. She's tired and grieving and lashing out. You're a handy target. Just let it go."

Leigh pulled away from both men and turned toward her bag. She took a moment—longer than the task required—to tuck away the boline. When she turned around, her face was schooled into calmer lines. "You're right. We're all stressed, but Bree most of all right now. We'll straighten this out later when we're both cooler and she's had some sleep."

Too calm, Matt thought. *Too controlled.*

Leigh rolled her shoulders before jamming her hands into the pockets of her blazer. "So what's next?"

"We'll finish the autopsy," Rowe said. "Then I'll leave Lowell to strip the bones to confirm that knife is our murder weapon."

"What about you?" Matt asked.

"I'm meeting with a Father Thomas from Our Lady of Mercy. He called the unit this morning after seeing this morning's newspaper article, which is likely the only useful thing to come from it. He said he might have some information for us."

"Can he identify the victim?"

"He thinks he can. Wells included a lot of detail, including the cross on the victim."

"Where is Wells getting all this information?" Kiko asked.

"I think from one of the firefighters. I wanted to discuss it with Bree, but . . ." Her shoulders hunched and she fretted with one of the buttons on her blazer. "Anyway, I'm headed over there now, and I'll see what I can learn that might lead to victim

identification or any possible connection to Moira Simpson."
She started for the door.

Matt noticed that she didn't meet anyone's eyes. "Give me a call later and let us know what you found out?"

"Sure." She turned briefly to Rowe. "Thanks for making this a priority."

"No problem."

And without a look at Matt or his students, she was gone.

CHAPTER SEVENTEEN:
UNPROTECTED OPENINGS

Unprotected Openings: openings in floors, walls, or partitions that allow the passage of smoke, flame, and heat between the floors of a building.

Friday, 3:46 p.m.
Rectory, Our Lady of Mercy Catholic Church
Salem, Massachusetts

"Thank you for agreeing to see me, Father Thomas." Leigh stepped through the door into the dim, quiet foyer. Constructed over a century earlier, the rectory was built of pale-gray granite blocks that shut out the sounds of the outside world when the heavy oak door swung closed.

"I want to help in any way I can," Father Thomas said. He was a young man, still relatively fresh from his vows, Leigh judged. His somber black pants and short-sleeved shirt were relieved only by the brief flash of white at his collar.

"If you'd come into the library . . ." He led the way down a short hallway of dark wood wainscoting. The wide oak floor planks, worn by decades of wear, groaned under each step. Above the chair rail, heavy wood frames enclosed small paintings of priests dressed in ceremonial vestments—a multitude of different faces, all with the same sober expression.

They entered a room that doubled as both parlor and library. A wide wood table sat near the door, half a dozen books spread open on its surface around a pad of paper covered with notes written in a broad hand. Towering bookshelves jammed tight with books surrounded the table. A stone fireplace, flanked by long windows that let in the last of the afternoon sun in wide swaths over the faded throw rugs, dominated the far end of the room. There wasn't a speck of dust and the room smelled faintly of lemon oil.

They settled into wing chairs on opposite sides of the cold fireplace. Father Thomas fiddled anxiously with the wooden crucifix that hung from a simple black cord around his neck. "I hope you'll excuse my presumption in calling this morning, but when I read this morning's paper . . ."

"No need to apologize, Father. You may be our first real lead as to the identity of the victim found in yesterday's fire."

"It was a detail in the article—the metal cross found with the victim. It made me wonder, so I tried calling Father Brian, but I didn't get any answer. I went to the rectory, but no one answered the door. And that's when I called the detective unit."

"And you think the victim is . . . ?"

"Father Brian Clarke. He was the pastor at Saint Patrick's up until the closing and he hopes to be back if the church reopens." The younger man flushed a ruddy red. "If he's still alive."

"If he's our victim, we can confirm his identify through dental records." Leigh pulled a photo out of her messenger bag—a scorched cross made of three intersecting nails on a chain of coarse links. "But this might help as well. Is this familiar to you?"

She handed Father Thomas the photo. As soon as he took in the image, he closed his eyes, making the sign of the cross as his lips moved in a silent prayer. "That's Father Brian's cross."

"You're sure?"

"Yes. It's unusual on this side of the Atlantic. He bought it at Coventry. It's a replica of the cross of nails made by one of the vicars using medieval nails from the remnants of old beams

176

after the cathedral was bombed during World War Two. Father Brian was never without it. He said it was the symbol of hope rising from the ashes of despair, lit by the love of God. With that hope, anything was possible. It buoyed his spirits, especially in the last year while Saint Pat's was threatened with closure. And then later when it actually happened."

"Why was it closed?"

"It was a financial decision made by the Boston Archdiocese as part of its process to reconfigure parishes that were struggling. Father Brian wasn't only the pastor at Saint Pat's; he also had fiduciary responsibility at another church, Saint Sebastian's. When Saint Sebastian's started to struggle financially, he transferred money from Saint Pat's in an attempt to keep both parishes afloat. An internal audit discovered the transfer, and since Saint Pat's was now the one in real financial difficulty, the archdiocese elected to close it instead of Saint Sebastian's."

"How did the parishioners feel about Father Brian after that?"

The younger man's head snapped up, a passionate fire blazing in his ice-blue eyes. "You think that someone in the parish was responsible for this?"

"I'm not saying that," Leigh soothed. "I'm just trying to get a read on Father Brian. Some of the parishioners must have been unhappy about the situation. After all, it seems Saint Pat's wasn't in trouble until Father Brian tried to help the other parish."

The priest stood, walking to the window to gaze out over the gardens beyond. Sunlight washed over him, broken only by the grid of the windowpane, one bar slicing darkly over his cheek. "Some were very angry, but most came around. Father Brian was very open and honest about his motives. His parishioners made the official appeal to reopen the church, but Father Brian was doing a lot of the work behind the scenes. Those who were still angry with him forgave him at that point. He'd been at

Saint Patrick's for over thirty years, so he had a lot of history with both the parish and with many of the parishioners."

"How do you know so much about this?" Leigh asked.

"I was the associate priest at Saint Pat's for nearly two years when this all started. For a full year before the church was closed, rumors circulated and several times the closure date was announced and then canceled. I was transferred from Saint Pat's to Our Lady of Mercy last January. He never said anything, but I think Father Brian put in a good word for me. He was happy I found a new position, leaving him as the only priest at the end. That was okay with him, because he was hoping to lead the parish once again when the church was reopened."

"He was certain it would reopen?"

"That's what he always said." Father Thomas returned to his chair, dropping loosely into it. "Between you and me, I think the chances were small, but I admired his determination. The church closed last March but the appeals process continued and might have gone on for several more years. In the meantime, Father Brian remained in the rectory, so there was someone on the premises to discourage break-ins." Propping his chin on his hand, he gave an unhappy sigh. "But now, with the destruction of the church, the archdiocese will likely decide that rebuilding is too expensive, even with the insurance. Because of the appeals process, many of the church's sacred objects were left in place, excepting the most valuable, which were removed to avoid the risk of theft. So nearly everything is lost."

Leigh steepled her hands together, her fingers tapping together rhythmically. "That explains it."

Father Thomas fixed her with a confused stare. "Explains what?"

"The fire itself. It struck me last night that it was a vigorous fire for what I thought was an empty church. If everything was still in the church, there would have been lots to burn."

178

The priest nodded. "Altar cloths, paintings, wooden statues, pews, furniture, and hymnals. The parishioners were hoping that they'd get the go-ahead to reopen and they'd literally be able to walk in and pick up their lives within the church."

Leigh suddenly froze. "Hold on. Only the valuables were removed. Does that mean that the church records were still on site?"

"Yes."

Leigh's shoulders sagged in discouragement. "And there goes our best way to connect victims."

"You're talking about the other fire? The 'Pentacle Killing,' as the newspaper coined it?"

"Yes," Leigh said flatly. She forced herself to swallow the irritation; between Wells and her earlier run-in with Bree, she was off balance today. "Did Father Brian have any dealings with the Witchcraft community?"

Father Thomas gazed at her steadily, his brow furrowed. "Not directly. We would occasionally come into contact with members of that community through our outreach programs. They're very active in Salem, working with various charities. So, we might run into them at a Thanksgiving food drive at the food bank, that sort of thing."

"Did he ever have any disagreements with any of them?"

"Never. You think there's a connection to the Witches because of the pentacle found on the front door of the church?"

"This is the second fire this week where a pentacle was found at the scene. We're searching for a connection between the two events." She extended a second photograph. "Do you recognize this woman?"

He took the photo, studying it for a long moment. "No, I've never seen her before. Who is she?"

"Moira Simpson. Her body was found in the first pentacle fire. I'm looking for any connection between the two fires."

"It's possible that Father Brian might have known her. I was only at Saint Pat's for a few years."

"And now we can't check the parish records," Leigh said. "What about longtime parishioners? Is there anyone who's been a member of the church for most of Father Brian's tenure?"

Father Thomas's eyes narrowed unseeingly on something over Leigh's shoulder. "I'm a little out of touch with the parish as I've been gone for nine months. If you can give me a day or two, I'd be happy to look up some members and see if they could help you."

"I'd appreciate it." She handed him one of her cards. "Please feel free to call my cell at any time."

The young man stood and took a few steps toward the door before stopping. "Do you mind if I ask how Father Brian died? Was it—" He stopped, cleared his throat and tried again. "Was it the fire? Or did he die of smoke inhalation?"

"He was murdered before the fire was set."

Father Thomas staggered back a step, and he grasped the back of the chair to steady himself. "Murdered? How?"

"His throat was slit." She didn't elaborate on the additional wound.

"And it was arson?"

"We think so. But the fire marshal's office is investigating."

"Blessed Mother Mary," he breathed. "I'll do what I can to help. Despite what happened between Saint Pat's and Saint Sebastian's, he was a good man. He didn't deserve this."

"They never do, Father Thomas." Turning, Leigh left the sun-warmed parlor, disappearing into the dark once again.

Friday, 5:38 p.m.
Boston University, School of Medicine
Boston, Massachusetts
Matt knew from the flash of Leigh's eyes as she came through

the lab door that she was tired, hungry and low on patience.

"Sorry I've kept you." She glanced at her watch. "We can do this another time if it's getting too late."

He motioned her further in to the lab. "It's fine."

Leigh's shoulders sagged slightly at his words.

"You've had the day from hell, haven't you?" When she glared at him through slitted lids, he chuckled. Grasping her arm, he pulled her over to the students' workstations and pushed her into an empty chair.

"What are you doing? I don't have time for . . . ohhhhhhhh-hhh . . ." Her groan bordered on sensual as Matt's hands settled on her shoulders, skillfully massaging the tight knots under her skin. "Maybe I have time after all." Her eyelids fluttered closed.

"You want us to come back in a few minutes?" There was a smile in Paul's voice and he winked at Kiko and Juka.

"No, I want you to tell Leigh what you've been up to since we got back to the lab."

Leigh's body went stiff under Matt's hands as her eyes flew open and she braced her hands on the arms of the chair, ready to spring. Steady pressure on her shoulders kept her off her feet as he leaned down to her eye level. "You stay in the chair. This is their show. I've been busy with the remains." He pointed a finger at Kiko. "Go."

Kiko swung around from her desk to face Leigh. "We know that you're under a lot of pressure right now. Especially with the media attention." She grinned when Leigh gave a soft snort. "So we thought we could help out. Matt wanted some solo time on the remains this afternoon, so we thought we'd help with your red phosphorus issue. We didn't think you'd had time to look into it yet."

"The second fire kind of got in the way."

"I bet. We went ahead and tracked down the chemical supply houses in the area that carry red phosphorus. Juka did most of the chemistry research so we could have an idea as to who the end users might be." She imitated Matt's pointer finger, passing the ball to Juka.

"Let's start with the basics. Do you know what phosphorus is?" Juka asked.

"Only from what I learned in high school chemistry and biology. My degree is in criminal justice. Not much use for phosphorus there."

Paul snickered. "I guess not."

Juka fixed him with a flat stare and then turned back to Leigh. "Elemental phosphorus exists in two main forms—white and red. Red phosphorus can be produced by heating white phosphorus or exposing it to light. Now, you likely already know red phosphorus from its main use—safety matches."

"Hold on. You mean the red ends of matches?"

"No. It's in the strike plate. That's about fifty percent red phosphorus. It heats up with friction and that sets the chemical compound caked on the match head on fire."

Leigh tipped her head back against Matt's hands, freezing his fingers in place temporarily as she looked up at him. "How did Bree describe it? The red phosphorus reacted with the latex to produce heat and that ignited the latex?"

"Yes. Add the oil accelerant and you've got yourself a fire."

"Red phosphorus can be dangerous," Juka continued. "But because of its use in the production of crystal meth, it's a controlled substance."

"Is that all it's used for? Matches and crystal meth?"

Juka shook his head. "There are many other uses: the production of pharmaceutical methamphetamines in diet pills or for treating ADHD, pesticides, rat poisons, welding alloys, fireworks, hazard flares, smoke bombs, caps for toy guys, and semiconductors."

"And, counterintuitively, in some flame retardants," Paul

added. "It's got a lot of legitimate industrial uses."

"All of which might have made our lives much more difficult if the DEA didn't have its hands all over it," Kiko said. "Because they're worried about it falling into the hands of illegal drug labs, they've made it a List I chemical." She looked down at the sheet of paper in her lap. "And I quote: 'As List I chemicals, handlers of these materials will be subject to CSA chemical regulatory controls including registration, record keeping, reporting, and import/export requirements.' Everyone who sells this stuff is required by law to have full records of every transaction."

"As much as we wanted to call the chemical companies in the area and tell them we were the cops and we needed info— OUCH!" Paul rubbed his shoulder where Kiko had smacked him. "Okay, okay, *I* wanted to call them and tell them I was a cop, but I got voted down." He handed Leigh a sheet of paper. "This is a list of eight companies in Massachusetts, Rhode Island, Connecticut and New Hampshire that produce and ship red phosphorus. For each one, we've listed product numbers and descriptions based on the purity of the phosphorus found at the first fire site. You should be able to get whatever warrants you need based on this pretty quickly."

Stunned, Leigh gazed down at the paper in her hands. "I don't know what to say."

Paul leaned back in his chair and crossed a high-top sneaker over his jean-clad knee. "Coffee and fresh baked goods say 'thanks' just fine," he hinted broadly, grinning.

"Deal." She looked up at Matt, her body swaying slightly as he dug his thumbs into a knot over her right shoulder blade. "You asked them to do this?"

"Nope, this was all them. But I thought it was smart. We understand the science and know what we're looking for. And you have enough to do. Now you have a little less on your plate."

He gentled his touch and ran his thumb lightly up the back of her neck, a subtle caress out of sight of his students. "Now, speaking of what's on your plate, how did you do at the rectory?"

Leigh quickly outlined her visit. "I think we're correct on our assumption of the second victim's identity. Father Thomas identified the cross and said the victim was never without it. The question then is why? And what's the link between the two victims?"

"What's next, then?" Matt circled around her to sit on the edge of Kiko's workstation.

"I need to find the link between our victims and identify who had access to the red phosphorus. What about you?"

"We'll confirm the murder weapon used on the second victim tomorrow. And I got the DNA results back this afternoon. I can go over them with you when you have time." He met her gaze, holding it, hoping that she realized that it wasn't just the DNA from Moira Simpson he was referring to. When her eyes widened slightly, he knew she remembered the envelope from her special delivery.

"Thanks. That would be great."

Matt pushed back his sleeve to check the time. "And now I'm kicking you guys out. It's Friday night. Go pretend you have lives. Go dancing, have a beer, watch the baseball game. But get out of my lab for fifteen or sixteen hours. It's like you live here or something."

Paul was already on his feet, heading for the door. "Don't have to tell me twice. I'll see you tomorrow."

Kiko and Juka rose, but hesitated. "Are you sure?" Kiko asked. "We could put in a few more hours."

"No, we're done for the day. Scram. Go remind your fiancé that he has a fiancée. Then sleep in tomorrow. We'll start at ten. That'll give me time to hit the water first."

Kiko grinned and started after Paul, Juka right on her heels. "Night."

The door closed behind them with a thump, leaving the lab suddenly quiet.

Matt turned back to Leigh. "How are you doing?"

Leigh sat back in the chair, exhaustion playing over her face. "Tired. It's been a crappy day. What did you mean—'hit the water'?"

"I want time out in the scull. I need to work off some of the stress from this case. Want to join me? We missed our chance at it Sunday. And the fresh air and exercise would be a good break."

"I miss being active. I try to climb a couple times a week, but the last month has just been hell on my schedule. I think I've made it there once."

"Rock climbing? You've never mentioned it."

Leigh shrugged. "Guess it never came up. Likely because it's been too long since I had time to go."

"You know, there's a great rock wall in the fitness center on campus. You could show me how it's done."

A slow smile transformed her tired face. "You'd like to try it?"

"Sure." He winked at her. "You know, I'll show you mine, then you show me yours. Besides, I've always thought it looked like fun, but never had the time to learn. Might be a good activity over the winter when the Charles is not so inviting." Leaning forward he picked up her hand. "Now, how about some dinner?"

"Only if you let me pay this time."

"Sure." Matt climbed to his feet, pulling her with him. "I'll just let Dad know he's on his own tonight."

She frowned. "That's not right. Why don't we take him with us?"

"You want to have a date with my father?"

"Buddy, you're not getting a date tonight. You're getting dinner and that's it. I'm too tired for anything else. Besides, I like your dad and I'd feel bad leaving him on his own on such short notice."

Tipping her face up, he pressed his lips warmly to her forehead. "You're a good woman, Leigh Abbott. I knew there was a reason I liked you."

She smiled back up at him.

Maybe the day wasn't ending so badly after all.

Chapter Eighteen:
Recovery

Recovery: the development, coordination, and execution of service- and site-restoration plans, and the resumption of government operations and services after a fire.

Saturday, 8:46 a.m.
DeWolfe Boathouse
Boston, Massachusetts

Leigh was laughing breathlessly when they glided up to the dock. Carefully raising her left oar to clear the wooden boards, she reached out with her free hand to slow their progress. One of the trainers jogged out of the boathouse, steadying the scull as they climbed out. She stood for a moment, out of breath and sweaty, but feeling deliciously alive from her workout.

Sunlight splashed over the Charles in bright streams, sparkling on the bobbing crests. Trees lined the river's edge in a dazzling array of flaming reds, oranges and yellows. Near the water's edge, a group of ducks paddled under the draping branches of an American elm, spinning the fallen leaves that floated on the river's surface. Under her feet, the dock pitched gently, rocked by the swift moving water below.

"Look out," Matt called.

Leigh stepped back as Matt and the deckhand pulled the scull from the water to carry it into the boathouse. Leigh followed along at a slower pace. Stepping inside, temporarily blind in the dim light, she was struck by the scents of sawdust, sweat, wax and lacquer. Blinking a few times, she peered into the storage room. Racing boats were stacked on metal racks four high, from short single-man sculls to massive eight-man shells. Beside the open doors, braces of oars stood blade up in neat lines, reaching from the floor nearly to the ten-foot ceiling. Through the floorboards overhead, she could hear the sounds of rowers working out on the fitness equipment.

Matt appeared at her side, two bottles of water in his hands and a windbreaker in Boston University colors draped over his arm. He wore a similar windbreaker already. He handed her one of the bottles. "Why don't we sit outside for a few minutes?"

She followed him back out onto the dock and over to a bench pressed up against the clapboard wall of the boathouse. He held out the windbreaker. "Here. The breeze is refreshing now, but it's going to be cold once you start to cool down."

Leigh pulled the windbreaker over her long-sleeved athletic T and sank gratefully onto the bench. She took a long gulp of water and then leaned her head back against the sun-warmed wood, gazing out across the water. An eight-man scull slid gracefully by as it arrowed under one of the arches of the Boston University Bridge, sixteen oars dipping in perfect time and barely making a ripple on the water. On the other side of the river, BU's Charles River Campus sprawled in an eclectic mixture of architectural styles that reflected campus growth after World War I. In the green space behind the buildings, students walked or lay on the grass, enjoying the last days of fall warmth.

"Penny for your thoughts."

Leigh lazily turned her head to look at Matt. He'd donned dark glasses and the wind ruffled his hair. Reaching out, she touched the ends that dangled in front of his eyes, pushing them aside. "You need a haircut."

"That's what you were thinking about?"

"No. Actually, I was kind of thinking about nothing. Just

enjoying the peace and taking a few moments to relax. You gave me a good workout."

He squeezed her biceps. "You did great out there."

She laughed and pulled her arm from his grasp. "Tell me the truth—you had to slow your pace for me, didn't you?"

"Okay, maybe a little. But not much. I didn't really expect that you'd be able to keep up with me. You're new at it and while you're in good shape—" His eyes ran over her body with an appreciative gleam. "—rowing is hard work."

"No kidding. And I underestimated how much legwork it was. How does your father do it?" she asked, referring to Mike's workout with Matt at the oars. Matt had told her about the specialized shell they had built so Mike could row without the use of his legs.

"You've seen what he looks like. When you can't use your legs, it's a total upper body workout. He's really strong now. I think he could bench-press more than me and he's twenty-five years older."

"He's amazing. I, on the other hand, have a bad feeling about what shape I'm going to be in tomorrow. I hope I don't have to chase down any bad guys, or I'm really going to be in trouble. I think I used muscles today I didn't know I had."

Matt laughed and rubbed her thigh in sympathy. "So . . . uh . . . speaking of bad guys . . ." He cleared his throat. "What's your next move with the information about your father?" His gaze searched her face, lines of worry deepening around his eyes. "You're covering it well for everyone else, but I can tell it's never far from your mind."

Leigh sighed, some the joy seeping out of her mood. A chill ran down her spine, but she doubted it was the breeze cooling the sweat on her skin. "I haven't had time to deal with it, other than getting you that sample to test."

"And that came up as a big fat goose egg. Must have been

one of those self-adhesive envelopes."

"There's no way I could have gotten so lucky as to get a hit with the DNA. The more I think about this, the more I think it had to come from within the department, and cops know evidence collection inside and out. We also know we're on file so our own DNA can be eliminated from a crime scene in case of contamination."

"What about a journalist? Could someone like that have a source inside the department who could slip them information?"

Leigh made a humming noise, deep in the back of her throat. "Maybe. But I keep circling back to why? If a journalist thought he had a line on a dirty cop, wouldn't he be more likely to investigate and then break it as a big story? That way he gets all the glory. That doesn't feel right here." She paused, taking a long sip of her water, trying to organize her thoughts. "Frankly, I don't know what feels right. None of it makes any sense. If it's intended as blackmail, why is there no request for money? If they want to go after me, why not just do it directly? What do they have to gain by ruining the name of a good man?" Her voice rose in pitch and the half-empty plastic bottle crumpled under the pressure of her fingers.

Matt pulled the bottle from her grasp, intertwining his fingers with hers instead. "You're angry and frustrated."

"Damn right!" When Matt's eyebrows shot up from behind his sunglasses, Leigh forced herself to calm down. "Sorry. Apparently we've hit a nerve here."

"No need to apologize. If someone was trying to do this to the memory of one of my parents, I'd be going crazy."

"But getting angry doesn't help. All it does is cloud my judgment and I need to think clearly. So, for now, I'm going to assume it's someone on the inside. There's nothing more to be gained from the first message, so I'm going back to basics. I'll start by signing out the case evidence from Dad's death."

"Do you think that's a good idea? That must leave some sort of paper trail."

"They know I'm going to look into it. Besides, it's either that or sit on my hands, and I'm not really the sitting-still type. So I'm going to start taking it apart. I've also got Dad's own files from back then."

"He kept personal files? You can do that?"

"Dad used to make copies of stuff to work on from home. When he died, all that stuff was on his computer. When I sold the family home, I kept a lot of his things. His hard drive was one of them. At the time I kept it because he had family photos on there and some personal documents, but maybe there'll be something relevant."

"It's definitely worth looking through. Can I help?"

She considered his request for a moment. "You could. Not your students though. I don't want them in on this."

"I agree. But I can be another set of eyes. You have enough going on. Let me carry some of this load."

"You do that a lot lately."

He rubbed the fingers of his free hand over the back of hers. "You know I'm happy to."

"And to think just four weeks ago I thought you were the most arrogant son of a bitch I'd ever met and wanted to kick your ass from here to Springfield."

Laughter exploded from Matt in a sharp crack that had the seagull perched on the edge of the dock rising into the air with an annoyed squawk. "And to think that just four weeks ago I thought you were a hardheaded, protocol-obsessed, controlling flatfoot with zero personality." He grinned. "Isn't it nice to be wrong?"

"In this case, yes." Leigh pushed back the cuff of the windbreaker to glance at her watch. "I'd better go. I want to talk to Flynn Simpson about the second fire. He may be able to see a connection between the victims that we're missing." She stood, looking out over the water as the wind whipped at her ponytail. "Thanks for this morning. It was a great break." She rolled her shoulders.

"We both needed it. But now . . ."

Their eyes met as they shared the same thought: It was time to get back to work.

CHAPTER NINETEEN:
REMEDIAL ACTION

Remedial Action: a permanent solution to prevent or minimize the migration of a hazardous substance after release into the environment.

Saturday, 10:45 a.m.
Salem Boatworks
Salem, Massachusetts
The tiny front office was only big enough to hold a filing cabinet and a counter with a computer and phone. Behind the counter hung a carved wood sign—*Salem Boatworks*—surrounded by glossy framed photos of beautiful custom-made boats.

"Good morning. Can I help you?" The young woman behind the counter greeted Leigh.

Leigh quickly flashed her badge. "I'm looking for Flynn Simpson. He told me I could meet him here."

The girl's face clouded. "This is about his mother's death, isn't it? Horrible tragedy. We tried to get Flynn to take some time off, but he came in to catch up since he missed the last few days." She leaned forward conspiratorially and her voice dropped to just above a whisper. "Have you got a line on the Pentacle Killer yet?"

Bloody newspaper articles. "I'm afraid I can't share that information with you. Mr. Simpson?" Leigh asked pointedly.

The woman straightened, her lips pursing in disappointment. "Just a moment. He's out back."

She disappeared through a door into the back room, leaving it open a few inches. Construction sounds drifted through the gap—men's voices punctuated by the punch of a nail gun, a saw roaring to life, followed by the scream of the blade biting into wood. Moments later, the receptionist returned. "He says to go on back, second office on the right."

"Thank you."

Leigh stepped through the door into the big boathouse. Overhead, fluorescent lights provided illumination and fat silver ductwork crisscrossed the high ceiling of the single large room. One wall was almost completely comprised of windows, allowing sunlight to flood in. Half a dozen boats filled the space, each in a different stage of repair or construction. Wooden struts supported an overturned boat, the unfinished wooden planks of the hull covering only halfway up ribs that protruded like spindly fingers. A heavy metal cylinder hung four feet off the floor, suspended from a long track bolted to heavy I-beam supports. Against the far wall, a crowded workbench was crammed with tools and cans of varnish, while nearby, a man wearing safety goggles manned a circular saw, the floor around him littered with sawdust.

A head briefly appeared above the side of a speedboat, stripped of all its fittings and windshield. At the questioning look, Leigh said, "Flynn Simpson?" and the man pointed to an open office door.

Leigh rapped lightly on the door. Simpson looked up from where he sat, head bent over a pile of paperwork. He looked worn and exhausted, and his mourning black further washed out his already pale skin. "Trooper Abbott, come in." He motioned to a chair on the opposite side of a desk covered in catalogs and paperwork.

"I appreciate you making the time to see me."

He sat back in his chair, his posture awkwardly hunched.

"You know what it's like—take some time off and the stacks on your desk mushroom by leaps and bounds." He lifted a pile of papers with his right hand and dropped them the few inches back to the surface. "Orders and inventories and billing. And everyone needs everything *now*." He sighed pensively. "I've been spending a lot of time planning Mom's funeral. I'd like it to be a beautiful service for a beautiful woman. She didn't outline anything in her will, but I hope she'd approve of my arrangements." Hope filled his expression. "Have you learned anything new about her death?"

"Nothing I can share at this time. When I can, you'll be the first to know. I actually have some questions about another death."

Hope melted away, leaving distress etched on his face. "The fire the other night?"

"You've heard about it?"

"It's been headline news for days now. The 'Pentacle Killer' strikes again. Were you able to identify the victim in the second fire?"

"We confirmed his identity this morning. His name was Father Brian Clarke. I was wondering if you knew him. Or know if your mother did."

Simpson's face grew thoughtful and one finger drummed lightly on the top of his desk. Finally he shook his head. "The name's not familiar. He was a priest?"

"The pastor at Saint Patrick's Catholic Church. You're sure your mother didn't know him? She didn't attend a Catholic church?"

He shrugged, an awkward one-sided gesture as only his right shoulder rose and fell. "I can't say for certain. I've been living away from home for about five years now. But she certainly never mentioned any Catholic priests to me. What if they were simply chosen at random?"

"The victims? To what purpose?"

"What purpose is there ever in taking someone's life? I read about the Bradford case in the papers. That was someone who was essentially playing games with peoples' lives."

He had her there. "That was more the exception than the rule. Ninety-five percent of the time murder has a very basic motive—greed, lust, jealousy, or revenge."

"Then the paper didn't get its theory on ceremonial sacrifice from you?"

For a moment Leigh simply stared at the twisted young man before her. "Ceremonial sacrifice?" The two words were enunciated clearly and slowly, disbelief ringing in every syllable.

"Killed with a Witch's blade and then cleansed by fire." Reaching over to the other side of his computer, Simpson held up a paper. "It was in this morning's *Salem Times*. According to them, the priest was killed with a curved knife." He scanned down the article. "A boline."

"Does it say how?" Leigh forced her jaw to relax so it didn't sound like her words came from between clenched teeth.

"Throat slit." He looked up. "That's different from Mom. Different weapon, different manner of death but the same sign on the door. When are you going to stop them?"

"Who?" Leigh asked coolly.

"The Witches. According to this article, tourists are thinking of leaving because of the risk of staying in town."

Leigh counted to ten before allowing herself to speak. "Don't believe everything you read, Mr. Simpson."

Simpson considered her thoughtfully for a moment before tossing the paper aside carelessly. "I guess you're right. You need to keep all your options open. But to save you from asking, I was with Aaron on Thursday. He came home early and we had dinner together and stayed in and watched a movie. It was memorable because normally he's out in the evenings showing houses, so when he's got the night off, we take advantage."

"Thank you, I'll make a note." Leigh rose to her feet. "Thanks for your time. If you think of anything else—"

"I'll be in touch. I have your numbers. Thank you, Trooper."

Once outside, Leigh took a deep breath of the tangy salt air rolling in off the harbor. She wanted to spend the afternoon following up on the list Matt's students gave her on the chemical companies, but she suspected they wouldn't be open on a Saturday. That was first thing on her list for Monday morning.

She turned her mind glumly to Jason Wells and the *Salem Times*. The information leak had to stop. She suspected she knew where the leak was and she was ninety-nine percent sure it wasn't in her own department. If the leak had come from the morgue, the juicy detail of the hamstringing would have been included in the article. She was now surer than ever that the leak must be in within the fire department and she wanted Bree's ear for five minutes to discuss it.

If she'll talk to me.

Leigh climbed into her car and closed the door with a muffled *thump.* She pulled out her phone and dialed Bree's number.

"Bree Gilson."

"It's Leigh Abbott."

There was a moment of silence, then Bree spoke in a quiet voice. "Hi. Um . . . look. I've been meaning to give you a call. I owe you an apology for—"

"No apology required," Leigh said, suddenly meaning it. With everything else going on right now, there was no room for egos in this case. They were all on the same team, after all. "I know what it's like, losing a colleague. Sometimes we need time to work through it. Don't give it another thought."

"Thanks." Relief layered thickly over the single word.

"I need to talk to you about something that's . . . a little awkward. Have you seen the articles in the *Salem Times*?"

"The ones written by Jason Wells? Have I ever. That little piece of—"

"We've got a leak. And based on the information that's getting out, as well as what isn't, I think it's coming from the fire department."

Silence.

"It's the only explanation," Leigh rushed on. "It's information our press officer isn't providing." Another pause. "What do you think?"

"I think if it's one of the firefighters, then they're going to answer to me. And the chief. And it's not going to be pretty."

"Look closely at the articles so you know what I mean. Can I leave it with you?"

"I'll get to the bottom of it."

"Thanks. I'm sorry to pile this on you along with everything else you're going through."

"No problem. It just gets added to the list. Anything new on the red phosphorus?"

"Not yet, but we're working on it. I'll let you know as soon as I have anything solid."

Leigh hung up, feeling better than she had since yesterday morning; she hadn't realized how much tension she'd carried because of Bree's outburst. And she was definitely looking forward to Jason Wells getting cut off at the knees.

Feeling energized, she started the car and merged into traffic, turning toward the unit.

Her mood abruptly darkened as she realized the next thing she needed to do—collect the evidence on her father's death. Her gut clenched with dread, but she wrapped her fingers tighter around the steering wheel, her jaw set.

She was going to get to the bottom of that too.

CHAPTER TWENTY:
ARCANA

Arcana: secret knowledge and mysteries known only to initiates; comes from the Latin words *arcanus* meaning "shut in" or "closed," and *arca* which is a "chest" or "safe." May also refer to the classification of the cards in a tarot deck.

Saturday, 8:25 p.m
Abbott Residence
Salem, Massachusetts

"This is everything on your father's death?" Matt asked as Leigh set two fat file folders on the coffee table.

"The paperwork's in the files. The physical evidence is in the box." Leigh nudged a cardboard file box on the floor with her toe.

"Can I see it?"

Leigh leaned forward to pull one of the folders toward her where they sat hip to hip on the couch. "There's really nothing useful in there. Everything we need is in the files."

"Hey." Matt wrapped his fingers around her wrist and she froze. "Nothing useful, or something you don't want me to see?" Leigh angled her face away the tiniest degree, her jaw locked as she stared unblinkingly at the paperwork. And then he knew. He gentled his voice. "Or is it something *you* don't want to see?"

"I've seen everything in that box." Flat, toneless.

Matt could practically see her defenses struggling to stay up

199

and his heart broke for her. He couldn't imagine the hell of having to examine the violent death of a parent in minute detail. "But you don't want to see it again. I get that." When she stayed turned away from him, he lay his hand on her thigh. The muscles were stiff under his touch. "But I can help better if you let me look. Maybe I'll see something you didn't."

She tried for a casual shrug, but the movement came off stiff and awkward. "Sure. Help yourself." She handed him the box.

He set it down on the floor by his feet and removed the lid. He rummaged through the contents, keeping everything below the lip of the box and out of Leigh's line of sight. He immediately saw why she didn't want to delve into the box. Two pistols lay on top, each in its own evidence bag. One was a .40 Sig Sauer, very similar to the firearm Leigh carried when she was on duty. The other was a Bryco .38 semiautomatic. *The gun that killed her father.* He continued sorting through the evidence. Two pairs of bagged winter gloves. Two bullets in individual bags—one slightly misshapen on one side, the other distorted into a mangled mushroom. *Her father's head shot.* His gaze flicked to Leigh. She was busily reading the content of one of the file folders, but her lips were pressed together so tightly they were almost bloodless.

There wasn't much more in the box after that, just the CI's unclaimed personal belongings in a single bag—clothing, wallet and cluttered key ring—and a second bag with Nate Abbott's clothing. There were none of Nate's personal effects, but Matt assumed Leigh had requested those once the case was closed and they were no longer evidence. He closed the lid and picked up the other file folder, sitting back on the couch. He leaned into Leigh. "What have you got?"

She held up a single finger while she finished reading. "The scientific reports. This is ballistics. I've already gone through the DNA reports. I also have shoe casts, fingerprints, and hair and fiber. Your folder has the crime scene photos and the autopsy report. We'll each go through a folder, then we'll switch. That way we won't miss anything."

"Are you sure? I can just summarize this for y—"

"Yes," she snapped. Then the file folder fell into her lap and she exhaled sharply. When she turned to look at him, her face was too pale and her eyes were sunken. "Sorry. I'm just finding this . . . difficult."

Matt set down his folder to take one of her cold hands in both of his, chafing the skin between his palms. "You're examining your father's death under a microscope. It's going to be difficult. So if I can do some of this for you, let me. I know you need all the facts, but give yourself a break."

She nodded, pulling her hand from his grasp. They both picked up their file folders and settled in to read.

Matt opened his folder, wincing at the sight of the crime scene photos on top. Nonchalantly shifting his left elbow onto the armrest, he purposely angled his body so Leigh couldn't see the contents.

He flipped through the photos slowly, taking time to examine each one. There were shots of the snowy alley from different angles and multiple shots of each body, including the one sent to Leigh the previous week. They'd clearly brought in lights and the snow sparkled cheerfully around the ruined bodies of the two men. The CI—Roger Tyson—lay face up, his dark eyes open and staring, a large red stain soaked into the front of his winter coat. *Straight shot, right through the heart.* A gun lay several feet from his right hand, scuff marks in the snow indicating it had been kicked out of the way, and boot prints straddled the body. Leigh's father lay face down in the snow, facing away from the CI, his legs twisted and his arms flung wide. Part of the back of his skull was missing and blood soaked the snow in a gruesome puddle. The dirty white brick wall behind the body was covered with a spray of blood and brain tissue, spatter from the fatal wound.

Matt felt the tangled knot in his chest ease slightly as he turned to the next page—the autopsy report. Both autopsies had been performed by Rowe, and Matt found comfort in the short, clinical reporting style. No emotion, just facts. Leigh's father had died instantly when the bullet penetrated the forehead near the right outer border of the frontal bone and exited through the back of the head, taking a chunk of bone with it in a ragged exit wound. Tyson's death took less than a minute after the bullet pierced his aorta. No sign of struggle with either man.

Matt flipped back to the photos, studying the two bodies again. Something uncomfortable was niggling at the back of his mind. The body shot in the CI made sense to him; cops were taught to aim for the middle of the torso to increase their chances of a hitting their target. But Nate Abbott's head shot was nothing short of pure bad luck. If the two men had shot at each other at the same time, the chance of the CI making that shot accurately was very small. Maybe he'd been aiming for Abbott's torso, had gotten hit the moment he pulled the trigger, and that had thrown off his aim. The bullet caught Abbott in the head, the force of the impact spinning him around so he fell face down in the snow.

Matt glanced at Leigh's bent head, keeping his thoughts to himself. If her father died from a bullet gone wild, he wasn't going to break the news to her.

The last document in the pile was the incident report, written by Detective Oakes. It told the story clearly and, in Matt's mind, left no questions unanswered. This also bothered him; in his limited experience in police cases, it was rare that every question got answered. From the outside looking in, it seemed very neat. Maybe too neat. Or was he simply trying to find answers for Leigh, even if they didn't exist?

He closed the file and looked up to see Leigh quietly watching him, the firelight painting one side of her face with a warm glow. "Already done?"

"Yes." She extended the folder. "Time to trade."

Matt's fingers involuntarily tightened on the file folder in his lap, but he forced himself to surrender it. He shifted on the couch, angling himself closer. They opened their files and started reading. When Matt took Leigh's hand, she didn't complain, even though it was awkward for both of them. Occasionally Leigh's fingers twitched in his, so he wordlessly held on a little tighter, stroking his thumb over the back of her hand until she relaxed. *Past the crime scene photos.* He read through his reports, but often glanced over at what she was reading, marking her progress through the information.

Finally, she closed the folder and he did the same, having been done for at least five minutes; he'd read that last page four times over.

"How about some wine before we take this apart?" she asked.

"Sounds perfect. Need help?"

"Sure."

Minutes later they returned to the living room carrying a chilled bottle of pinot blanc and two slender stemmed crystal wineglasses. Sitting back down on the couch, Leigh poured two very generous portions, faint notes of pear and citrus wafting into the air.

"Let's review," she said. "The shooting looks very straightforward. Dad and Oakes were supposed to meet Tyson outside a bar in The Point neighborhood at nine o'clock, but Tyson didn't show. After waiting for fifteen minutes, they agreed to split up and look around."

"According to the report, Oakes was going through a building the city had marked as condemned when he heard two nearly simultaneous shots," Matt continued. "It took him a few minutes to find them in an alley between two tenements. He knew at first glance that your dad was gone, so he went to check Tyson. He kicked the gun clear, then pulled off his gloves and checked for a pulse, got nothing. Called it in."

"There's nothing about this scene that looks out of place to me," Leigh said. "Trace evidence and DNA point only to Dad and Tyson. Oakes's boot prints were around Tyson's body, but he was checking for signs of life. Ballistics is clear—the bullet from Dad's Sig Sauer killed Tyson, the bullet from Tyson's .38 killed Dad. There are smudged fingerprints on both guns, probably from the last time they cleaned their weapons—Dad's on his weapon; Tyson's on the Bryco. Their winter gloves both tested positive for gunshot residue. The incident report is clear." She shook her head in frustration. "Why is someone sending me this material? Just to torture me? Clearly it's all here. The picture I received is part of this file. It's not new. What am I supposed to see?"

"I don't know. But I think our next step is to look into the case he was working on. The case that required meeting the CI."

"I can easily get the case file. But I'm not going to request evidence for now so it stays under the radar."

"What about talking to Oakes? Is he still with Salem PD?"

"Last I heard, yes. I thought about talking to him, but the moment I do, it all goes public. So for now, I'd like to hold that in reserve."

"Then get that file and we'll go through it. Maybe what we're looking for is there."

"Maybe." Leigh's voice clearly conveyed her doubt. "It may have to wait until this case is closed though." She reached over and turned off the lamp, letting the warm glow from the fire light the room. For long moments they simply sat, with only the *whoosh* of flames and the crackling logs to break the silence.

Matt relaxed back on the sofa, propping his head on his hand. "So . . . I'm kind of curious about something."

"What?"

"The whole tarot thing."

She cast him a sidelong glance. "Why are you curious about that?"

He shrugged. "It just seems . . . interesting."

She sat up and pinned him with a laser stare. "You're telling me that you, the scientist, are going to believe what a random drawing of cards will say?"

"Not even remotely, I just thought it would be fun, especially after all this." His open palm indicated the folders on the coffee table. "Come on, you said that you could do a reading. Show me." He picked up the wine bottle, topping up their glasses. "Tell me my future."

Leigh picked up her glass, swirling the wine inside, watching it dance in the firelight. "Just for fun?"

"Yeah." He gently elbowed her ribs. "Come on," he wheedled, putting on his best puppy dog expression.

She laughed, her first easy sound in over an hour, and pushed him back a few inches. "All right, you win. I just need to find my cards since I haven't touched them in years." After searching through several cabinets in the living room, she disappeared into the hallway beyond.

Matt propped his feet up on the coffee table, as he sipped his wine, lazily watching the flames flickering in the grate.

"Ah ha!" Leigh's voice filtered down from somewhere over his head.

"Found them," Matt murmured. Pulling his feet from the table, his gaze fell on the file folders. His motivation for a tarot reading wasn't simply curiosity, it was also to distract Leigh from her father's death. She was keeping her chin up, but the stress and sadness shone in her eyes nonetheless. Short of carrying her upstairs to linger over her in bed for several slow, intense hours—and as much as he wanted to do that, Leigh wasn't mentally in the right place for their first time together tonight—this was what sprang to mind as a lighthearted distraction. He picked up the file folders, laid them on top of the box and pushed everything behind the couch. She'd find it later tonight or tomorrow, but for now, out of sight, out of mind.

He reclaimed his wine just before Leigh reentered the room, carrying a small box. Opening it, she slid out an oversized deck of cards. The cards were Gothic in style, the backs jet-black with a scrolling design in gold, each front bearing a stylized oracle. A parchment illustrated above each figure named it in medieval calligraphy.

Matt picked up a card entitled *The Siren*. On it, a voluptuous mermaid held her arms open wide in a gesture of welcome. Gold bracelets twined around her upper arms and wrists, and her long dark hair trailed down to cover her naked breasts. But her eyes were vacant and her body glowed a watery blue. "Beautiful artwork, but I have to say, this gal looks like she could steal a man's soul."

Leigh plucked the card from his hand, slid it back into the deck and started to shuffle. "She's definitely trouble. She's the embodiment of temptation and enchantment. Of foolish risk and losing yourself in another's influence."

"So not one you want to get," Matt said.

"Or at least one that you want firmly in your past since I'll be reading your past, present and future. Now, instead of the classic tarot deck, I've chosen a smaller oracle deck."

"What's the difference?"

"It's a different form of divination but it still uses cards in the same way. It's been a while since I've done this, so I thought a less complex reading might be a good idea. It can take months to learn tarot in depth and I've forgotten a lot over time."

Leigh stopped shuffling and laid the first card out on the table, face down. "This is you." Matt reached out to turn the card over and she smacked his hand. "Not yet."

"Can't blame a guy for trying." Matt grinned at her.

Leigh laid out a single card above the first, then below. "North and south." On either side. "Then west and east." She continued laying out cards until nine lay face down on the table, in a three-by-three grid. "Now we look at them one at a time. The cards are set up in three vertical rows that are your past, present and future but we'll read through them in a specific order." She touched her fingertips to the center card. "As I said, this card is you, in your present circumstances." She turned the card over and laughed.

Matt sat up straighter. "What's so funny?"

"I should have known." She handed him the card.

Under the title *The Wizard* was an old man in a pointed cap and royal-blue robes trimmed with a line of Celtic knots. He stood straight and tall, a heavy staff in his left hand, the top of which formed a claw that held a brilliant blue ball. "I'm Gandalf?"

"Don't play your geek card so early in the game. You're the philosopher, the adviser. The practitioner of the sciences. You use your skills to help others." She slid the card from his fingers to look at it. "It's a good call, actually. This one is right on."

"What's next?"

"The north card. This one represents what you aspire to do or to be."

She turned over the card and Matt let out a laugh. "I like the skull. Maybe it means I'll get tenure at BU." The card depicted a tall, slender woman in a flowing strapless red gown, delicate angel wings bursting from her back. She cradled a skull in her cupped hands, gazing at it almost lovingly. He glanced at Leigh to find her staring at the card with narrowed eyes. "What?"

"This is *The Spirit*. It represents your need to be a watchful protector. You protect those you hold dear, even at risk of your own life. Your students, family, friends." She thoughtfully set the card down. "Now the south card represents your earthly present pursuits and material concerns." She turned over the card. In tones of orange, a horizontally bisected, upside-down triangle lay in the center of a circle marked with the names and Greek symbols for Capricorn, Virgo and Taurus. "*The Earth* oracle," Leigh said. "This represents someone who is logical, practical and grounded. Someone who is always dependable."

Matt set his glass down near the edge of the table and leaned in for a better look at the cards. "For someone who says she can't do this, this is pretty accurate. Did you stack the deck?"

"No." But the set of her mouth told Matt that something here was making her uncomfortable. "I'm sure the card saying that you're a two-faced deceiver is coming up next to balance all this out." She set the card down. "Next is the west card, the Oracle of the Past Realm." She turned it over. A center star burned outwards in an explosion of smaller starbursts, all glowing a ghostly blue. "*The Stars*. They represent a great journey in your past. It could include a separation and a reunion." She turned slowly to meet his eyes.

"My deployment overseas. Afghanistan. Separation from my mother forever, but a reunion with my father." The words sounded clipped and distant, even to his own ears.

"You know, maybe this isn't such a good idea. You wanted a fun diversion after a stressful evening and if it's just bringing back bad memories—" She stopped when Matt's fingers closed over her wrist.

"Keep going," he coaxed. "I can handle it."

"Are you sure? We're getting into the future stuff now."

"Yup. Do it."

"Okay, the east card tells you what is to be." Leigh took a deep drink from her wineglass, then reached for the next card. Her breath caught when she turned it over and Matt leaned forward for a closer look.

A jet-black raven with blood-red eyes sat atop a skull, its talons biting into the bone. Its wings were unfurled and the mouth was open in a silent scream of warning.

"*The Raven,* a creature of the shadows. The harbinger of ill portent. An omen. Darkness lies ahead."

Ice sluiced through Matt's veins. *Darkness. Death?*

A log suddenly settled in the fire with a shower of sparks, breaking them both out of their frozen stares.

Matt laughed and reached for his wine. "Look at us. We're like twelve-year-old girls at a slumber party telling ghost stories."

Leigh's fingers hovered over the card, not quite willing to touch it. "This is a very dark card."

"That was randomly drawn out of a deck. Come on, Leigh, this is supposed to be for entertainment. There's no way a card can determine the future. But keep going. Maybe it'll tell me I'm going to win the lottery next."

Leigh slowly pulled her hand away from *The Raven.* "The northwest card. This one represents a past spiritual or romantic influence in your life." She turned the card over.

Matt picked it up, studying it. It was entitled *The Golem.* On it, a knighted figure wearing burnished armor held the hilt of a mighty sword, his eyes glowing greenish-blue in an otherwise shadowed face. "Definitely not a past romantic influence. This guy looks kind of scary."

"Actually, that's a good card. *The Golem* represents a loyal friend and stalwart companion. One who will aid you in times of trouble. Unless you abuse him; then he can become the instrument of your destruction. Who in your past fits that role?"

Matt closed his eyes for a moment, then it came to him in a

flash. "Of course . . . Colin."

"Who's that?"

"You remember that I told you about the chaplain who was with our unit in Afghanistan? That was Colin. A good man and a loyal friend. There were days when everything went wrong over there, when it felt like he was the only one holding onto our sanity. Even those of us who weren't religious. He knew when to be a priest and when to be a friend."

"Sometimes you just need someone to talk to."

"Yeah." Matt tapped the card against the flat of his hand. "I wonder what ever happened to Colin."

"You two lost touch?"

Heat flushed his face and he fought the urge to drop his gaze. "I lost touch. On purpose. When I came back, I was busy with Dad's rehab and, frankly, I didn't want to think about my time in-country. So I cut all ties. Looking back, maybe that wasn't the smartest thing I ever did. I haven't thought about Colin in years. I wonder what ever happened to him."

"You should look him up sometime. Maybe the VA could help you get in touch."

Memories of Afghanistan flooded Matt's mind like a slide show on fast-forward. Standing at the back of a full tent, eavesdropping on Mass when his spirit was particularly low, Colin in desert fatigues at the front of the group, a Navy chaplain's stole draped around his neck. Playing beach volleyball with the men during a lull in the fighting, Colin, shirtless like the rest of them, at his side. Sitting together quietly on the edge of his bunk, grieving the loss of a friend. Colin by his bedside after the explosion.

He absently touched the tough scar tissue at his temple as if it was a talisman. "Yeah, you know, I really should do that." Looking up, he grinned at her. "See, not all bad."

"Good." She took a deep breath. "The northeast card. This is a future spiritual or romantic influence in your life." She turned the card over and then simply stared at it as a blush bloomed over her cheekbones.

Matt found himself fascinated by the warm color flushing her face, but he pulled his gaze away. "My future romantic or spiritual influence is a knight?" The card depicted a rearing stallion draped in red and gold. Seated astride the horse was a knight in full armor, wielding a sword and shield emblazoned with an eagle rising in flight. "Is he going to save me from myself?"

Leigh's gaze stayed fixed on the card. "*The Knight* is the symbol of the warrior. The champion of justice and the triumph over adversity. Honor. Truth. Valor."

Clarity slammed into Matt with surprising force. He cupped his fingers under her chin, turning her face to his. Her eyes rose slowly. "That's you," he said softly. "You're my warrior." She shook her head but he leaned in and pressed his mouth to hers briefly, feeling the soft breath of her sigh against his lips. When he pulled back, she ducked her head, but he tipped her chin back up. "You're embarrassed."

She pulled away from his hand and this time he let her go. "No, of course not. Why would I be embarrassed?"

"Because, as you said only a few weeks ago, you don't do the spotlight. You're more comfortable doing the right thing offstage than being in the limelight taking credit for it. The thought of being a knight in shining armor actually makes you uncomfortable." Her stiff body position made him smile, but he let it go. "Okay, I promise not to tell anyone or Paul will start calling you 'Sir Not-Appearing-In-This-Film.' " He chuckled when Leigh stared at him in confusion. "Forget it. I was referring to Paul's love of Monty Python, but it went right over your head. Okay, two more cards."

Leigh looked relieved to return to the task at hand, the

spotlight shifting once more to Matt. "The southwest card—a past physical influence in your life regarding health or money."

"Well, I haven't won the lottery yet, so that must be in my future," Matt quipped.

Leigh turned over the card. On it was a Wyvern—a winged creature with only two legs bearing both the head and tail of a dragon. "*The Wyvern* is the keeper of secrets. It can also reflect conflict or guilt."

Matt's smiled drained away and he shifted uncomfortably. The cards were hitting a little too close again. "Yeah, I get it. My scars. Afghanistan. Coming home and changing careers."

"Don't think about that card. That's the past." Leaning forward, Leigh tapped the *Earth* oracle again. "This is the card that's more important."

Logic. Practicality. Dependability.

"Or better yet, this card. Your future influence concerning health or money." She flipped the final card over. A golden chalice was the centerpiece, a graceful cup embossed with delicate swirls and leaves. She smiled and handed him the card. *"The Chalice."*

"This is good?"

"Very. *The Chalice* represents fulfillment. Rejuvenation. The attainment of a goal and the end of a quest." She turned the Wyvern face down and tapped the card in his hand. "Look ahead, not back."

Look ahead.

Matt's gaze trailed over to the two future cards sitting on the table. "I like the Knight card. I like that future. Our future." He turned to meet her gaze. "We have a long way to go still, but I'm looking forward to the journey."

When he smiled at her, she returned the gesture.

His gaze fell upon *The Raven* and his smile fell away. He reached for it. "And then there's this guy."

"You don't mean to say that you actually believe this do you?" Leigh asked.

"My mind knows it's all chance. I watched you shuffle the cards, watched you deal them out. Watched you turn over cards that somehow had meaning for me. Every single one. Sure, you could find meaning in them for everyone, I suppose. But still . . . this one. This one somehow bothers me."

They sat, side by side on the couch, lit by the fire's glow.

Foreboding prickled along Matt's skin.

Darkness. An omen. But of what? Betrayal? Injury? Death? And for who?

Chapter Twenty-One:
Drafting

Drafting: using water drawn from a pond, swimming pool or other source when no fire hydrant is available.

Sunday, 2:34 p.m.
Boston University, School of Medicine
Boston, Massachusetts

Paul staggered into the lab carrying a stack of boxes which he slid onto one of the few remaining empty sections of benchtop.

"Are those the last of it?" Leigh asked.

"Yeah." Matt came through the door with a single box and nudged the door closed with his boot. He rolled his eyes at Paul's dramatics when the younger man slid down the wall to sink into an exhausted tangle of limbs. "It wasn't that bad."

"Those boxes were heavy," Paul moaned. "And there was a ton of them."

"Of which you only carried a quarter because the rest of us did our share." Matt set down his box and turned to Kiko who was bent over a tray scattered with small pieces of cranial bone. "That's coming along nicely." He moved to stand behind her, taking in the gradual shaping of the tiny, fragmented newborn skull she'd brought from the Old North Church a few days before the case started.

"It's slow work because of all the open sutures, but I'm getting there. Do you need me to give you a hand?"

Matt's gaze flicked to Leigh and she nodded. "I know you're trying to catch up on your project, but if you could take a break, we could certainly use your help."

Kiko rose from her stool, stripping off her gloves. "These bones aren't going anywhere; I can come back to them later. What have we got here?"

"We're not sure yet," Leigh said. "Father Thomas contacted me before Mass this morning. He'd been calling around to Saint Patrick's parishioners when one of them mentioned to him that they had a bunch of church records. There were too many boxes to load into my car, so Matt was kind enough to drive up and give me a hand."

"Why would records like that be kept outside of the church?" Kiko asked, skimming the labels on the boxes. "Don't get me wrong, it's great that they escaped the fire, but why were they ever taken off church property?"

Leigh opened the lid of the nearest box, labeled *Adult Education,* and winced at the jumbled chaos inside. "This is going to take forever if everything looks like this." She closed the box and turned away from it. "From what I understand, once a church is closed, some records are considered to have historical relevance and should be kept forever, while most administrative paperwork can be discarded after a few years. Financial papers are kept for a certain number of fiscal years. This parishioner offered to take the papers home and sort through them, separating them into different categories based on their content."

Paul's voice drifted up from the floor. "I have a sneaking suspicion they never started. Once they realized what they were getting into, they probably put it off, hoping the church would reopen and they'd be off the hook."

"They're back on the hook now," Juka commented. "They have to get the job done. The church is gone."

"They're probably hoping we do it for them," Matt said. His

gaze scanned the boxes. "Let's get started." He held out a hand to Paul and hauled him from the floor. "This is going to take a while. Grab a box, find some bench space and start reading."

"You guys know the names in this case, but to refresh your memory—" Leigh proceeded to list every name associated with the case thus far. "Victim, clergy, parishioner, Witch. Any names jump out at you, speak up. I'd rather do a lot of extra reading than miss what could be the key to this case and the link between our victims."

Leigh grabbed a box and carried it over to a bench on the far side of the lab. She pulled out a sheaf of papers and started to scan them.

Matt settled at the other side of the bench from her with his own box.

Their eyes met through the open shelves over the bench, in the gap between an alligator skull and a giraffe vertebra. Matt recognized the hopeful gleam in Leigh's eyes—*please let the answer be here*—then her gaze dropped as the room went silent and they all got to work.

Sunday, 4:07 p.m.
Boston University, School of Medicine
Boston, Massachusetts

"Did you ever say what Moira Simpson's husband's name was?" Kiko's voice broke the nearly oppressive silence that hung over the lab.

Leigh looked up cautiously. There had been a handful of false starts already—mostly names that sounded similar but were unconnected—so by this point, Leigh was looking at all interruptions with a jaundiced eye. "Probably not. He died nearly thirty years ago so I didn't think it was relevant to the case. His name was Stephen."

With a triumphant grin, Kiko closed the worn cover of the

notebook she was reading, marking her place with a finger tucked between the pages. The cover was of worn leather, with faded gold lettering on the front—*Endowments.* "This book contains a running list of all the items that were gifted to the parish, usually in memoriam. It starts in nineteen twenty-eight." She opened the book again. "There's an entry here from nineteen ninety-two: Repair and restoration of the vandalized Holy Family stained-glass window, in memory of Stephen Simpson by 'THE FAMILY.' "

Kiko spread the book out flat on the countertop so everyone could see as they gathered around her. The entries were handwritten in different hands and inks, but she indicated a single entry near the top of the page. "This one. I guess the real question is how common is the name Stephen Simpson?"

Matt leaned back against the counter, crossing his ankles. "It could be common if Simpson is an old family name in this area."

"We can look at birth and death records." Leigh's gaze scanned over the boxes. "I haven't found an actual roster of parishioners in any of the boxes I've gone through. Has anyone else?"

There was a chorus of *no.*

"Of all the things we needed, that was it. But that was likely in the church offices still. Most of what I've found has been historical records dating back at least twenty years."

"Same for me," Matt said. "Most of mine has been correspondence or reports—the Altar Society, letters from the bishop, diocesan awards, that kind of thing."

"Let's assume that really is Moira Simpson's husband. What are the chances she'd make a gift like that to a church she didn't belong to?" Paul asked.

"I can't see it," Kiko said. "What would be the meaning in that? It was a memorial after all."

"Then the real issue," Juka interjected, "is why would Flynn Simpson lie about any connection between his mother and Father Brian?" He swiveled on his lab stool to face Leigh. "Father Brian was at the church by that time, right?"

"Yes, and had been for at least a decade. Simpson not only denied any knowledge of Father Brian, but also said that there wasn't any connection to Saint Patrick's." She stared sightlessly at the page in the book, her thoughts drifting back to her interview only two days ago. "Now that I think about it, he couched it in present terms—not to his knowledge was his mother attending a Catholic church. I'll ask him about any previous connection."

"Could he have been too young at the time to remember?" Paul asked.

"It's possible, I suppose. If he was young and the connection to the church didn't last long."

"Don't forget, he was sick then too," Kiko said. "That would have been around the time his FOP was diagnosed. He may have been in the hospital or housebound."

"What if he's protecting his lover?" Matt asked.

Kiko swiveled on her lab stool to face him. "You're thinking about the fact that the lover was connected to the site of the first murder."

"Yes. What if the connection between the killings is Flynn Simpson himself? If we don't think Dodsworth killed for money, what if the motive is Simpson himself? And what if Simpson's lying to protect his partner?"

"You're suggesting that Dodsworth is the murderer, Simpson knows, is okay with it, and is covering for him by lying about Father Brian?" Leigh asked.

Matt shrugged. "I'm not sure where I'm going with it. But that connection with Dodsworth is still there and I think we'd be foolish to ignore it."

"I can't argue with that. But the first thing we need to do here is figure out if this is the same Stephen Simpson. If not, then we're just spinning our wheels."

"But if it is . . . ," Juka said.

"Then we need to take another look at the connection between Moira Simpson and Father Brian," Leigh said firmly. "Whatever binds them together is there, we just need to find it."

Chapter Twenty-Two: Multiple Attack Lines

Multiple Attack Lines: use of multiple hoses to fight a fire.

Sunday, 6:55 p.m.
Lowell Residence
Brookline, Massachusetts

The comforting aroma of roasted meat greeted Matt and Leigh as they entered the kitchen. They found Mike seated at a lowered countertop, slicing a medium-rare prime-rib roast. The older man smiled at their guest's arrival, the crow's-feet around his eyes crinkling in delight.

Leigh bent down and kissed him on the cheek. "Thanks for inviting me for dinner. I brought some Italian pastries for dessert. I hope that's okay."

"Thank you, that was very thoughtful."

Hands on her hips, she scanned the kitchen. "I feel bad that you went to all this trouble."

"It's no trouble at all. And we're men—we go out of our way for an excuse to buy a nice piece of red meat." Mike winked at her.

Matt scanned the countertop, seeing it through Leigh's eyes—almost every square inch was covered with food and dishes. He was used to his father's cooking sprees, but after so much time on her own, cooking for one, the extent of the meal must seem extravagant. "Don't let him fool you. He loves having company over to eat. He kicks me out every time and does the whole

220

thing himself. He won't accept any help."

"You can do the dishes," Mike said dryly. "Now, Leigh, why don't you sit down? Matt, pour her a glass of wine."

Leigh settled in one of the kitchen chairs and Teak immediately wandered over to sit at her side.

Matt eyed her surreptitiously as he poured three glasses of red wine from the heavy crystal decanter on the counter. She looked worn, the usual sparkle missing from her eyes. He knew the case was intense, especially now with a firefighter lost in the second blaze; she not only had her own department looking to her for answers, but Salem FD as well. But he suspected it was more than that—her father's death could never be far from her mind now.

Leigh's head was bent, one hand lost in Teak's thick, ruddy fur as the Belgian Malinois leaned against her knee, an expression of pure bliss on his face as she stroked him. "You know, if you keep that up, he'll never leave your side." He handed her a glass.

"That wouldn't be so bad. Man's best friend and all that." She took a sip of her wine. "Nice. Really hits the spot."

Matt could practically see the wine spreading warmth and relaxation through her.

His father interrupted his study. "Matt, a hand please."

Leigh set her glass down on the table and started to rise. "Let me help."

Matt gently pushed her back into her chair. "You sit and relax. The old man would have my head if you helped. Besides, you're already helping by keeping Teak out from underfoot."

Matt and Mike spent the next few minutes carrying food to the table. Matt kept an eye on Leigh as he worked, noting with satisfaction when the tightness seemed to ease from her shoulders and her laugh became easier as they bantered back and forth.

Finally he sat down and his father pulled his wheelchair up to the open side of the table.

Leigh's gaze scanned the mountain of food set out on the table. "This looks absolutely amazing. But there's no way we can eat all of it."

Matt laughed at his father's disconcerted expression. "I always tell him he makes enough food to feed the average Army regiment."

"Where did you learn to cook like this?" Leigh asked.

Mike started passing dishes. "After the accident, I was housebound." Color flooded Leigh's cheeks, but Mike reached across the table to lightly pat her hand. "Don't be embarrassed. It happened, there's no point in beating around the bush."

"Matt told me about the accident."

"It's hard, losing the love of your life. One moment there she was, large as life, laughing with me in the car on the drive home. The next minute I was waking up in the hospital, Matt was at my bedside and I'd lost days. And my wife."

A whirlwind of emotion swept through Matt at the rush of memories: Applying for and receiving his hardship discharge from the Marines. Flying home from Afghanistan in a panicked rush, fearing his only remaining parent would die before the plane touched down. Going right to the hospital, still in combat fatigues and carrying his duffel. His father's broken body in the bed. The devastation in his father's eyes when he broke the news of his mother's death. His own overwhelming sorrow.

Matt reached for his glass and took a deep swallow, but the wine didn't ease the pressure in his chest.

"That must have been horrible." Leigh's quiet words broke into his thoughts at the same moment her hand touched his knee. He looked up. Her eyes were fixed on his father, but she'd reached out to him under cover of the table, knowing his discomfort with these memories. He laid his fingers over hers, squeezing her hand in a silent gesture of thanks.

"It was. But Matt's told me a little of your background so I know you've experienced it yourself. You grieve, but then you pick yourself up and you go on. Part of my healing process was learning to cook."

Matt suddenly found himself the focus of his father's warm gaze.

"There we were," Mike continued. "Two bachelors with no woman to take care of us. We were totally lost without Susan. Matt was readapting to life back home again and I was learning how to get along without my legs." He chuckled at the memory. "We were both miserable and out of our element. We nearly poisoned each other a few times. After that, I decided one of us better learn how to cook or we'd both starve. And since Matt was going back to school, it needed to be me. I discovered I actually enjoyed cooking and was good at it. It was therapeutic, and it gave me something to concentrate on and small victories to mark." Mike patted his flat stomach. "It's a good thing we picked up rowing or else I'd be fifty pounds heavier. I ended up being *too* good."

"I couldn't ask for a better wife," Matt quipped.

The older man waved an index finger at his son in a mock scold. "Careful. Or I'm cutting you off from those pastries Leigh brought."

Matt glared at his father. "That's low. Pass the potatoes."

For a moment there was quiet as everyone filled their plates and settled in to eat.

"Matt's told me a little of the case," Mike said. "How's it coming along?"

"It was a lot stronger when we only had one fire," Leigh said. "It seemed much more straightforward then. We had a woman who definitely ruffled some feathers in a coven, and we had several pieces of evidence that pointed to a connection within the Craft with both the murder weapon and the pentacle left on the door of the shop."

"You thought it was someone in the coven that murdered her?"

"That was my initial direction. But every string I pulled seemed to unravel in my hand. She left the coven after a disagreement with one of the other Witches. But that Witch has been out of state on business for the last two weeks. I interviewed two other Witches who left the coven because of Moira Simpson's behavior toward them. They're so happy in their present group, they're actually grateful that she drove them away. No one else seemed to have any significant issues with her and all but three of the remaining members of the Circle of the Triple Goddess have alibis for the night of the murder. And I don't buy any of those women as the killer." She turned to glance at Matt. "I've talked to all the Witches since the second fire. None of them admit to knowing Father Brian, so there's no obvious connection there either. Of the three Witches that had no alibi for the first fire, all have an alibi for the second." She paused to have another bite of prime rib, her face thoughtful as she chewed. "And that's our real problem. We can't find a workable link between the two killings."

"You're sure they're connected?" Mike asked.

"Both fire scenes had a pentacle nailed to the front door. Both murder weapons originally belonged to Moira Simpson. On the surface, they're linked, but look a little deeper . . ."

"Assuming that the information about the memorial gift is correct, then you know the victims are connected," Matt pointed out.

Leigh paused, looking up from buttering her roll. "If so, that connection goes back over twenty years and probably has no relevance to her time in the coven during the last ten months."

"For the sake of argument, let's assume it's her husband's

memorial," Matt said. "We have a priest and a parishioner who knew each other decades ago, but then cut ties sometime later. Certainly, Father Thomas didn't recognize her so she hasn't been a parishioner in recent years. But I'm not sure how a twenty-year-old link will lead you to your murderer."

Mike picked up his wine and stared into the ruby liquid thoughtfully. "But don't you agree that any parishioner making an expensive donation—like the refurbishment of a hundred-year-old stained-glass window—would have significant ties to the congregation?"

"They must," Leigh said.

"Then is the son lying about his mother's connection to Saint Patrick's?" Mike asked.

"We tossed that around," Matt said. "But we have to remember that he was a sick seven-year-old back then, who'd just been given the news that his life would never be normal because of his disease. Maybe he wasn't really a part of the parish."

"That's the bone disease you were telling me about," Mike said. "The one that turns muscle into bone?"

"Yes. Fibrodysplasia ossificans progressiva."

"Then I think it all depends on how long she was a parish member. But that kind of gift says 'long-term commitment' to me. And if she was there long-term, surely he was part of the parish too." Mike set down his glass. "Let me play devil's advocate. Let's say the memorial is for Moira Simpson's husband, and Flynn knew about it and wanted to throw you off the scent, so he denied any connection."

"If you look at it that way, he's the concrete link between the killings," Matt stated. "Someone familiar with both victims."

"Normally, family is the first group that we look at," Leigh said. "More homicides are committed by family members than any other subset. But this man is handicapped. He couldn't have done it."

"What if it was done for him?" Matt cast a quick glance at this father. "His partner, Aaron Dodsworth, has been tied to this case from the beginning."

"You think it's Simpson's motive that's driving this, but Dodsworth is actually the killer?" Mike asked.

"If it's Simpson's motive, then we haven't figured it out yet. The last time I talked to him, he was going on and on about his wonderful mother and . . ." Her voice trailed off as she turned toward Matt. "Oh, that was subtle. So subtle I nearly missed it. He offered me an alibi for both himself and Dodsworth for the second killing. I didn't ask him."

"You'd assume he was covering his own ass, but was he really covering for his partner?" Matt asked.

"That's a damned good question." Leigh sat back in her chair. "Partners have certainly been known to lie to cover their lover's tracks before." Suddenly she stiffened and her hand clamped down on the edge of the table.

Matt's heart stuttered at the look on her face. "What?"

"It couldn't be . . ."

"What?"

"What if he wasn't just providing an alibi for his partner, but was helping him with the murders instead?"

"Only we could be that cursed." The thought made Matt's mouth go dry, but he forced himself to reason it through. "What are the chances that we'd catch two cases like that?"

"I can't imagine they'd be good, but you can't deny the possibility," Mike said. "Is there any evidence to link the son back to the killings?"

Leigh shook her head. "Nothing. But once we work through the Witchcraft angle, we don't have any solid ties to anyone. The fires have done a great job of destroying all the usual evidence we depend on—hair, fibers, epithelials."

"He could have had easy access to her Witchcraft tools though," Matt said. "He could have taken them without her knowledge."

"Dodsworth could have had the same access through Simpson. They had her spare key," Leigh said. "And there's always the possibility that she may not have wanted them anymore. We know they weren't sold through any pawn or Witchcraft shop, but that doesn't rule out a private sale we're unaware of. To Simpson's credit, he looked wrecked and he always talks about Moira affectionately. He makes her sound like the most devoted of mothers."

"It would be very stressful to have a sick child like that," Mike said. "I can't imagine how hard it would be. We were lucky that Matt was never ill, but we did have some worrisome moments."

"Like when I fell out of the tree and broke my arm?"

"That was one of those times. We thought you broke your neck, the way you laid there so still." Mike looked across the table at Leigh. "He's got a hard head, so we were lucky. He was just stunned."

"I've butted up against that hard head a few times." Leigh softened her words by smiling at Matt.

"But from a parent's point of view, you would do whatever was needed to make your child healthy. If there was nothing you could do, it would be horrible to stand by helplessly and watch your child suffer."

An idea suddenly blossomed in Matt's mind, an idea so horrific it made his stomach clench. He turned slowly to Leigh. "Can we get his medical records?"

Leigh blinked at him in confusion. "Flynn's?"

"Yes."

"I'd have to have a damned good reason for it. No judge is going to just give carte blanche permission to look at private health records. Why do you want to see them?"

Matt stalled for time as he ran the scenario through in his head again, trying to decide if it was too outlandish to be possible. To cover, he ate several bites and washed it down with the last of his wine without tasting either. "Something's been bothering me since I first saw him. I won't know if it's a possibility until I see those records but I think his disease is too progressed for his age. And that makes me wonder why."

For a moment, questions clouded Leigh's eyes. Then they went wide with a mixture of clarity and horror.

But it was Mike who spoke first. "You're suggesting he was abused?"

"I'm probably way off base here and grasping at straws. He could have been a clumsy child; some kids aren't very coordinated. And with every fall or bump, he'd lose mobility, making him more uncoordinated."

"But if someone was abusing him, wouldn't that show?" Leigh asked.

Matt shook his head. "Not necessarily. Sometimes abuse can be subtle. If you know where to place a blow, it can be hidden by clothing. Then threaten worse harm if the child tells."

"Are you thinking the priest abused the child?" Mike asked.

"It's been known to happen. Maybe he told his mother and she didn't believe him."

Leigh leaned back in her chair, drumming her fingers on the table. "So you want the medical records to go toward establishing motive. Giving Dodsworth a reason to take revenge on his lover's abusers since the lover isn't capable. That's the first motive I've heard that makes sense."

"But will it convince a judge?"

"I'm not sure, but I'll give it a try tomorrow. If we're successful, it could take a day or two to get our hands on the records."

"If it's Dodsworth, then why the pentacle on the door?" Mike asked.

"To throw blame on the Witchcraft community," Leigh said. "Worked pretty well too. Between the pentacle and the athame from the first killing, those were the only suspects we were looking at. The problem there was that nothing panned out as a lead for us, but the killer doesn't know that, not the way the *Salem Times* keeps ragging on this story." She pushed her empty plate away and relaxed back in her chair. "That was wonderful, Mike. Thank you."

Matt surveyed the food. During the conversation they'd all cleaned their plates, but there was still plenty left. "See what I mean? Army regiment."

"And yet somehow nothing ever gets thrown away," Mike said.

"That's because you send it in with me to the lab, and Paul and Juka inhale everything in sight." Matt glanced over at Leigh and rolled his eyes. "Grad students."

She laughed and pushed back from the table. "Don't forget, you were one of those once. Let me help you clear this up." When Mike protested, she held out a hand to stop him. "I insist."

Mike reluctantly conceded with a slight bow of his head. "Then we can have those lovely pastries you brought. And Matt's going to make cappuccino."

Leigh stood, stacking the plates and carrying them to the sink. "No more shoptalk. It's time to give all of us a break from death and mayhem. Tell me more about Matt falling out of the tree."

Matt stopped abruptly, halfway to the counter, a large salad bowl in his arms. "You *don't* want to hear stories of my childhood."

"I certainly do."

She grinned at him, and, in that moment, he would have shared every embarrassing story to see her so easy and relaxed. But he put on a good show nonetheless. "Fine," he grumbled. He glared at his father. "But not the one about getting stuck on Heather McDonald's roof."

Mike let out a booming laugh. "I'd forgotten about that. Oh, Leigh, you're going to like that one. One of the better stories of Matt's teenage years."

Their moods buoyed, they cleared the table as stories and laughter flowed freely.

Chapter Twenty-Three:
Rekindle

Rekindle: restarting of a fire several hours after it was extinguished because of residual heat or hidden embers remaining after improper or incomplete overhaul.

Monday, 5:05 p.m.
Essex Detective Unit
Salem, Massachusetts

Leigh practically jogged through the unit corridors toward the bullpen. She knew from checking earlier that several of the chemical companies she'd talked to that morning had already replied. Those emails would contain lists of all the companies in the area that purchased red phosphorus in the past two years. She knew she was throwing the net wide, but she preferred getting too much information rather than wasting time having to go back and ask again.

She was just passing the conference room when her phone rang. "Leigh Abbott."

"It's Bree. I've plugged your leak. Permanently."

Leigh stopped at the doorway to the bullpen. "Really? No more screaming newspaper headlines?"

"I don't know about that, but I can guarantee there won't be any more information coming from the fire department. That weasel will have to find another snitch for his information."

"It was one of the Salem boys?"

"Yes." Disgust coated Bree's tone. "One of the rookies is the younger brother of some guy Wells went to school with, so he's known Wells for years. All Wells had to do was take him out for a few beers and he told Wells everything he knew. I had words with him, and then the chief had a go at him. Let me assure you, he won't say a damned thing to a reporter ever again. He may not speak for the next few weeks period, because I think he swallowed his tongue while I was reaming him out."

"I'm sorry I had to stick you with this, but thanks for getting to the bottom of it."

"My pleasure. I really hated my mornings starting with a bang, so now maybe I can go back to enjoying the newspaper with my coffee again. Talk to you later."

Leigh rounded the corner into her cubicle with a smile on her face. But the smile melted away the moment she saw the envelope lying neatly on her desk. The sudden adrenaline rush had her stomach clutching and her heart tripping unevenly in her chest.

Leigh quickly looked around the bullpen. Two other detectives were in their cubicles, but they had their heads down. One of them was on the phone while the other pecked at his keyboard with both index fingers, occasionally cursing when he hit the wrong key. Leigh lowered herself into her desk chair, relieving legs that suddenly felt unsteady. She braced damp palms on the edge of the desk and gave herself a moment to study the envelope.

Manila, eight by ten inches. Her name and the detective unit's address in black marker. Handwriting identical to the last time. Boston postmark again. No return address.

She closed her eyes just for a second, pulling herself together.

A biting curse from beyond her cubicle reminded her that she wasn't alone. Ripping a sheet off the scratch pad on her desk, she used it to pick up the envelope and jam it into her messenger bag. Then she sagged back in her chair as the piece of paper drifted from her fingers and fell unnoticed to the worn carpet below.

Another one.

But this time she wasn't alone. She speed dialed Matt. "I've just received some information I want to discuss with you," she said brightly when he picked up. She sat up a little straighter, peering over the top of her cubicle. Two dark heads, both bent over their work. No doubt they were totally ignoring her but she wasn't about to let on. "But you need to see it in person."

"Information? Can you be more specif—" Matt cut himself off. "Damn it, you got another package. Same as last time?"

"I believe so, yes."

"You sound funny. Is someone else there?"

"Yes. Is this afternoon convenient for you?"

"Of course it's convenient for me. I'm just coming back from the Old North Church so I'm already in the car. I'll meet you at your place."

"All right."

"We do this together, Leigh. Don't start without me. I'll be there as fast as I can."

Leigh ended the call and surged to her feet. To her surprise, the shock of the initial discovery was melting away and determination now stiffened her spine.

I'll be there as fast as I can.

She wasn't alone anymore. She had a partner willing to work shoulder-to-shoulder with her.

Together, they'd figure this out.

Monday, 5:31 p.m.
Abbott Residence
Salem, Massachusetts
Leigh sat on her front step, flanked by a large russet chrysanthemum and a tumbled pile of mini-pumpkins. In the distance, the

sky darkened and anvil-shaped thunderclouds signaled a coming storm. The wind whipped her unbound hair around her face and she impatiently tucked it behind her ear. To occupy herself while she waited, Leigh pinched a single bloom from the chrysanthemum and focused on pulling individual dark-red petals from the head, scattering them like bloody teardrops around her feet.

The flower tumbled to the ground at the sound of gravel crunching as Matt's SUV pulled to the curb in front of her house.

She met him halfway down the front walk. "You got here fast."

"I figured you could fix my ticket if I got caught speeding." He caught her by both shoulders, his hazel eyes serious as they searched her face. "You okay?"

"Yeah." She laid her hands on his hips and allowed herself a moment to just hold on. "I feel steadier this time. Part of it is knowing I'm not on my own."

"No, you're not. And if I'm not enough, you know Dad or the students will do whatever you need." Turning her, he slid an arm around her waist and walked her up the front path. "Like it or not, you're part of this group now. And we take care of our own."

"There's that watchful protector coming out in you."

They stepped into the quiet house and Leigh pushed the door closed against a particularly blustery gust of wind. She led the way into the kitchen, where her bag sat in the middle of the table beside a long, thin letter opener.

After donning latex gloves, Leigh slit open the envelope. She took a deep breath and peered inside.

There were two items—a blurry photograph and a sheet of paper. She removed the photograph first, angling it for Matt. The image was black-and-white with the grainy appearance of security footage. The photo was time-stamped 01/13/2008, 10:49 p.m. and showed two men talking in the shadows. Over their heads, a neon light spelled out *Bruno's Tavern.*

Matt leaned into her, studying the photo. "I don't recognize the people or the place."

Leigh pointed at the man who was angled toward the camera. He wore a heavy coat and a cap pulled down low over his brow, his shoulders hunched against the cold. "That's Dad." She pulled the photo closer, studying it. "I can't tell who the other person is. That bit of profile isn't enough and his hat's pulled down over his ears."

"That's significant?"

"Ears can be as individual as fingerprints in making an ID. There might be enough facial features in this picture to confirm identity if we can get a lead on who this might be, but it's certainly not anyone I recognize." She flipped the photo over. "No message on the back this time."

"Is this close to your father's death?"

"The month before. This looks like a meet to me. Maybe an informant?"

"Someone inside the drug ring they were investigating? Where's Bruno's Tavern?"

"North Salem. We've had some trouble in that area before."

"Drug trouble?"

"Which then led to other trouble, like assaults. Dad was investigating one of the deaths."

Matt studied the photo again. "I don't see anything else here. I think you're supposed to know who the other man is."

Leigh glanced over her shoulder to meet his eyes. "Or I'm supposed to find out."

"What's on the other page?"

Leigh picked up the paper, holding it between them. "It's a phone log from a cell carrier." A long string of calls with associated dates, call times and destination numbers filled the page. Three individual calls were highlighted in fluorescent yellow. "It's the summary from a phone subpoena."

"Some of these calls go to your cell." Matt pinned her with an intense stare. "Why are you on this list?"

She was silent for several seconds, her eyes locked on the call log. Then she set the page down on the table. "Because these calls all originated from my dad's cell phone. Of course he'd call me."

"Then whose is the number in yellow? Do you recognize it?"

"No."

"It's got to be something related to all this. Maybe it's the man in the photograph."

"Maybe."

He reached over and nudged her chin with one finger, tilting her face up toward his. "You shutting me out?"

The concern in his eyes warmed her. She reached up to stroke her fingers over the back of his hand. "No, just thinking. Trying to connect some of the dots."

"What do you mean?"

"Remember what the previous picture said on the back? *Your father wasn't the hero you think he was. He was a dirty cop. Soon the world will know it. And you'll be the one to pay for his crimes.*"

"Like I'm going to forget that," Matt muttered.

"Whoever is sending this is trying to make it clear my father was dirty." She tapped the photo with a gloved index finger. "This looks like a deal going down."

"A drug deal? Do you mean to say—"

"I don't." She said it quietly, but with absolute certainty. "My father and I meant the world to each other. I knew when something was bothering him, when he had a good or bad day. And he knew the same about me. If he'd been doing this, I'd have known."

"Are you sure? As much as we don't like to admit it, sometimes we don't know the people in our lives as well as we think we do."

She swiveled to face him so quickly he took a half step back in surprise. "Would you know if something was off with your dad?"

"Sure, I would because . . ." The light went on behind his eyes. "Because we're all the family we have left for each other. The connection between us is vital." He nodded in understanding. "I get your point, but I also hope you get mine. I wasn't saying that your dad was dirty. I'm just trying to look at all the possibilities."

"He was a good cop, and he was clean. Someone is trying to frame him for this." She looked back down at the list. "But whoever sent this may have just tipped his or her hand."

"How?"

"Because you can't just ask a cell carrier for this kind of information. You have to subpoena it. That not only limits the number of people who can request it, it also leaves a paper trail." She smiled as she met his eyes, some of the weight in her chest falling away. "We've got our first lead."

Matt grinned at her. "Hot damn. Besides looking into the subpoena, you'll trace that highlighted number?"

"Absolutely. We'll also check for fingerprints and you can run DNA again."

"You have to know that whoever is sending you this material isn't going to be pointing you in a direction other than your father's guilt. You know if you stir this up, it might end up sullying his name."

"Clearly that's what someone wants. So my job is to find out the real truth—" She threw a splayed hand out over the table. "—because this isn't it. For starters, I don't even know if this log is real. It could be mocked up, based on a real copy of his records. My guess is that the highlighted number will come back connected to someone in that last case he was running. It will have something to do with those deaths. But until we know what story they're trying to sell us, we can't uncover the real truth. So that's where we start." She bent over the table and repacked the envelope, sealing it an evidence bag before discarding her gloves. "By the way, I heard from Father Thomas today. He found a longtime parishioner of Saint Patrick's to talk to me about Father Brian. I'm going to see her first thing tomorrow morning. Apparently she's ninety years old, sharp as a tack and the church busybody. And she's been a member of the church long enough to predate Father Brian."

"She's going to be useful, then."

"I think so. And next on my list for our case today is running through the companies that sent reports on red phosphorus sales. Time to start narrowing down the possibilities there." She turned to him, stepping into him to wrap her arms around his waist. "Thank you for coming all the way up here to do this with me."

Reaching up a hand, he brushed the back of his fingers against her cheek. "I'm happy to do it."

She pushed up on tiptoe, closing the few inches between them to press her mouth to his. She started to drop back down again, but he caught her waist in his hands, holding her still. The color morphed in his eyes, warm hazel-green shifting to a deeper gold.

She knew that look.

She had only a second to reflect on it before she was pressed against his chest, her lips under his again. His mouth was greedy, drinking her in even as his hands slid up her torso to stop just below her breasts. His fingers twitched against her, as if he was struggling with himself to not to push her further.

We've both been dancing around each other for long enough.

Maybe it's time to stop.

As if to test him, she slipped her left hand under the edge of his shirt to run her fingers over the puckered skin at his side, waiting for him to hesitate under her touch. He simply pulled her in closer, his tongue slipping over her bottom lip to slide slickly against hers.

Definitely time.

She stepped back from him, a small smile curving her lips when he moved to follow her, reluctant to break contact. She wedged her hands between them and pushed him back a couple of inches. His eyes stayed on hers, intense and watchful. Then they dropped as she held out her hand to him.

A single eyebrow arched, his gaze flicked from her hand to her eyes. "What's this?"

"You know what it is. Come upstairs with me."

His eyes darkened further, desire warring with responsibility. "What about the reports you wanted to read?"

"I can print out the lists here and work on them later tonight. I work a lot of overtime, so I can take an hour—" Her warm gaze dropped from his eyes, down over his chest. After a leisurely moment, they skimmed back up to his face again. "—or two off the clock. Then maybe you could help me catch up afterward."

A slow grin curved his lips.

He took her hand and let her lead him up the staircase, into the dimness above.

CHAPTER TWENTY-FOUR:
HESSIAN CRUCIBLE

Hessian Crucible: an alchemist's pot that could withstand the feverish heating and stirring required to transmute base elements into gold.

Monday, 5:56 p.m.
Abbott Residence
Salem, Massachusetts

Leigh pushed open the door and led Matt into her quiet bedroom, their fingers still entwined.

She turned to him, reaching up to slide her fingers into his hair, guiding his mouth down to hers for a soft, slow kiss. Their earlier urgency in the kitchen was gone now, replaced with the need to explore. Wrapping one hand around his neck to pull him closer, her other hand slipped under his shirt. Her fingertips whispered over his skin, the low groan in the back of his throat encouraging her. Her hand swept higher, but his shirt quickly frustrated her exploration, hampering her movements. She stepped back, pulling out of his arms to grasp the bottom of his shirt and slowly draw it off.

She turned back to him, giving a hum of appreciation. Stretching up on her toes, she looped one hand over his shoulder as she ran the tip of her tongue from the hollow of his throat nearly to his jaw, smiling against his skin when his body jerked in response. She pressed her face to the hollow of this throat to inhale the scent she now associated only with Matt—

the spice of sandalwood, overlaid with hints of citrus. A shudder ran through her, followed by a flood of warmth. "God, you smell good. Right from the start, I always noticed that." Her voice was muffled against his skin.

Matt gave a choked laugh. "I had no idea it was such a turn-on for you."

"Oh, yeah."

He tugged impatiently at her blouse and Leigh reluctantly looked up. "Don't get me wrong. I love what you're doing, but you're killing me here." He tugged again. "Off."

She lifted his hands to the button of her blouse, silently giving permission. He immediately went to work, spreading the material wide to slide it off her shoulders and to the floor as he looked his fill. Reaching out, he ran the back of his fingers over the side of one lace-covered breast, his gaze flicking to her face at her involuntary shiver. Then his hands slid to her waist, holding her still as he dropped his head, his lips just skimming the scalloped edge of her bra.

The softness of his lips contrasting against the slight roughness of the calluses on the hands sliding up her torso was intoxicating. His tongue slipped under the edge of the material, lightly teasing as she instinctively arched her back. Supporting her with one hand, his free hand rose to cover her other breast, his thumb gently stroking her nipple though the silky fabric. Her breath caught raggedly and her hands closed over his biceps. She was grateful for the support a moment later, holding on tightly when his teeth gently raked over the nipple through the fabric as her knees went weak.

Then his hands were gone, skimming down her body to her waistband. His fingers made quick work of her button and zipper, darting beneath the material to push it down to pool at her feet. She gazed at him in surprise when he dropped to his knees to help her step out of her clothes.

Kneeling at her feet, his gaze slowly traveled up her body. Then he pressed an openmouthed kiss gently to her hip as his fingers stroked lightly up the back of her legs. Her eyes slid closed and she dropped one hand into his hair with a gentle sigh.

That simple touch broke his control. He surged to his feet, his hands at her hips, boosting her up into his arms. Suddenly off balance, her legs instinctively wound around his waist even as her arms locked around his neck, holding on as he carried her to the wrought-iron four-poster bed under the open window. Bracing one knee on the mattress, he lowered her down, following her onto the bed. Then his body was on hers, cradled between her thighs as his mouth covered hers. There was nothing slow or tentative about this kiss—it was wet and frantic and full of heat. She brought her knees up, cradling him closer as her hands explored his back.

Matt's mouth slid down her throat, nipping softly. But, just as her hands were darting under his belt, he inched his body lower, chuckling at her groan of disappointment as he slid away from her.

Pushing back, he knelt between her thighs, making short work of the clasp at her back before slowly drawing off her bra and dropping it off the side of the bed. He sat back on his heels, giving himself a moment to take her in.

The memory of his first, nearly clinical examination of her flashed in her mind—the two of them facing off in the cold, damp basement at the Old North Church, his detached, scientist's gaze cataloging her features. This examination was as different from that as night from day. Now, the heat in his eyes nearly scorched her.

Then his gaze fell on her scar, and a little of the desire in his eyes cooled. He dropped down to his right elbow, his warm breath washing over the scar just before his lips touched it. It was a gentle kiss, almost a benediction. She reached up one hand, stroking her fingers over his cheek. His gaze rose to hers for just a moment, then his head dropped and he kissed it again, but this time it was a hot openmouthed kiss that he carried down over the curve of her breast. When his mouth closed over her, she gasped, her fingers twitching spasmodically against his shoulders.

The room suddenly darkened as if a light had been quenched and the low rumble of thunder vibrated the air around them. The gauzy drapes billowed over their heads, the cool air wafting over Leigh's naked skin like a whisper over silk.

She threaded her fingers through his hair as her head fell back on the pillow, cradling him to her breast as his lips and tongue explored her skin, alternately tasting and tormenting her with small nips.

When his mouth started to trail down her stomach, her eyes flew open again. He made fast work of her thong, easing it slowly down her legs as his lips followed. When he nipped at her hip she nearly came up off the bed.

He grinned. "Ticklish?"

"A little."

He chuckled. "I'll have to file that one away for later. But for now . . ." His mouth dropped again, this time taking care only to soothe and rouse.

He took his time with her. When she shifted under him impatiently, he slowed his caresses. When his fingers delved deep and she cried out, he eased back. When her hands fisted in his hair, trying to draw him down, he slipped from her grasp and continued to tease.

Tension spun into a tangled knot within Leigh, desperation winding it tighter. "Please . . ." The single whispered word sounded desperate, even to her own ears.

Matt must have sensed that he'd pushed her to the wall

because he moved in, finally covering her with his mouth. With a low moan of relief, she threw her hands over her head, her fingers wrapping around the swirling metal curves of the headboard as her back arched off the bed. She was already teetering on the edge and it seemed to take only seconds to push her over the brink. With a cry, she arched against him. His fingers bit softly into her hips, holding her still for him, forcing her to accept more. Her breath sawing, she was helpless to do anything but ride out the storm.

Afterward, she lay boneless, her lips parted as she simply tried to draw air into her lungs. She was limp, momentarily drained of energy. She became aware of him slowly moving up her body, his lips gently grazing over her hip, then her belly, then all the way to her collarbone and throat before dropping over her mouth, stealing what little breath she had left. Her hands came up to frame his face, her fingers trailing over his temples and sliding into his hair as she sighed into his mouth.

Pulling back finally, he pushed the damp hair from her forehead and smiled down at her. "Need to catch your breath?"

"Nope. Got it back already." She caught him off guard, rolling with him to straddle his hips. Lying below her on the bed, his head on her pillow, he looked up at her, his gaze skimming over her naked torso hungrily. His brow furrowed for a moment when she reached over, sliding open the drawer of her bedside table and pulling out a small, silver-wrapped square which she laid on the tabletop.

"Aren't you prepared," he said with a grin.

"Mostly just hopeful that we'd get here." She leaned down, her breasts brushing his chest as she pulled his earlobe between her lips, nipping at it with her teeth. Her mouth slid down his throat and over his chest, feeling the muscles quiver under her lips and tongue. His hands tangled in her hair, encouraging her on with his touch and his harsh breathing.

But his body stilled, his fingers tightening subtly when she shifted to straddle one thigh, her head drifting toward his damaged side. "Leigh . . ."

"Shhhh . . ." She quieted him with a gentle whisper, pulling his hand from her hair to twine her fingers with his. He squeezed back hard enough to tell her that part of him was uncomfortable with this level of intimacy. He stiffened further when she pressed her lips almost reverently to a hard mass of scar tissue. She repeated the action again and again, touching each ridge and furrow, feeling his body gradually loosen under her touch. When his body finally lay lax, she looked up at him. His head was angled on the pillow to watch her, his eyes fixed on her, but his expression was relaxed, all tension gone.

The first drops of rain started to fall, striking the roof over their heads sharply, the wind a haunting cry outside the window.

She gave him a sly smile and bent over him to drop a kiss just over the button on his jeans. When she looked back up, his eyes were closed, his lips parted on a breath. She undid the button and slid down the zipper.

"Lift up," she said softly. He lifted his hips off the bed and she shimmied his jeans and boxer briefs down his legs. As he had, she allowed herself a moment to sit back and take him in for the first time. But when she reached for him, he surprised her by grasping both of her wrists and pulling her up so she sprawled over his chest.

"What—"

"You're killing me here," he repeated.

"You felt free to tease me."

"You've been teasing me for weeks. It wasn't intentional, but the result is the same." He reached for the condom on the bedside table. "Time to end the torture."

She didn't need to be told twice. Taking the package, she quickly ripped it open and then sheathed him in one smooth motion. Bracing herself on her hands, she settled herself over him, then rocked back and forth, letting him glide slickly against her several times. She smiled when his eyelids fluttered closed and his fist closed around the bedsheet. Coaxing open his fist, she caught his hands, entwining their fingers. Pushing their joined hands back to the sheets at his shoulders, she leaned forward over him, skin to skin, her lips just barely grazing his. He pressed up from the pillow trying to catch her mouth but she eluded him, keeping his hands pinned to the bed. Instead, she kissed a line along his jaw, his late-day stubble pleasantly rough under her lips, each kiss punctuated by a languid stroke of her hips. Only when he relaxed back onto the pillow, his fingers loosening around hers, did she finally kiss him, simultaneously changing the angle of her hips. This time when she slid back, she took him in, her own gasp matching his as he finally slid home. She held still for a moment, drawing out the pleasure for both of them.

Thunder crashed, echoing through the quiet room as the heavens opened and the rain pounded like hail on the roof over their heads. Wind swirled into the room, bringing with it the smell of damp earth, fallen leaves and the last of summer's flowers.

She moved slowly at first and he let her take the lead, but she knew his control was fraying rapidly from the strength of his grip. Damp palms pressed together, her hair falling like a curtain around them, his movements became jerky. Sensation was building again, but she was determined to stay with him to the end. When he couldn't hang on any longer, he released her hands, clasping her hips instead, bracing her as his thrusts became stronger, more powerful. Relinquishing control, she leaned over him, cupping his face in her hands as she poured herself into one more kiss.

With a last hard thrust, she shattered, gasping into his mouth as her nails bit into his shoulders. One of his hands rose to wind into her hair, crushing her mouth down on his. With a low groan, his body strained against hers, and he joined her in the fall.

Chapter Twenty-Five:
Flue

Flue: also called a "windway," a passage for air in a chimney that allows smoke to move away from a fire. The pollutants in flue gas are a signature for what has been burned.

Tuesday, 10:03 a.m.
Kent Residence
Salem, Massachusetts

Leigh lifted the cat off her lap, setting it gently on the floor beside two other cats that wound around her ankles. "I appreciate your assistance, Mrs. Kent. Father Thomas told me that no one in the congregation knows the church's history like you do."

She sat in a tiny living room, which burst at the seams with knickknacks and trinkets. She was reluctant to turn around or make any sudden move, terrified she'd knock something over. The apartment had a thick, cloying scent: mothballs, potpourri and too many cats seemed to close the room in even further. It made Leigh thankful she didn't suffer from claustrophobia.

"I'm the longest-living parishioner." Mrs. Kent set a bone china teacup and saucer precisely in the middle of the tiny doily-draped table at Leigh's right elbow. The table swayed ominously, sending the tea in the cup washing from side to side before finally settling. Mrs. Kent lowered herself gingerly into a matching chintz armchair opposite Leigh. "Is this about the fire those Witches started?"

"We don't actually have any proof to connect this to the Witches, Mrs. Kent."

"But what about the pentacle? I've read all about that in the newspapers."

"Of course you did. But we need more than that to actually charge anyone." The older woman started to draw breath as if to speak, and Leigh rushed to cut her off. "I have some questions relating to the fire at Saint Patrick's Church. There's been two fires in the area and I'm looking for a connection between them." Leigh suddenly found her lap full of fluffy tricolor cat again as it launched itself from the floor back into her lap. When she wrapped her hands around its middle, razor-sharp claws expressed displeasure by piercing the soft wool of her dress pants. Leigh hissed in a breath.

"Don't mind Patches, dear. She just loves company."

Company is allergic to Patches, Leigh thought sourly, but resigned herself. The cat kneaded her thigh painfully. She gritted her teeth and continued. "You've been a member of the church since before the arrival of Father Brian?"

"Yes. I was baptized at Saint Patrick's in nineteen twenty-five. Father Brian didn't arrive for about another fifty or sixty years." Mrs. Kent smiled with pride, her oversized glasses magnifying her watery blue eyes, making them appear disproportionately large in her wizened face.

"I'm hoping you'll be able to help me, then." Leigh passed a picture of Moira Simpson across to Mrs. Kent, the cat in her lap digging in further as she shifted. "Do you recognize this woman?"

Mrs. Kent squinted at the photo for several seconds, the wrinkles in her papery skin crinkling even deeper with concentration. Then she tapped the photo with a knobby trembling finger. "I remember her. She was much younger then, of course, but that's Moira Simpson."

Jen J. Danna

Leigh froze. *Here's the connection we needed.*

The old woman was still staring at the photo. "Is she dead?" Her shrewd eyes studied Leigh's face. "You're from the police. She's either dead or missing, or else you'd be talking to her."

"She was killed in a fire earlier this week. How did you know Mrs. Simpson?"

"She was a member of the church . . . let me think." Her eyes took on the unfocused gleam of memory. "It must have been twenty-five or thirty years ago that she joined us. A young mother, a widow. With that sweet little boy."

"Her son, Flynn."

Mrs. Kent slapped her knee enthusiastically. "Of course. Flynn. Sweet child. He was always sickly though."

"That must have been hard on Mrs. Simpson."

"She was lucky to have Father Brian."

Awareness pricked like icy thorns over Leigh's skin. Mrs. Kent's words were innocuous enough, but there was a thread in the tone behind it that hinted at . . . what? Envy? Scorn? "She knew Father Brian, then."

"She was a favorite of Father Brian. All the . . . let's say . . . *generous* contributors were."

"She gave freely to the church?"

"Oh yes. There'd been some sort of settlement when her husband was killed and Moira was very generous to the church. And Father Brian was always very . . . appreciative."

"You say that like he was only appreciative of those who gave to the church?"

Anger flashed in the older woman's eyes. "Are we all not children of God? Do we not all give what we are able? Doesn't Mark say, 'And calling his disciples together, he sayeth to them: Amen I say to you, this poor widow hath cast in more than all they who have cast into the treasury. For all they did cast in of their abundance; but she of her want cast in all she had, even

250

her whole living'?"

"Did Father Brian give preferential treatment to those who were especially generous?"

The older woman's eyes seemed to sink even deeper into her face as she studied Leigh. "Back then, yes."

"But not later?"

"He went on a spiritual retreat one summer, digging wells and building a school in Africa. That trip changed him. Made him the man he is today." She jerked slightly as she belatedly caught her own words. "Or was, if the rumors are correct. Even an old woman, mostly shut away, hears murmurs. Was Father Brian the victim found in Saint Pat's fire?"

"Yes. So, Mrs. Simpson was a particular favorite of Father Brian's when she was with the church. When did she leave?"

"It was after Father Brian's trip to Africa. When he came back, he no longer paid her the same attention and deference as before. I think she felt slighted." She sat back in her chair and picked up her teacup, a sly smile curving her lips. "She didn't stay long after that." Her nose wrinkled. "Which is something he likely regretted later when this business with church finances became a problem. He could have used her money then."

"I've heard a little about the church's financial problems from Father Thomas. How did you and the other parishioners feel about Father Brian?"

Mrs. Kent's lips pursed and she shifted in her chair. "You must understand that we all loved Father Brian. He was a man of God and was most devoted to us."

"But he put your parish at risk trying to save another. Surely there must have been some bad feelings about that," Leigh said.

"There were." Mrs. Kent reached down to pet a Siamese cat that rubbed against her thick ankles. "For a while, things were quite tense at Saint Patrick's. But then Father Brian preached a few sermons on the Catholic Church's mission and caring for your fellow man, and most of the parishioners realized that even if it hadn't worked out well, he had the very best of intentions at heart when he tried to save the other parish."

"Most?"

"Well, there were some that left the parish, angered over the situation. But they were gone six or eight months ago. I can't imagine them coming back after all this time to murder Father Brian. Or Moira Simpson." She said her final words with just the tiniest trace of a sneer.

"I get the impression that you weren't overly fond of Mrs. Simpson."

The delicate bone china cup froze almost to the older woman's lips and her eyes went sharp. "Am I in trouble? Do I need a lawyer? I watch crime shows, you know. I know how things work on *Law and Order.*"

Leigh quickly schooled her features, keeping her face solemn when her lips threatened to twitch. The idea of this frail old woman hamstringing a man thirty years her junior was simply ludicrous. A strong wind would knock her down. "No, ma'am, I'm not accusing you of anything. I'm simply trying to understand her connection to the pastor. And how that might have been viewed by the congregation."

"We saw her as an attention-seeker. She used that poor child to garner sympathy for herself. And since, at the time, Father Brian was willing to pay more attention to those that generously supported the parish, he was constantly at her beck and call. As the little boy grew, that need only seemed to grow along with him. He had some sort of rare disease, I believe."

"He has a bone disorder." Leigh felt a heavy weight against her lower legs. She looked down in time to see a huge cat with a drooping belly collapse over her shoes to lounge against her shins. She was doomed. In about twenty minutes, she was going to be sneezing up a storm.

"I probably knew that at the time, but some things just don't stay with me anymore." Mrs. Kent gave an airy wave of her hand. "I do remember he was a clumsy child though. Always falling over this or banging into that. And he was often in the church. There were many days when I'd come in to light a candle for my dear mother, and there they'd be in the pews, praying for the little boy's health. For hours at a stretch sometimes."

Leigh's body went rigid and she covered for it by reaching again for her cup and trying to make her voice casual. "So Flynn Simpson wasn't housebound?"

"No, not at all."

"And he used to spend a lot of time at Saint Patrick's?"

Mrs. Kent stared at her as if she was slightly dense. "Didn't I just say that, dear?"

"I was just confirming." Leigh's mind was whirling and she took a long, slow sip of tea to buy herself a few extra seconds. If Simpson was willing to lie about Saint Patrick's to cover for his partner, then he could have lied about Father Brian. Leigh set down her cup. "What was Flynn's relationship with Father Brian? Were they friendly?"

Mrs. Kent's eyes took on an unfocused look and she was silent for several seconds. "Nothing stands out in my memory. Father Brian was very considerate of both Flynn and his mother."

"You never saw him lay hands on the boy? Perhaps even just to grasp his arm?"

Mrs. Kent stared at her in shock. "Are you implying that Father Brian mistreated him?"

"I'm not implying that at all. I'm just trying to establish their relationship."

The older woman made a *tsking* noise. "I know some priests have reputations for . . ." She paused, clearly searching for the most diplomatic way to express herself. "*Interacting* with some of the young boys. But Father Brian was never like that. He was always perfectly appropriate."

"Thank you, Mrs. Kent. You understand that I have to ask these questions as part of the investigation. It's important that I do whatever is necessary to find Father Brian's killer."

"Of course." Mrs. Kent regally bowed her head in either forgiveness or understanding, Leigh wasn't sure which.

"Moira Simpson must have been a very devout Catholic, seeing as she spent so much time in church," Leigh said.

"She seemed very devout until things didn't go her way. Then she dropped out of the parish fairly quickly. But . . ." Mrs. Kent paused and made show of fiddling with the small silver cross she wore on a slender chain around her neck. "Well . . . I don't like to speak ill of the dead."

Leigh simply waited. The eager gleam in the older woman's eyes clearly said that she was quite willing to speak ill of the dead.

Mrs. Kent gave a gusty sigh of resignation. "Since this is for a police investigation. Moira was more about showiness than actual faith."

Elanthia's voice rang in Leigh's head—*It became clear almost immediately that Moira was all about the symbols, rather than the substance of our Craft.* "What do you mean by that?"

"She always dressed impeccably for Mass and gave beautiful gifts to the church. She even paid for the repair of one of the sanctuary windows after someone threw a rock through it. She made the donation in memory of her husband. And the rosary she carried. It was very beautiful—hand-tooled silver with gemstone and pearl beads."

"Let me guess . . . custom made?"

Mrs. Kent pulled back in surprise, her tea cup rattling in her saucer. "Yes. How did you know?"

"I'm seeing a general trend. Mrs. Simpson had expensive taste and the money to support it."

"Let's just say she wasn't too modest to show off what she could afford. She had a very expensive silver crucifix she wore everywhere as well that matched her rosary. I always assumed she had it made by the same silversmith. But there was something in her that didn't seem genuine to me. I'm not sure I could even put my finger on what that was. But it wasn't a surprise when she suddenly stopped coming to Mass."

"Once Mrs. Simpson left the church, did you ever see her again?"

Mrs. Kent shook her head. "Never in the church. Maybe occasionally around Salem, but that was all. I never saw the boy again, although by the time they left, he was likely in his mid-teens. Poor twisted soul."

Leigh had been studying the cat in her lap with a jaundiced eye, but her gaze shot back to Mrs. Kent. "What do you mean by that?"

Mrs. Kent pressed a hand to her breast. "Oh no, dear, not that. I didn't mean he had a twisted mind. I literally meant that his body was twisted. Whatever that disease did to him, by the time he left the church, the effects were clear. He hunched on one side and his back was twisted and stiff. I believe he also didn't have full control of his left arm. He was a lovely boy, very polite and quiet spoken. And his mother was very attentive to him. They were practically inseparable."

"Thank you for clarifying. How long was Mrs. Simpson with the church?"

The thin lips pursed. "I would guess about seven or eight years."

Leigh made some quick calculations in her head. "She left in the mid-nineties?"

"Yes, that would be about right."

"To your knowledge did she have any contact with Father Brian after that?"

"Not that I know of. You might ask Father Thomas about that though."

Leigh took a final sip of tea and drained her cup to set it gently down on the wobbly table. "I've spoken to Father Thomas. He was the one who gave me your name. He'd never seen Ms. Simpson before." Ignoring the protesting yowl, Leigh lifted the cat from her lap, tugging until the claws finally released. She set the cat on the floor and then stood before it could hope to reclaim her lap. Gently coaxing the other cat from her feet, she stepped free of the furry mass. She could feel her eyes starting to water and a sneeze starting to build behind her nose. *Too late.*

She turned to Mrs. King. "Thank you for your time. You've been very helpful." She extended a card and the older woman took it with shaking fingers. "If you think of anything else, please let me know." When Mrs. King started to try to push herself out of her chair, Leigh waved her back down. "I can see myself out. Thank you for the tea."

Then, with one last look at the passel of cats, she fled.

CHAPTER TWENTY-SIX:
K-12 SAW

K-12 Saw: a circular saw that can be fitted with different blades to cut through wood, metal or concrete. It's an all-around tool that can take the place of an ax, chain saw, or the "Jaws of Life."

Tuesday, 4:14 p.m.
Boston University, School of Medicine
Boston, Massachusetts
Working alone at his desk, Matt looked up at the sound of the door opening. When he realized it was Leigh backing through the door with her arms nearly overflowing with files, he sprang to his feet to relieve her of half the load. "What's all this?"

"Flynn Simpson's medical files. You asked for them, you got them. In spades." They eased everything onto the cold stainless steel of an open gurney. "You need to look these over carefully. *Very* carefully."

Something in Leigh's tone had the hair on the back of Matt's neck standing up. "What's going on?"

"I think we're getting close."

"What makes you say that?"

"Remember I had that interview this morning with Mrs. Kent? She recognized Moira Simpson right away. Said that she was a dedicated member of the parish until about fifteen years ago." She paused and met his eyes. "She remembers Flynn Simpson, remembers him in church often with his mother."

Matt whistled. "That son of a bitch. He lied. He wasn't

housebound and even if he'd been young, he'd remember something that was such a major component in his life."

"Exactly. We're assuming he lied to cover the lover's tracks, but so far we have no proof and no obvious motive. We need to find both."

Matt tapped the files with an index finger. "If the motive is here, we'll find it." He glanced at his watch. "Kiko, Paul and Juka should be back from the charnel house any time now. There's a lot of material here, but they can give us a hand." He paused when her brows drew together. "What?"

Leigh held out a placating hand. "I know they're good, but I really want your eyes on this. They might miss something and—"

"I'll read it all, don't worry. But they might help find something a little faster." His gaze skimmed over the towering piles of paperwork. "This is a lot of information. Where did it all come from?"

"I started at the hospital. It seemed the reasonable place to begin since we knew from Simpson himself that they did surgery on him for cancer, only to find out it was FOP. I got all the records from his orthopedic surgeon, who then referred me to the family doctor, so I got those too. And it looks like there are copies of files from other specialists as well. On top of all that, I received the last of the chemical company reports so I need to go through those while you're going through this. Since there was nothing obvious that we found in the reports we went over last night, I'm hoping something pops for us here."

"Speaking of last night . . ." Matt stepped into her, feeling something lighten in his chest when she slipped her arms around his waist. It wasn't exactly uncertainty, but he felt like he was trying to find his footing in the transition from being lovers last night to colleagues this afternoon. "How are you today?"

She flashed him a cocky smile. "Fantastic. I thought I might be tired due to someone not letting me sleep very much last night, but strangely enough, I'm not. How about you?"

"Never better. I didn't even get a lecture when I got home this morning."

Leigh laughed. "You thought your father would lecture you? A grown man?"

"You never know with Dad. But he seemed remarkably chipper this morning."

"He's probably just happy to see you with someone. I bet—" She stopped suddenly, her head cocked slightly to one side.

Then Matt heard it too. Familiar voices, coming from down the hallway.

When Kiko, Paul and Juka entered the lab, they found Matt and Leigh standing on opposite sides of the gurney, leafing through stacks of paper.

"Good, you're back," Matt greeted them. "Flynn Simpson's medical records are here as well as a stack of reports from chemical companies." His gaze flicked to Leigh. "How about Paul helps you with the chemical reports, and Kiko and Juka help me with the medical records?"

"That works."

It didn't take long for Matt to find exactly what they were looking for. "Got something already."

Leigh looked up from the thick report she was reading. "That was fast."

"Well, I started with the orthopedic surgeon because the big issues will mostly be in here." He pulled an X-ray from the folder and took it to a light box on the wall. Flipping on the light source, he slid the film into place. "Ouch."

Leigh came to stand beside him. "What are we looking at?"

"This X-ray was taken of eight-year-old Flynn, after he'd fallen off his bike." He pointed to the narrow, double-curved collarbone with a clearly misaligned fracture near the shoulder joint. "That's a type-three distal fracture. And that's his left side."

She winced. "The side that's nearly immobile."

"Yes. When this healed, extra bone likely built up from the damaged soft tissue at the joint, immobilizing it."

"You said he was eight when that happened?" Kiko asked from across the lab.

"Yeah."

"Here's one from four years later." She held up another film. Matt waved her over, and Kiko replaced his film with hers on the light box. "Fracture of the distal ulna," she said. "He was skateboarding."

Leigh stared at the X-ray aghast. "What on earth was he doing skateboarding? Even if he was capable of it, the risk of injury would be too great. Is that his left side again?"

"Yes."

"He probably couldn't keep his balance with that kind of fusion already starting in his shoulder," Paul said.

Leigh turned to where he sat at his writing station. "What do you mean?"

"Think about skateboarding," he said. He stood up and set his feet like he was on a skateboard, his knees bent and his arms slightly spread from his sides. "You have to be able to constantly adjust to keep your balance as you board." He mimed taking a curve. "Every turn, every bump. He wouldn't have been able to if his shoulder was fused."

"No," Matt said, slowly. "He wouldn't." He stared at the X-ray, his lip starting to curl in distaste. An idea was forming in his mind, and he didn't really like the implications.

Leigh touched his arm. "What are you thinking?"

He pulled his gaze from the X-ray to find her intent green eyes fixed on his face. "Not sure yet. Let me work it through."

She stared at him curiously, but finally nodded.

It was Juka who found the next piece of the puzzle. "I found something too."

"Another break?" Matt asked.

"No. Nothing that dramatic. He had a cavity filled."

Leigh set down her report. "What does that have to do with anything?"

"A lot, unfortunately," Matt said. "What happens before your dentist drills?"

"They freeze your mouth?"

Matt simply held out both hands in a *there you go* gesture.

"The needle? An injection is enough to do damage?"

"Yes. Anything that causes soft tissue injury."

"God almighty. This kid never had a chance."

"No, he didn't."

Shaking her head, Leigh turned back to her report. She found the connection they'd been looking for less than five minutes later, drawing Matt's attention when her hand slapped down on the countertop in triumph. "I've got it!" She grinned at him. "I got a connection to Simpson." The triumph in her voice was infectious.

He abandoned his notes immediately. "What is it?"

"Look at this. This is the report from Graves Chemical Corporation, out in Worcester." She ran her finger under an entry.

Matt's gaze skimmed over it, from the date, to the product number to . . . "Salem Boatworks. Simpson's company ordered the red phosphorus."

"I can go one better than that. I saw his office and what he does. Simpson ordered it himself. Now, this is last May, but he could have kept it since then, or there may be another order. I'll keep checking. But this is our first real connection. Our first piece of *real* evidence."

"There must have been a legitimate reason for them to order

it. Surely someone would have questioned it between last May and now otherwise."

"A custom marine shop ordering phosphorus? No one would question that."

Both Matt and Leigh turned to Juka who sat on a stool in front of the gurney, papers spread out before him. "Why not?" Matt asked.

"Did you see a smelting furnace there?" Juka asked Leigh, ignoring Matt's question.

"A smelting furnace? I'm not sure that I'd recognize one if I even saw one. They had a lot of equipment in the building and . . ." She closed her eyes for a moment as she pictured the back workspace. "Would the furnace have a crucible?"

"Yes."

Her gaze swung up to Matt. "There was a heavy cylinder suspended from an I-beam frame so it could run down the length of the workspace." She turned back to Juka. "Could that have been it?"

He nodded. "It's a custom boat shop. If they do custom fittings, then they'd smelt their own metals on site. Phosphorbronze is a mix of copper, tin and phosphorus, in this case, red phosphorus. They'd likely heat the crucible in the furnace and then, if it was suspended, they could move it down the line, filling molds for the parts of the fittings. Now you don't use much phosphorus in phosphorbronze; it's less than one percent of the total mixture, but if they make enough of it, they might still order quite a bit."

"Enough that a few missing grams might not be noticeable over the long run," Matt said. "What you put in is never what you get out, depending on your scale's calibration, so no one would think twice about small amounts that were unaccounted for. But what are you thinking? That Dodsworth knew about the phosphorus and managed to secret some out of the shop?

Or that Simpson was in cahoots with him and he stashed it away? If it happened months ago, then no one would connect the missing materials simply because of the time frame."

"No one but us. I'm going to keep looking. There may be other orders, or there may be orders from other companies. Then I'll get copies of the invoices and, if possible, the delivery receipts to the company. We need this tied up neatly."

They went back to work, but with clearly increased enthusiasm.

Matt broke the silence again a few minutes later. "I have two more fractures. A supracondylar fracture of the elbow. Bad one too. And a scaphoid fracture."

"Those breaks are classic fall injuries," Kiko said. She held out her left arm, tilting toward the floor as if she was falling, her arm outstretched and her open hand flexed, her fingers spread. "If he was falling and tried to catch himself, his weight landing on his palm and the force radiating up his arm would do it. How did he fall? Does it say?"

"He was knocked off the porch steps by his dog, a Tibetan Mastiff."

"That's a big dog. How old was he at the time?" Leigh asked.

"Nine. Combined with the other injuries, this would have finished off his left arm for sure. I'll bet he was looking at complete fusion by the time he was thirteen or fourteen." He flipped through a few more pages. "There are lots of comments here about bumps and bruises. That's something that would never make it into anyone else's medical records, because they'd simply heal normally, but not with Flynn Simpson. Every bruise could become a new area of ossification."

"Mrs. Kent commented that he was a clumsy child. Actually, come to think of it, Simpson referred to himself the same way."

Matt carried the elbow X-ray to the light box and stood staring at it for a long moment. *Could it be? Still . . . who would do such a thing?* It disgusted him, but he knew such things really happened.

"I have a theory," he finally said. "It might explain motive."

"You're still thinking abuse?" Leigh asked.

"Yes. But with a horrific twist." He blew out a long breath and laid his cards on the table. "I'm thinking Münchausen. More specifically, Münchausen by Proxy."

Leigh closed her report with a snap as she swiveled around in her chair. "I've heard of that before. Isn't that—" Her breath caught in her chest in horror as understanding dawned. "Isn't that when a parent hurts their own child, simply to bring attention to themselves?"

"Yes."

Kiko's shocked gasp sounded behind him, and Matt let silence hang heavily in the lab for a moment, giving everyone a chance to absorb his theory. "Think about it. What's the one thing that everyone has consistently said about Moira Simpson? That she was all flash and no substance."

"She was a member of the parish and made large donations to the church, but only as long as Father Brian was showering her with attention. Once that stopped, she left," Leigh said.

"She joined the coven, and bought all the expensive tools of the trade, until she realized there was no hierarchy to climb and no one was listening to her ideas," Kiko said. "Then she left."

"She used her own son to attract attention to herself?" Disbelief and horror laced Paul's tone. "Münchausen is bad enough for any child, but in this case, she was doing permanent physical damage."

"It's a nightmare to think about, but look at the injuries he suffered. By the time the serious injuries started, Simpson was already diagnosed. Yet he was riding a bike and skateboarding, two activities he never should have been allowed to do by a responsible parent."

"And the dental work," Kiko said. "She *must* have been told by the doctors that any injection would cause inflammation and that in turn would stimulate ossification. If she'd passed that on to the dentist, surely he would have found another way, maybe used an inhaled anesthetic." She whirled on Juka. "What about vaccinations. Did he get those?"

"Hold on, let me look." Juka flipped back through his paperwork. "Yes, several. Mumps, measles, rubella, polio. Some were before his diagnosis, some weren't." He paused squinting down at the notes. "This doctor has terrible handwriting, but I think it says that he counseled that Simpson not receive the injection and Mrs. Simpson insisted."

Matt looked over at Leigh to find her staring off into space, but he could tell from her unfocused eyes that her mind was going a mile a minute. He walked over to her, laid his hand lightly on her shoulder and waited until she looked up. "Got something?"

"I'm just trying to put the pieces together. I think it's a sound theory. But what if it all started before Flynn Simpson's birth? Moira's husband was killed in an industrial accident. What if it all started there? There she was, widowed and pregnant. That probably attracted a lot of attention. What if she decided she liked being the sympathetic figure?"

"Simpson's diagnosis would have only strengthened it then. Imagine the attention she got once they figured out it was FOP," Paul said.

Matt suddenly found Leigh's green eyes narrowed on him accusingly. "What?"

"I'm just remembering your reaction to him. You totally checked out during that discussion, you were so floored by his condition."

"Well, sure. Most osteologists will go through their entire careers never seeing a clinical patient like that."

"That's exactly my point. I'm sure they called in specialists and made a big deal out of him."

Matt could imagine the reaction and the response. "And all the time they fussed over Flynn, they fussed over Moira too. She caught the limelight tangentially, and that only strengthened her desire. And since she didn't work, she could devote all her time to him."

"Remember that Simpson said she was devoted to him and totally involved in his health care. That she told him she felt responsible for not being able to find the right treatment for him—meaning a cure, I assume—so she kept taking him to different specialists."

"There is no cure," Juka said.

"I understand that. I bet she did too, but every new doctor was a new ear, and a once-in-a-lifetime clinical opportunity. I'm sure they were all very sympathetic to her plight, as well. She could have played the part of the loving mother, and everyone would feel terrible for her because there really wasn't anything anyone could do. And then all those injuries happened."

"Requiring more visits to doctors and trips to the ER," Kiko said, shaking her head in disbelief. "If it's true, it was cruelly subtle. She should have ensured he stayed safe. Instead, she provided sports equipment he wasn't physically able to handle because of his existing disability, thereby causing further injury."

"The dog is an interesting touch," Paul interjected. "Don't buy anything small. Buy a large dog, something that could be a guard dog for a single woman and her child, but one that Flynn wouldn't be able to handle. Restraining a dog of that size would be the only way to keep Flynn safe, but that clearly didn't happen. So he gets injured and ends up back at the doctor's office. And then likely again and again during the healing process. All those visits must have been crazy expensive, but it sounds like she had the money to afford it."

"If we're right, her money simply allowed her the leeway to keep all those doctor appointments." Leigh stood up and wandered over to the light box to stare thoughtfully at the X-ray. "I'll bet the child never even knew he was being abused. It wouldn't have been anything as obvious as a slap or a punch. If any of the doctors had asked him, he would have been able to genuinely say that his mother never mistreated him. In fact, she appeared to be a very loving, protective and involved parent."

"And his injuries lined up nicely as expected accidental fractures," Matt said. "There are typical pediatric fractures that are associated with child abuse—skull fractures, for instance, tend to be common, so are rib fractures—but none of Simpson's fractures would automatically raise an alarm since they aren't typical abuse fractures."

"Okay, so we've potentially identified the mother as the abuser. How does that explain the priest? Why would he be a target?" Paul asked.

"What if the priest knew?" Leigh asked. "What if Flynn Simpson figured it out himself as he got older and went to Father Brian as a trusted adult, but the priest didn't believe, or maybe didn't help him?"

"Wouldn't Father Brian have been required by law to disclose that information to the authorities?" Juka asked.

"Today he would," Leigh answered. "But it would depend on when he found out. He might not have been required by law back then."

"Only by morality," Matt muttered. "Let's run with this. Let's say that Father Brian was aware of the type of subtle abuse going on, but didn't do anything to step in or even talk to Moira Simpson. Why? Because of her donations to the church? He didn't want to kill the goose that laid the golden egg?"

"Possibly," Leigh conceded. "If so, then Flynn Simpson was sold out by a man of God for money."

"If that was me," Paul said, "I'd be pissed off. If it's true, then Father Brian allowed Moira Simpson to go on causing irreparable damage. Essentially, he was allowing her to slowly kill her son."

"So the whole time Simpson's been singing his mother's praises, it was all part of the cover," Leigh said. "He was deflecting attention away from himself and, therefore, away from Dodsworth because there was no motive for revenge. And in the meantime, Dodsworth was killing for him."

Matt raised a finger and started to say something, then abruptly pulled back, suddenly unsure.

"What?" Leigh asked.

"What if it's not Dodsworth doing the killing?"

"If not him," Kiko said, "then who?"

"What if it's Simpson himself?"

Leigh simply stared at him. "But he's not capable of carrying out those murders. You saw for yourself how little mobility he has. You were the one who told me I wasn't giving his disease enough credence when I first suggested him."

"I know." Matt paced up and down along the length of the bench. "And I'm kicking myself for it now. Did I dismiss him out of hand because I know too much about his disease? Do you remember when we first discussed him that I said his disease was more progressed than I expected for someone his age? Sure, some of that's because of the abuse, but what if some of it's an act?" His eyes stayed on Leigh, watching her turn the idea over in her mind.

"We discounted him from the start because we didn't think he'd have the strength and mobility," she said. "But from the beginning, we were considering women because the victims were incapacitated. Maybe they had to be incapacitated so he had time to make a clean kill."

"Exactly. And while we were thinking that Simpson was alibiing his lover, what if it was the other way around? Dodsworth was alibiing Simpson? And then when we look at the red phosphorus, it wasn't Simpson getting it for Dodsworth to use, but for himself."

"But why is Simpson doing this now?" Kiko asked. "Assuming that we're onto something here, why did he wait so long to exact his revenge?"

Leigh shrugged. "I'm not sure. There might be an angle of this that we're not seeing yet."

Matt went back to his files and flipped through some of the later entries. "Maybe it's something very basic. Maybe he's simply losing his ability to take action. As it is, he has to incapacitate his victims before killing them. What if he suspects that in another few years he'll be so trapped inside his own skeletal cage that he won't be able to avenge himself?"

"You may be on to something." Leigh checked her watch. "I need to go talk to Simpson."

"I'm coming with you." At her pointed look, Matt glared right back, not willing to back down. "Remember Bradford. In the end, it was our teamwork that took him down."

"Good point." Leigh turned back to Matt's students. "Thank you for your help. Can you guys—"

"We'll handle it," Kiko said. "Go."

Matt and Leigh didn't need to be told twice. They were already running out the door.

CHAPTER TWENTY-SEVEN:
FLAME FRONT

Flame Front: outermost boundary or edge of the fire.

Tuesday, 5:27 p.m.
Simpson Residence
Salem, Massachusetts

"I'm sorry; Flynn's not back from work yet." Aaron Dodsworth checked his watch, then looked back at Matt and Leigh standing on his doorstep. "The shop doesn't close until six, so I don't expect him home until about six thirty."

"We'll check back another time then, thank you," Leigh said.

"Is there anything I can help you with?"

"Now that you mention it, I did want to ask you about the key to the antique shop again."

"What about it?"

"You mentioned that you kept the commercial keys here at the house."

"Yes."

"How are those keys labeled?"

"Each has its own tag with the name of the property and the address."

"Did Mr. Simpson know where you kept them?"

Blood drained from Dodworth's cheeks as his mouth sagged open briefly, but he recovered quickly. "I never showed them to Flynn and he doesn't have a personal interest in my individual listings, so I'm sure he doesn't know where they're kept."

"I see. One more question then while I have you. Can I ask where you were last Thursday evening?"

She saw it only because she was watching specifically for his reaction. Just the tiniest of clues: His eyes widening ever so slightly as they flicked up and to her left. His weight shifting to his off foot. The speed of his answer.

"Flynn and I were here on Thursday night."

"Are you sure?" Leigh pressed. "Most people need to think about where they were the week before."

"Yes, I am. It was somewhat memorable because evenings like that don't happen very often for us." He laughed lightly and threw a hand out toward the dining-room table, covered with paperwork and house brochures. "I don't often get an evening off. So when I actually do have a night off, we try to enjoy it. Flynn came home early, and we had dinner and then stayed in and watched a movie."

"Thank you for your time and cooperation, Mr. Dodsworth." Leigh stepped onto the front porch and briskly strode down the front walk.

Back in her Crown Vic, Leigh glanced up at the house. Dodsworth stood frozen in the open doorway, watching them with an unreadable expression. She pulled into traffic. "You might not have caught it, but Dodsworth just made a mistake."

"You mean besides nearly panicking when you asked him about the keys? Did I miss something?"

"It's not so much that you missed it, it's that you weren't there when I interviewed Simpson. It's their story—Dodsworth had the night off, so they had dinner and stayed in and watched a movie."

"Yeah. Isn't that our main problem for this case because they alibi each other out?"

"It might be except their stories don't match. They do partly—they had dinner and stayed in and watched a movie. In fact, that part matches so well it sounds rehearsed. As in *This is our story, let's go over it again* kind of rehearsed. When you talk to subjects, even if they tell the same story, if it's unrehearsed, they always use different wording. But rehearsed stories always match a little too well—they use the same wording or the same cadence because they've practiced it together over and over. But they contradict each other on an important detail. Simpson said that Dodsworth came home early. Dodsworth said Simpson came home early. One of them isn't telling the truth. Or, more likely, both of them."

Matt grinned at her. "Nice catch."

"Thanks." She turned toward downtown. "He gave it away before that though. I caught his reaction the moment I asked him to confirm Simpson's alibi. His body language definitely said 'deception' to me."

"Would this stand up in a court of law as evidence?"

"I wouldn't put money on it. A good lawyer would run circles around it. I was the only one to hear Simpson's alibi and there's no record of it. Still, it might be enough to start to put doubt in the jury's mind. But let's not try to make this all we've got."

"We're going to the Boatworks, then? To hit Simpson and follow up on the red phosphorus?"

She grinned at him and gave the car more gas. "Oh yeah. Let's nail his ass to the wall."

Tuesday, 5:52 p.m.
Salem Boatworks
Salem, Massachusetts

"I'm sorry, you just missed him."

Leigh planted both hands on the reception counter. "What do you mean we just missed him? He's supposed to be here until six."

"Yes, that's right. But he got a call about ten minutes ago. I transferred it back to him and then the next thing I knew, he was flying out the door." The receptionist colored and bit her lower lip. "Well, you know what I mean. Flynn doesn't fly anywhere because of—"

"Yes, I know." Impatience whipped out the words with more edge than Leigh intended. "Where did he go?"

"He didn't say and I didn't ask him since—"

"Does he drive?"

The woman stared at her in confusion. "He drives the sedan his mother bought him—"

"Thank you." Leigh spun, grabbing Matt's arm and pulling him after her. Once outside, they hurried back to the car.

"What just happened?" Matt demanded.

"Dodsworth must have given him the heads-up that we stopped by," she nearly snarled. "He guessed—correctly—that we'd head straight here." Her open palm smacked down hard on the steering wheel. "Damn it, now he's in the wind."

She looked up when she felt Matt's hand on her arm.

"Let's think this through," he said. "He's less than ten minutes ahead of us. Let's assume that you're right and Dodsworth called him and told him that we were at the house asking about the key. Now he's on the run. Surely he wouldn't go home. He knows we'd look for him there."

Leigh heaved out a frustrated breath and sat back in her seat, forcing herself to slow down and think. "The only reason he'd run is because he thinks we're on to him."

"Which we are. But where would he go? With his disability, he simply can't melt into a crowd. People will remember the stooped man with the frozen left side. And he can't drive to another state and pick up some odd job you don't need references for. He's not capable of manual labor."

"He's distinctive, so he can't disappear. What about . . ." An idea washed over her like a bucket of ice water. "Oh, no."

"What?" From the alarm in Matt's voice, he was picking up on her apprehension.

"What if he's not done? What if he wants to finish off the next person on his list before he gets caught?"

"You think he's got more?"

"I don't know but what if he does? We're running on the theory that he's killing those responsible for his physical condition—his mother—or those that didn't step in to stop his injuries—like the priest. Who else would he go after? Friends of the family? Distant relatives who weren't in the picture to help? His family doctor?"

"What about the doctor who saw him most often?" Matt suggested. "Not the family doctor, but the orthopedist?"

"Didn't he see a lot of specialists?"

"He did. But from what I saw in those files, Moira kept coming back to one in particular for his regular care. There were a large number of doctors involved, but this orthopedic specialist was the one he saw the most. Until a few years ago, that is. Then he didn't go to him anymore. I suspect that's when he moved out and started to call his own shots. Maybe there was a reason he went somewhere else for his care."

Leigh dug her phone out of her pocket. "You're talking about Dr. Robert McAllister at Mass Gen? The one I got the records from earlier?"

"Yes. Think about it—surely the doctor who treated him consistently might have suspected some sort of subtle abuse."

"Or maybe Simpson tried to confide in him and wasn't believed there either. Something happened to cause that break between them." She picked up her Bluetooth earpiece from the dash and slid it into place, quickly dialing 4-1-1. "Boston. Massachusetts General Hospital."

She flipped on lights and siren as she sped down the crowded street, cursing the increased tourist traffic at this time of year as cars reluctantly pulled over to get out of her way. "This is Trooper Leigh Abbott of the Massachusetts State Police. I need to contact Dr. Robert McAllister in orthopedics." She blew through a red light. Out of the corner of her eye, she saw Matt grab the side handle of the door as they lurched around a corner.

After a brief conversation with the receptionist at orthopedics, Leigh pulled her notepad and pen out of her pocket and tossed them to Matt.

"What's going on?" he asked.

"McAllister is off today, but I'm the second person to call in the last ten minutes looking for him. She won't give me his address but I've talked her into giving me his phone number. She's gone to look it up. I need you to write it down."

When the receptionist returned, Leigh repeated the number out loud for Matt, then ended the call. Matt was already reaching for her phone to enter McAllister's number.

The phone rang four times then went to voice mail. "Dr. McAllister, this is Trooper Leigh Abbott of the Massachusetts State Police. I need you to call me back immediately upon getting this message. I'm concerned your life may be in danger." She rattled off her phone number and clicked off, then pulled off the road into a convenience-store parking lot.

"Now what do we do?" Matt asked.

"We go to him." She took her phone from him, speed dialing a familiar number. "It's Abbott. I need an APB out on a vehicle and I need an address. No, don't put me on hold. I need it now. There's a life at stake."

Chapter Twenty-Eight:
Advancing a Line

Advancing a Line: progress made by fire crews as they move a line of hose forward and away from the engine while fighting a fire.

Tuesday, 6:21 p.m.
McAllister Residence
Marblehead, Massachusetts

They spotted the black sedan the moment they turned onto the street. Leigh immediately pulled to the curb and cut the engine.

"Is that him?" Matt asked.

Leigh squinted at the license plate. "It's too far away. Let's check it out. We'll confirm when we get closer."

As they hurried down the sidewalk, Leigh unbuttoned her jacket and ran her palm over the butt of her gun. She needed to be ready, just in case. But even knowing she was ready didn't quiet her suddenly thumping heart.

The sun had set over thirty minutes earlier and the deepening gloom of twilight threw long shadows over the sidewalk and street. The silvery light of a nearly full moon flickered overhead through the branches of trees dancing in the cool breeze. Tomorrow was Halloween, and all up and down the length of the street, grand historic houses were dressed for the occasion—filmy white ghosts floated from roof lines, cobwebs dripped from spindly tree branches, and gravestones jutted from front lawns, a skeletal hand reaching from beyond as if to snare the ankle of a passerby. When a sudden gust of wind whistled around them and a branch over their heads groaned, she nearly jumped.

Calm down. They're just Halloween decorations; no one is going to jump out at you. Besides, you're armed.

Then her gaze settled on the stuffed raven perched on top of a gravestone a few feet away. A chill ran down her spine as her own words rang in her head: *The Raven, a creature of the shadows. The harbinger of ill portent. An omen. Darkness lies ahead.*

She resolutely turned away from the shadows and looked down the street instead. "There is it. Number fifty-nine." Leigh pointed to the large clapboard house that sat close to the street. Three stories tall and nearly two hundred years old, it was a huge house with more than a dozen windows across the front face of the building and clustered around a grand, glass-paned front door. An intricate wrought-iron railing ran from the squared porch down steps covered with a tiered cascade of colorful chrysanthemums.

Grasping Matt's arm, she pulled him back against the trunk of a century-old tree, hiding them from view of the house. "That's the right license plate. I'm calling this in. I want backup."

"It's like Hershey's house all over again," Matt said, his eyes locked on the sedan at the curb.

Her gaze flicked to his stony face. Neither of them would ever forget what happened only weeks ago in John Hershey's kitchen. Or the resulting fallout.

If Matt noticed her searching look, he didn't comment on it. "We can't wait for backup," he continued. "Simpson could have McAllister dead and a fire set by the time they get here. We have to go in now."

"I know." Leigh pulled out her cell phone and quickly made the call, giving their location and asking for backup from both

State and local police. "They're on their way," she told Matt. Quickly going down on one knee and pushing up her pant leg to reveal an ankle holster, she freed a snub-nosed pistol and handed it to Matt. "Your Glock's at home. Until the real backup arrives, you're my backup and I want you armed." She unholstered her service weapon. "Let's go."

Keeping to the shadows as much as possible, they crept forward. A short, wrought-iron fence separated the house from the street, and Leigh vaulted over it at the corner. Matt followed, trailing behind her as she crept low under the front windows. She froze for a moment, one hand held out, signaling Matt to stop.

Several seconds passed, but there was no sound or movement from within.

Leigh jerked her head sharply toward the door and was about to step forward when Matt grabbed her arm. She turned back to him, and the expression on his face made her blood freeze. "What?" she hissed.

"Do you smell that?"

She stared at him, remembering another moment when his sharper sense of smell had saved their lives. Then she caught it, just a whiff of a sweet oily scent. "What is that?" Her voice was barely above a whisper.

"It's been a long time since I went camping, but I swear that's kerosene."

"To start another fire? But why change MO now?"

"Maybe we cut him off from his supplies. Maybe he was keeping the red phosphorus at home and couldn't go back for it. Kerosene is readily available and will make a damned big fire without the explosive danger of something like gasoline. He wants to set a fire, not blow the house into a pile of matchsticks with himself still inside."

Leigh was already pulling out her phone, kneeling down on

the grass to stay out of sight, pulling Matt down with her.

"Bree Gilson."

"It's Leigh Abbott. We have a situation on our hands. I think our arsonist is Flynn Simpson and he's about to strike again."

Bree's voice came over the line crisp and no-nonsense. "The first victim's son?"

"Yes. It's a long story and I don't have time for details but Matt and I are in Marblehead outside the home of Simpson's orthopedic surgeon and we can smell kerosene."

Bree swore. "You think he's going after the surgeon next?"

"Yes."

"How strong is the smell?"

"Not that strong outside, but assuming he's using it inside, if we can smell it out here there must be quite a bit. We're going in now, so we'll know more shortly."

"Whoa. Wait a second. You can't go in. If he's using accelerant, that thing could go up like a tinderbox."

Matt's gaze was fixed on Leigh's face, following the conversation even if only from her end. The set of his jaw alone told her he was with her. "We don't have any choice. Police backup is coming, but we need your guys down here." She quickly rattled off the address.

"I'll get them out there ASAP. But be careful. One spark of any kind and you're in big trouble. That includes gunshots."

"Thanks for the tip. Hurry." She hung up, not even waiting for a response. "She's not happy we're going in."

"I'm sure she's not. But she's both cop and firefighter—part of her understands what we have to do."

"She also made one point very clear—a gunshot might produce a spark big enough to burn the place down. The gun's just for show unless you have absolutely no other way to defend yourself."

They crept the rest of the way to the front steps and then up to the front door. Leigh tried the handle—locked. Making a snap decision, she flipped the gun in her hand, grasping the barrel. "Watch yourself."

"What are you doing?"

"Door's locked and we have no time to waste. We have the right to enter as we suspect someone is in jeopardy." She shattered the pane of glass nearest the door handle in a single strike. Several sharp taps knocked out the remaining shards and she slipped her hand through, throwing back the dead bolt with a *click*.

"Unless Simpson's deaf, he now knows we're here, and he might be armed. Stay behind me," she ordered.

She eased the door open, and stopped momentarily in the doorway, listening intently for any sound. When only silence met her ears, she eased open the door a little further and slipped through the gap, Matt right behind her.

They stood in an open foyer, flanked by living and dining rooms. The decor clearly spoke of wealth and quiet class. Old money at its finest.

A scuffling noise from upstairs drew her attention to the main staircase.

Leigh's heart stuttered and her mouth went dry.

Liquid spilled down the stairs in a thin stream to pool on the floor below. *Kerosene.* When the fire started, it would instantly spread to engulf the house, and it would block any hope of exit. Tapping Matt's arm, she held her finger to her lips and then pointed to the trail of kerosene. His lips parted on an intake of breath, but he made no sound.

She pointed upwards and then picked her way quietly to the foot of the stairs. She looked up into the gloom above them, then cast a furtive glance back at the front door. Their only means of escape potentially cut off by flames and a trail of accelerant. *We'll just have to prevent the fire from happening.*

Pressing her back against the wall and holding her gun in front of her, Leigh carefully eased up the stairs, testing each tread before trusting her weight to it. Simpson might know that someone was in the house, but he didn't know where they were and she wanted to keep it that way. She carefully stepped around the kerosene trail. If it got onto the soles of their shoes, it could be a death sentence.

They were halfway up the stairs when they heard more scuffling and a low moan. Leigh froze, using her free hand to press Matt back against the wall. They stood motionless for several seconds, but the sound wasn't repeated. Leigh continued her slow stalk up the staircase, Matt a shadow right behind her.

The final step gave away her position, quietly squeaking under her weight. She quickly moved off it, but the damage was already done.

Matt joined her at the top of the stairs. The second floor was dim, only a single light was on in a bedroom down the hall; the rest of the floor was quenched in twilight. Near the top of the stairs, a one-gallon metal kerosene can stood near the wall, the lid missing. Leigh nudged it gently with her toe. *Empty.*

"Come on in, Trooper Abbott."

Leigh jerked, the gun wavering only for a second as she swung toward the voice, gripping her firearm in two hands. "I know it's you, Simpson. I know you're responsible for the fires."

"I knew you were onto me. Aaron called me and told me you were asking questions. That's why I came here."

"Where's Dr. McAllister?"

"He's here with me. He's got a gun under his chin, so no fast moves or he dies."

"I'm coming in," she said. "Don't hurt him."

"Too late for that." There was a note of satisfaction in Simpson's voice that made her heart race in alarm.

Turning quickly to Matt, she laid her palm on his chest

281

mouthing *Stay here.* Unless Simpson had seen them, he might think she was alone and they might be able to use that fact to their advantage.

She half expected him to balk, but he was already a few steps ahead of her, silently moving past her to press his back against the wall near the open doorway, staying outside the light that flooded out onto the carpet. Leigh nodded in approval. Now she just needed to find a way to keep Simpson distracted so Matt could come through the door.

Easing forward, gun extended, Leigh stepped toward the open doorway.

It was a bedroom, richly furnished like the rooms below, a large king-sized bed dominating the space. It was the small puddle of blood, soaked into the plush beige carpet in a brilliant splash of color that caught Leigh's eye first. Her stomach dropped—was she already too late?

Taking a deep breath, she stepped into the room.

The first thing she noticed was the smell. A vaguely familiar, sickly sweet odor. *Gasoline? Why use that in here when he'd used kerosene on the stairs?* Then Matt's words from only moments before came back to her—*Kerosene is easily available and will make a damned big fire without the explosive danger of something like gasoline.*

He'd used both accelerants to ensure a catastrophic fire.

They were in very big trouble.

Flynn Simpson stood near the foot of the bed. An older man, wiry, thin and balding, stood in front of him, his eyes blinking dazedly as he swayed slightly. His head tilted back at an awkward angle, forced into position by the barrel of the gun pushed into the soft flesh under his chin. A slow stream of blood trickled from a gash on his temple, winding down his cheek and jaw to drip off in a steady slow rhythm. It splashed hollowly onto a red plastic gas can, tipped onto its side at Simpson's feet.

Tap, tap, tap.

One quick glance around the room told Leigh everything she needed to know. Bedding. Draperies. Carpet. Pillows—all branded with wet splashes. The fumes in the room told her the rest, nearly making her head swim.

The gasoline was his *pièce de résistance.* All it would take was a spark. The house would go up in a heartbeat and they'd all be trapped. Or blown into splinters, the kerosene consuming anything else that remained after the explosion.

A shudder ran through her as memories tumbled unbidden over each other, flashing through her mind in Technicolor. *Fire behind the windows of the church and licking up the tower. Charred flesh, dark and horribly curled, lying on damp grass. Blackened muscle, peeling back to reveal stark white bone. An unrecognizable face, contorted in a scream of agony.*

She brutally pushed the memories away. If she became paralyzed by fear, they were all dead. She needed at least ten minutes until Bree and the fire department arrived.

Leigh fixed her sights on the middle of Simpson's forehead. She didn't dare take the shot, but she wanted Simpson's attention focused on her. She inched further into the room, hoping to turn Simpson so the doorway—and Matt's potential entrance—wasn't directly in his line of vision.

"Looks like we're at a stalemate here, Flynn. If you shoot Dr. McAllister, I'm going to have to shoot you, then I'm the only one who walks away. Why don't you put down the gun and we can talk this out?"

Simpson shook his head, a mulish set to his mouth. "No. You put the gun down. I don't have any desire to hurt you. You haven't done anything to me."

"The firefighter in the Saint Patrick's fire didn't do anything to you, but he died."

Remorse layered with sorrow flickered over his face. "I never meant for anyone else to die. They just should have let it burn. There was nothing they could do for the priest. He'd already found his justice."

"Is that what you're doing? Meting out justice?" While she talked, Leigh's gaze slid to Dr. McAllister, trying to judge his coherency and whether he could help himself in any way. With a sinking heart, she realized the man was only barely conscious. He'd need all the help she and Matt could give. "This isn't the way to go about it. I know what they did to you and why you want revenge. If you want justice, I can get it for you."

Interest and hope swirled briefly in Simpson's eyes but then slowly faded. "No, you can't. Even if you charged someone, it would be years before it went to trial and by that time I'd be trapped inside my own skin. I'd literally be a piece of evidence." His voice went hard. "I've been a spectacle and an object of pity all my life. It won't happen again. They were killing me slowly, so I was going to kill them first. Besides, it would always be my word against theirs. You have no idea what I went through."

Leigh let all the sympathy she felt for him fill her expression and her voice. It wasn't hard. She didn't approve of his methods, but what had been done to him was cruel beyond measure. "I don't, because I'll never be able to experience what you did. But I know what your mother did to you, how she changed your life forever."

Simpson's hand jerked, belying his calm.

Got his attention. Now keep it and win his trust.

"Your mother suffered from Münchausen by Proxy," she continued. "She had a child with a rare disease and she played you and the doctors for the attention it brought her."

"She 'suffered'?" Simpson nearly spit the word, his fingers tightening in a white-knuckled grip around the butt of the gun. With a spurt of horror, Leigh realized her mistake. "You make it sound as if she wasn't responsible for her actions."

Leigh held out a hand, placating. "Of course she was. You were the victim, Flynn. In your mother's desperate bid for constant attention, she put your safety, your quality of life, at risk." *Keep stalling.* Eyes locked on the finger on the trigger under McAllister's chin, she went for a different tack. "How old were you when you figured it out?"

"When I . . . ?" Simpson trailed off to stare at her blankly.

"You were only a child when it started. Look at the type of abuse: Biking and skateboarding accidents, a dog too big for you to handle. Dental appointments, immunizations. It was subtle, but unmistakably vicious."

Simpson swallowed jerkily. "How do you know all that?"

Leigh ignored him and pushed on. "Dr. McAllister was an adult. He should have seen the incidents for what they were. And then you told Father Brian about your concerns and he didn't help you either. But this isn't the way."

"What other choice did I have?" Simpson's voice cracked on the last word. "No one would listen. No one cared. Not until Aaron."

"Is Aaron involved in this too?"

For the first time, panic flashed in Simpson's eyes. "No. He's innocent. No matter what evidence you find, he's not responsible."

"What evidence would I find, Flynn? You can tell me. We're going to work this all out."

"He's a realtor. He had a key to the antique shop on the wharf because the owner was getting ready to sell and he needed to be able to show it. I knew where it was and I took it. He had nothing to do with it."

"How did you get your mother to meet you there?"

"I asked her to come down and see it. I knew she'd quit the coven and had time on her hands. I told her she'd be perfect running a boutique store where only the best of the best shopped. By the time she agreed to come down, she was already planning her career as the darling of the wharf. And, of course, when she came she brought that damned dog," he snarled. "I hated that dog from the first time it bit me."

And the dog certainly paid for it. "Why did you pick that shop?"

"It was accessible and basically unconnected to her. That location and the fire completely erased her identity, giving me time to move on to my next victim. I never meant to get away, you know. I just wanted time to kill them all. I always knew how this story would end."

Leigh noticed Simpson's right arm start to shake with the strain of holding the gun at such an awkward angle. She moved further into the room, trying to give Matt more leeway. "And how will it end?"

"With my death."

Alarm shot through Leigh. A murderer who didn't care about his own outcome was a dangerous man indeed.

"It doesn't have to end that way," she said soothingly, easing another inch to her right. Out of her peripheral vision, she caught a glimpse of Matt creeping around the door frame, still out of sight of Simpson, but clearly reacting to his threat of suicide.

"Stop!" Simpson barked.

Matt and Leigh both froze.

"Move another inch and I'll shoot him right now. And there are enough fumes in here that the gunshot could set the whole house ablaze."

Leigh knew it was the adrenaline rushing through her veins that caused a tremor in the hand that gripped her gun, but she resolutely steadied it. "Okay, Flynn, it's all right. I'm not going anywhere." Not daring to look at Matt for fear of giving him away, she dropped her left hand casually out of sight behind her thigh, signaling him to wait. The situation was simply too volatile. If Matt suddenly appeared they could catch Flynn off guard and overwhelm him, or he could kill the doctor and start an inferno. Then there was no telling how many of them would die.

She latched onto the one weakness she'd seen in Simpson thus far. "You know, Aaron is still in trouble. He alibied you for Thursday night when you know very well you were at Saint Patrick's killing Father Brian. He put himself on the line for you."

A sad smile curved Simpson's lips. "He loves me. He'd do anything to protect me. But he lied because he thought I was protecting him."

Leigh was baffled by the sudden turn in the conversation. "Protecting him? Why would you need to do that if he wasn't involved?"

"He's not. But he was out with his lover on Thursday night."

His lover? "And you were okay with this?"

"He only did it for the sex." Simpson's voice was flat and matter-of-fact. "I can't . . . participate like that in our relationship anymore. I know he sees other men. He tries to hide it from me, but I know. He's young and healthy and has needs. I have his heart; they can have his body. He thought I was home that night and was making sure he was alibied because he had access to the antique shop. He didn't realize that he was alibiing me instead."

"So was he out with his lover when you killed your mother?"

Simpson shook his head, his right shoulder slumping as guilt settled over him like a dark cloak. "No, I slipped him a sleeping pill early that night. Once he was out, I got the key and went down to the wharf to meet my mother. I told her it had to be late as her seeing it ahead of time wasn't exactly on the up-and-up, so we met at midnight. She loved it. It was like she was playing spy. So we spent some time going through the shop."

The light left his eyes, leaving his face frighteningly blank. "Then when she turned away I hit her with an antique candlestick and she dropped like a rock. Her demon dog went nuts, so I bashed its head in too."

"Then you stabbed your mother with her own athame. But there's something I don't understand. If she was killed shortly after midnight, why did you wait so long to start the fire?"

"Because the shop is right by the marina and several restaurants. And at this time of year with all the tourists, I didn't dare start it until after everything was closed and everyone had gone home. It was crucial that the fire get a good start. If it was noticed too soon, the fire department might put it out and her identity might have been discovered sooner. So I waited for hours, until I was sure that all was quiet and no one would see me slip out the back. It worked like a charm."

Leigh tried to imagine the patience required to sit in the dark with the dead body of your mother, waiting for just the right moment. Maybe all those years waiting in doctors' offices had taught him the art of stillness.

"Did you talk her into bringing the athame with her?"

"No, I already had it. I'd taken it from her house the week before one afternoon I knew she'd be out getting her hair done. She told me she'd boxed up all her things and never gave them a second thought. She never even noticed it was missing."

"The boline as well?"

"And her wand. That's how McAllister was supposed to die. Her fancy sculpted metal wand, slicing right through his heart. Which would be justice since his affair of the heart sealed my doom." At those words, the doctor suddenly found the strength to struggle, squirming in Simpson's unsteady hold. Simpson cruelly pushed his head further back, compressing his windpipe with the gun, leaving him gasping for air and twitching help-lessly.

Leigh used the break in the conversation to listen, hoping to hear sirens. Nothing. She forced herself to ignore the older man's plight, trying to keep Simpson in the conversation. "An affair? With your mother?"

"Yes. They were having an affair even though he was married. At first I think the appointments were an excuse to see more of her, so he didn't worry too much about why I kept having them, but later, as things started to fall apart between them, he stayed silent. My theory is that she threatened to expose the affair if he exposed her . . . habits." Simpson's gaze skimmed over the expensively furnished room. "Big house, fancy wife . . . if she found out that he was carrying on, she'd have taken him to the cleaners and he'd have lost everything. So he stayed silent and I was just collateral damage. I was always collateral damage," he sneered. He jabbed the gun harder against McAllister's throat and the older man spluttered and groaned. "The wand is hidden at home and I couldn't take the chance that you'd circle back there and catch me if I went for it. Lucky for me, I was smart enough to start carrying a gun after our last conversation. I had a feeling that you weren't buying the Witchcraft angle."

"There simply wasn't enough evidence to support it."

"I didn't need evidence," Simpson snapped. "Just time."

"Were you keeping the red phosphorus at home too? Is that why you've switched to kerosene and gasoline?"

"How did you—"

"I know all about it. I know you ordered it through the Boat-works, but kept some back for yourself and no one ever noticed. You didn't need much, just enough to start the reaction in the balloon. It was really brilliant. If our fire marshal and her men weren't so good, I think it might have been missed. How did you learn that trick?"

"I had a buddy in college whose father was a firefighter in Malden. He used to pass on interesting stories sometimes. They had an arson case a decade or more back that used that same trick. It was simple and original enough that it stuck with me, and had the added bonus of a time delay, allowing someone who wasn't fast or graceful on their feet time to set it and disappear. Who knew that it would be such a useful piece of information years later?"

Far off in the distance came the sound of a siren.

Desperation flashed in Simpson's eyes. "Who did you call?"

"Cops and firefighters. Take your pick. It's over, Flynn. Let's end this peaceably."

"No. Let's end this like I planned."

Dread filled Leigh when his eyes went flat and dull, all emotion simply evaporating. Her gaze flicked to Matt and she gave him a sharp nod. *GO!*

It all happened at once.

Matt came through the door, crouching low and headed straight for Simpson. Simpson jerked in surprise and McAllister took advantage of the younger man's delayed reaction to break free and throw himself toward Leigh, knocking the gun from Simpson's weak grasp with his shoulder. But McAllister's sudden move put him directly in Leigh's line of sight, blocking the shot she was about to take despite the risk involved. In a flash of panic, she stopped herself from killing the wrong man—and perhaps causing an explosion in the process—just in time. But McAllister was stunned and unsteady on his feet, and he reeled toward Matt who lunged to the side to get out of the way while still trying to catch the older man.

"Freeze!" Leigh yelled, finally getting a clear shot at Simpson. Simpson stood stock-still by the bed, his right fist extended outward, as if willing the gun on the carpet at his feet to leap back into his hand. Leigh held her gun on him, steadily clasped in both hands.

"Matt, you okay?" she asked, not taking her eyes off Simpson.

"I'm fine. And I've got McAllister. He took a good knock to the head and is probably concussed."

"Get him out of here."

"I'm not leaving you."

"We'll be right behind you. You need to help Dr. McAllister. Go," she insisted.

There was a moment of silence—Leigh could imagine the battle going on in Matt's mind—and then he started to walk Dr. McAllister toward the door.

"Now, Flynn, let's just—"

That's when she saw it.

Simpson had opened his hand. Clutched in his fingers, suspended over the gasoline-soaked bedding was a squat, silver lighter.

He'd lost his gun in the struggle, but now held a much deadlier weapon.

Leigh's reflexive gasp had Matt turning back even before he reached the door.

"Stop! You're going to kill all of us."

Simpson shook his head. There was neither madness nor cruelty in his eyes, just resignation. "I'm not going to jail. I won't live out the rest of my days locked in the dual cages of this body and a cell. If you don't want to die with me, you'd better run."

Leigh glanced at Matt but he was already turning to Dr. McAllister. "Can you walk?"

The older man gave a wobbly nod.

Matt pushed him toward the door. "Get out now."

As the doctor staggered from the room, Matt turned back to Simpson. "You don't want to do this, Flynn."

"Yes, I do. You most of all know what my life will be like."

Matt inched slowly closer. "It will be tough, but you could have years left. Maybe decades."

"That's bullshit and you know it," Simpson spat. "I'll be in a wheelchair within a year or two and dead from pneumonia a few years after that. Or from a fall. There's no hope."

Leigh saw the tiny remaining flicker of light go out of Simpson's eyes and knew it was too late. "NO!"

Matt launched himself toward Simpson, just as his thumb scrolled over the flint wheel and a single bright flame danced to life.

The room exploded into the flames of hell.

CHAPTER TWENTY-NINE:
FLAMEOVER

Flameover: occurs when fire gases trapped at the upper level of a room catch fire and spread flames across the ceiling.

Tuesday, 6:44 p.m.
McAllister Residence
Marblehead, Massachusetts
Matt realized the danger as soon as the flame burst to life. Simpson wouldn't need to set the bedding on fire. The vapor that permeated the room was far more lethal.

The air seemed to ignite even as Simpson let go of the lighter. With a *whoosh*, tendrils of flame rushed through the room, riding a cushion of air just above the floor as the heavier-than-air vapor ignited.

Matt abruptly checked his forward momentum, throwing himself sideways toward Leigh instead, scrambling to stay on his feet as his balance shifted. He struck her hard, his arms wrapping around her waist as they hit the wall with enough force to nearly wind them.

He didn't see the explosion of flames; he didn't need to. He could hear it as heat bloomed with fiery intensity at his back. Spinning around, he saw the curtains were alight, flames racing higher and higher to kiss the ceiling. The bed was totally engulfed and fire crept steadily along the carpet toward them.

"Simpson, we've got to get out!"

But Simpson simply stood on the other side of the room,

unmoving, his eyes almost dazedly fixed on the dancing flames. Mesmerized.

Leigh tugged on his arm. "We need to get him out of here. Can we carry him?"

Matt was already jamming the gun into his waistband at the small of his back, freeing his hands. "We can try. But if he fights us, we're going to have to let him go, or we'll die with him."

She opened her mouth as if she might argue, but then sharply nodded. He understood how torn she was. Her instinct was to save lives, but he wouldn't allow it to be at the cost of her own. If Simpson wanted to die that badly, Matt was willing to let him go. In many ways, he understood his choice. Even respected it.

But they'd make the attempt first, navigating the rivulets of gasoline that were already alight. Darting around a patch of flaming carpet, they headed toward Simpson.

Suddenly there was a small burst of fire at the floor around Simpson's ankles, and then the flames were racing up his legs. Cold horror coursed through Matt as realization struck—Simpson must have splashed some gasoline on himself as he spread it around the room.

The expression on Simpson's face was one of joy and relief. Release. His suffering would finally end.

The flames shot up his body, greedily licking and biting and suddenly the body before them was an inferno. Joy melted from the face even as a blood-curdling scream filled the rapidly overheating air and he fell to the carpet, shrieking in agony.

Matt looked around frantically for anything he could use to smother the fire, but Simpson had set every piece of material in the room ablaze. His gaze fell back to the form writhing on the floor.

And then he noticed the gas can.

Matt grabbed Leigh's arm with a force that would leave bruises. Flames were licking around the edges of the can. It was tipped on its side, the cap off, but whether it was empty or not, he couldn't be sure.

If even just a few ounces remained, that can was a bomb.

"Run!" He jerked Leigh toward the doorway. She was startled but didn't question, falling into step with him, sprinting for the hallway.

They'd just cleared the doorway, careening into the corridor and around the corner when there was an explosion of heat and a huge fireball blasted through the doorway into the hall. The fireball quickly receded, leaving thick black smoke rolling out from beneath the lintel and spreading down the hallway.

Breathless, Matt leaned against the wall for a moment, his head hung low and his breath sawing as his heart pounded in his ears. It was a very narrow escape—four feet closer to the door and they would have been caught in that fireball. Killed instantly.

If the flames hadn't killed Simpson, the explosion surely had. He was beyond their help now.

Leigh's gasp of fear brought his head up. His brief relief at escaping the maelstrom in the bedroom instantly dissolved into the smoke around them.

Everything was in flames.

The carpet was on fire, sending thick smoke into the shadowy second floor. Flames trailed down the main staircase and licked up the spindles of the carved wooden banister. Light flickered in each open doorway along the hall and smoke roiled in thick waves along the ceiling, billowing in dark, smothering swirls.

The acrid smoke stung his eyes, making them water. Matt swiped at them, blinking as he searched for a way out.

The flashes of red and white lights pulsing through the thickening smoke from the second-floor windows told him that Bree and her men were outside. But he had no idea if they'd be able to find them before either the smoke or the flames killed them.

They needed to get out. But their way down was blocked and every doorway led to a window guarded by flames.

"We need off this floor." His body was wracked with harsh coughing. Desperation spun his adrenaline reaction higher as smoke inhalation suddenly became a very real concern. "Wait, where are you going?"

Leigh was running down the hallway, toward a dead end. A narrow door was set into the wall, closed tight.

She was headed for . . . a linen closet?

Cursing, he bolted after her. She was struggling with the door handle. "Help me!"

He pushed her out of the way. The handle was old, possibly original, and the door—which appeared to open inward—was stuck tight. He put his shoulder against it and pushed. With a groan, he felt the wood shift minutely.

"What is this?" he asked through gritted teeth, taking a step back to get more leverage. He hit the door hard and there was the high-pitched screech of wood scraping against wood as the door gave another fraction of an inch.

"I think it's an old servants' staircase."

"I hope you're right." Matt threw all his weight behind one more strike at the door and it abruptly gave way. Forward momentum carried him into the darkness and he had the brief thought that it wouldn't be the fire that killed him because the fall down the stairs would break his neck. Then he felt Leigh's hand lock around his wrist and he latched on hard as she yanked him back into the hall. "Thanks."

She was already patting the wall beside the door, finally finding an antique light switch. Two lights flickered on dimly, one at the top and another at the bottom of the stairs. "Thank God. I was sure we'd be doing this blind."

The air inside the staircase was stale, but blessedly free of smoke. The space was narrow, clearly meant for the female household staff, and Matt had to angle his body slightly sideways to keep his shoulders from brushing both walls.

"You should have left with McAllister," Leigh tossed over her shoulder as they clattered down the worn wood stairs. "Then you'd be out of here."

"And leave you alone to deal with Simpson? No chance in hell."

Leigh stepped off the last step onto a worn stone floor. "If you wanted hell, it looks like you got your wish."

Matt eyed the door at the end of the narrow corridor suspiciously. The hinges looked like they were made around the time Lee surrendered to Grant at Appomattox. "If that doesn't open, we're in big trouble. And it's got to come toward us."

"I know."

Leigh cast a worried glance back up the stairs and Matt followed her gaze. Flames roared at the doorway. They were cut off. His gut clenched. They were either going through this door, or they'd die together here. "Let me by."

He squeezed past her, her slight groan at the tight quarters whispering in his ear, and then he was free. The brass door handle felt sturdy and relatively cool, and there was just enough room for him to wedge his boot on the door frame for extra leverage. "Give me some space."

Leigh moved back up several steps.

Heart pounding, Matt gripped the handle. If the door was jammed they were done. Or if the handle came apart with one good yank. Or if—

He made himself stop thinking of all the ways they could die.

He took a deep breath, held it and then turned the handle and pulled slowly, trying not to stress the hardware.

For a pulse-pounding moment of terror, the door didn't

move. And then it started to slide toward him. He blew out the breath he'd been holding and pulled again. A half inch. Then another.

Then the door popped open and Matt found himself staring at hell itself.

He slammed the door shut.

Shit.

"What?" Panic backed Leigh's voice.

"The house is engulfed. We'll have to go through it." He could hear his own fear in the rapid staccato of his words. He pulled off his jacket, balling it in his hands. "Take off your blazer. We won't be able to breathe out there without some sort of filter. And stay low. Ready?"

Even in the dim, flickering light, her face was sheet white under the light smudging of soot already coating her skin. She pressed the material to her mouth and nose and nodded resolutely.

"Whatever happens, we stick together."

She gave a curt nod of agreement. "Do it."

Suddenly the lights went out. Matt wasn't sure if that was the fire department cutting power or the lines burning through. Either way, they needed to get out now.

He whipped open the door. Then he grasped her free hand with his and they stepped out into the inferno.

Flames rolled across the kitchen ceiling in living, writhing waves, sliding sensuously into every corner. The acrid stench of melting plastics and burning wood filled the room. Smoke hung at the ceiling in thick oily clouds and the heat level alone would roast them if they didn't get out quickly.

Matt scanned the room—the cabinets and center island were aflame and the wide picture window over the sink was framed by burning curtains.

The only potential escape was a door on the far side of the

room. Gripping Leigh's hand, he ran through the kitchen, bent as low as he dared while still trying to peer through the thick gloom.

Flames licked at his arms and the heat was unbelievable. He was sure his hair was starting to singe. Choking smoke slithered through the material pressed against his lips, and his lungs burned, straining for oxygen, but finding only noxious chemicals. The air was only minimally clearer this close to the floor; he could feel the particulates in the smoke coating the inside of his nose and lungs, and tears ran down his cheeks as his eyes stung and watered.

Somewhere ahead of him came the crash of something heavy collapsing, followed by glass shattering. Around them, the flames cracked and popped, slithering ever closer.

Leigh was coughing, the force of the shudders wracking her body and shaking his where they gripped hands. The doorway in front of him wavered and he blinked furiously.

Flames outlined the door frame and poured under the lintel in an undulating wave. Beyond it, the room was engulfed. But on the far side Matt thought he saw French doors. Leading out to a ground-floor patio?

The ceiling above them gave an ominous creak and their eyes met in alarm. If the ceiling collapsed on them it was game over. The flames roared and screamed around them and the air nearly sizzled.

He looked back at Leigh. Soot from the smoke stained her face, and the tears from her watering eyes had washed furrows through it. Pale fine lines radiated from her eyes, delineated in the darkness of the soot.

He dropped his jacket; it wasn't helping anyway at this point and he needed his hands free.

Coughing shook him again and he felt his head start to swim.

He wasn't getting enough oxygen. They were running out of time.

He pointed through the flaming doorway toward what he hoped really were French doors; either that or his mind was playing tricks and sketching a mirage through the thick smoke. Unable to speak, Leigh grasped his hand more firmly in acknowledgment.

They both leapt forward at the same time, sprinting through the doorway and into the next room. There was a line of flaming carpet in front of them, but it was go straight through or die. Forcing himself to ignore the inferno around them, Matt kept his gaze fixed on the doors—real ones, thank God—on the far side of the room. Escape from this hell. In ten feet. Five.

The roar around them became a deafening crescendo as they pelted through the wall of fire. The heat was excruciating and Matt felt Leigh's death grip on his hand clamp even tighter. Aiming for the separation between the doors, he threw his arm up to protect his face and hit them with all his weight. There was a sound of shattering glass and splintering wood as the doors burst outwards.

And then he was dragging fresh air into his starving lungs. The air was so thin it was almost painfully sharp.

But he was off balance as they hit the patio, still half crouched and angled to take the door with his shoulder. He let go of Leigh's hand as he tried to stop, tried to straighten, but then something was underfoot and he was flying through the air. He hit the earth with a *thud,* rolling through cool, damp grass until he came to rest, lying on his back. When he opened his bleary eyes, the stars winked down at him through the bare branches of a tree.

"Matt!" Leigh fell to her knees beside him, her head blotting out the stars. "You okay?"

Wincing, he pushed up to his elbows, a groan breaking from

his lips. "Yeah, just . . . hit hard." He had to stop to gasp in more oxygen. "What happened?" he rasped.

"You tripped over a planter . . . on the patio." She braced her hands on her knees, her head dropping as she drew a ragged breath. "You did the whole 'stop, drop and roll' routine." She tugged on the tail of his shirt, the edge of which was charred and still smoking. He'd been on fire and hadn't even noticed, but his fall had extinguished the flames.

Leigh sagged down into the grass beside him. "I can't believe we made it."

He raised a hand to her cheek, using his thumb to stroke away the wetness from under her bloodshot eyes, but only succeeded in rearranging the soot into a dark smear. "You had doubts?"

She laughed, but it instantly turned into a hacking cough.

He sat up, wrapping his arms around her and rubbing her lower back until her coughing finally trailed off.

"Oh yeah," she croaked.

"Me too. We cut it pretty close in there."

He dropped his head down to touch his forehead to hers, feeling a tremor run through her body. He knew he was shaking himself in a combination of adrenaline, fear, overexertion and lack of oxygen, so he gave into the urge to take a moment for both of them.

His lifted his head at the sound of their names.

Bree was sprinting over the grass toward them in full turnout gear.

"We're okay," he called out, his voice cracking and breaking.

"You were spotted making your grand exit. I heard it when it came over the radio." She unclipped her walkie-talkie. "Trooper Gilson to command. I have Trooper Abbott and Dr. Lowell."

The radio crackled. "Message received."

"We got Dr. McAllister. He made it out the front door just as we were getting our lines set up. He's being treated now. What about Simpson?"

"Dead," Matt said. "He never intended to escape."

"You're sure?"

Matt's stomach rolled at the memory and he closed his eyes for a moment, hearing again the terrible shriek of agony as Simpson went up in flames before their eyes. "Yes. He went up like a roman candle."

Matt thought he heard Bree mumble *good riddance* as she put the radio to her lips again. "Trooper Gilson to command. Cancel rescue." She pocketed the radio and held out a hand. Leigh slapped her hand into Bree's and let herself be pulled to her feet.

Matt followed next, giving himself a moment to get his balance, swaying slightly.

"Come out front," Bree ordered. "I want you guys to get some oxygen."

They followed her around the house to what was becoming a familiar sight: Engines and ladder trucks lined the street, and firefighters swarmed all over the site. Charged lines snaked from engines over the sidewalk to drape over the short fence that surrounded the house. Black soot stains were smeared over the windows, and flames still licked through the broken glass while smoke and steam billowed in huge clouds into the night. Water sprayed into every window, and ladder trucks streamed water through holes in the roof.

Together, Matt and Leigh sat on the bumper of the ambulance as medics milled around them, fitting oxygen masks over mouth and nose, and checking pulses. He glanced sideways at her and she threw him an exhausted smile from behind her mask. Turning his eyes back to the house, he watched the flames consume and destroy anything they touched. Wood. Cloth. Flesh.

Simpson had been as much of a victim as the people he killed.

His life had ended almost before it started, and he'd taken his revenge. And then paid for his crimes in the worst possible way.

There would be another body to autopsy and Matt had both a personal and professional interest in the ravages of Flynn Simpson's corpse. But for now, for the first time in over a week, they could rest.

The case was over.

CHAPTER THIRTY:
SAMHAIN

Samhain: the Wiccan New Year, celebrated October 31, is one of the four Greater Sabbats, and it divides the year into winter and summer. Since winter and the New Year both begin on the same day, it is a time of beginnings and endings, change, and looking to the future. Witches perform rituals to prevent past evil and negative influences from tainting the future.

Wednesday, 8:32 p.m.
Salem Witch Trials Memorial
Salem, Massachusetts

Candlelight flickered from hundreds of white candles, giving the open space an almost holy glow.

The crowd gathered in the green space under the spreading branches of a cluster of locust trees. When that area proved too small, people flowed outwards to stand at the edges of the seventeenth-century Charter Street Burying Point, peering over the fieldstone walls.

They'd made their way from Gallows Hill, the park named in honor of the location of the eighteen infamous Witch hangings in 1692. Salem residents knew this wasn't the actual site of the executions, and local lore whispered of the true location, but the park remained their annual gathering place. From there, hundreds of people had walked silently, lit only by flickering flames, down into Salem and into the lush green landscape of the Salem Witch Trials Memorial. As the crowd gathered, some had stopped briefly at one of nineteen roughhewn stone benches, leaving small tokens—a spray of flowers; a crystal; a card with a personal note; the stub of candle, its flame dancing in the breeze—beside the names of the lost.

Bridget Bishop, Hanged, June 10, 1692.

Rebecca Nurse, Hanged, July 19, 1692.

Martha Proctor, Hanged, August 19, 1692.

Giles Corey, Pressed to Death, September 19, 1692.

The Witches of Salem's many covens formed the inner circle, men and women of the Craft gathering together on their most holy of days—a day when the veil between the spirit and the material worlds was at its thinnest, allowing for communication with the spirits. They were all in black, accented with jewelry and symbols in silver or gold, or the oranges and reds of flame and fire.

Standing just outside the circle, Leigh stood next to Matt. Warm candlelight flickered over him, highlighting the planes and angles of his face. When he transferred his candle to his left hand to slip his fingers through hers, she squeezed back in return.

They were flanked by friends who had come to pay their respects for those who had gone before them. Bree stood to her right, and on Matt's far side were Paul, Juka, Kiko and her fiancé, Greg. Each held a thick white candle, the flames casting a soft glow over their faces.

Leigh thought she'd never want to see fire again, but, somehow, the purity of the candlelight mixed with the intent of the ceremony served to wash away all negative connotations.

She recognized several faces in the crowd—the young woman from Draw Down the Moon on her second visit, as well as Jocelyn and Sherry. And then Elanthia stepped forward into the center of the circle, and the crowd hushed.

She cast a circle with her wand as she walked clockwise

around the ring. "I cast around us now a circle of power, inviting all Spirits that are correct for this rite to be with us this Samhain night."

Others joined the ceremony—some dressed in elaborate masks, some forming an archway of boughs for celebrants to pass through, others shook bells, their silvery peal ringing out into the clear, dark night. Crescent-shaped sabbat cakes were blessed and shared by the participants. Winter was embraced as summer's passing was marked. *For in death is life, and in life is death, and the Wheel is ever turning.*

Then Elanthia spoke again. "Mother Goddess. We raise our voices to you, in memory of those who have gone before us. We honor them. We remember them. We commit them to your peace."

Elanthia stepped back toward the circle, and the Witches instantly separated, taking her back into their ranks.

Around them, voices murmured the names of those they'd loved. Those they'd lost.

Matt's arm slipped around Leigh's waist, drawing her closer, and she tipped her head against his shoulder, both comforted and comforting. "Nathaniel and Grace Abbott," she murmured.

Matt bent his head, pressing his lips to her forehead. "Susan Lowell," he whispered into her hair.

Down the line came quiet murmurs in turn.

"Cody Buchanan." Bree's voice was rough, as if she was struggling hard to contain emotion.

"Hoor Ahmadi," Juka said, casting his eyes skyward.

Paul raised his candle. "Tracy Kingston."

"Flynn Simpson," Kiko whispered.

Voices rose around them, adding names of loved ones and those that were missed, sending them out into the star-drenched night sky.

Somewhere, in a tiny part of Leigh's heart, she hoped that

her father was watching. *See, Dad? I'm not alone anymore. I still miss you, but I'm part of a group now. I'm going to be okay. And Matt and I are going to make sure no one smears your name.*

There was still work to do—paperwork to close the case, evidence from yesterday's fire to go over, possible charges to file against Dr. McAllister. Her father's case to investigate.

But not now. Not tonight.

She pressed her face against Matt's shoulder. She felt the answering stroke of his thumb against her side and a warm pressure as he dropped his cheek against the crown of her head. She sighed quietly, at peace.

Everything else could wait.

Tonight was for memories. Of parents. Lovers. Friends. Victims.

So she stood under the night sky, awash in candlelight. And remembered.

ABOUT THE AUTHORS

A scientist specializing in infectious diseases, **Jen J. Danna** works as part of a dynamic research group at a cutting-edge Canadian university. However, her true passion lies in indulging her love of the mysterious through her writing. Together with her partner **Ann Vanderlaan,** a retired research scientist herself, she crafts suspenseful crime fiction with a realistic scientific edge.

Ann lives near Austin, Texas, with her three rescued pit bull companions. Jen lives near Toronto, Ontario, with her husband and two daughters, and is a member of the Crime Writers of Canada. You can reach her at jenjdanna@gmail.com or through her website and blog at http://www.jenjdanna.com.